Jellyfish
DREAMING

D. K. McCUTCHEN

Leapfrog Press
New York and London

Jellyfish Dreaming
9 8 7 6 5 4 3 2 1

First published in the United States by Leapfrog Press, 2023

Leapfrog Press Inc.
www.leapfrogpress.com

First published in the United Kingdom by TSB | Can of Worms, 2023

TSB is an imprint of:
Can of Worms Enterprises Ltd
7 Peacock Yard, London SE17 3LH
www.canofworms.net

Cover and text design: Jim Shannon and Prepress Plus, India

US Edition ISBN: 978-1-948585-750 (Paperback)

UK Edition ISBN: 978-1-911673-40-8 (Paperback)

The Forest Stewardship Council® is an international non- governmental organisation that promotes environmentally appropriate, socially beneficial, and economically viable management of the world's forests. To learn more visit www.fsc.org

LEAPFROG GLOBAL FICTION PRIZE

Past Winners of the Leapfrog Global Fiction Prize

2022: *Rage and Other Cages* by Aimee LaBrie
2022: *Jellyfish Dreaming* by D. K. McCutchen
2021: *But First You Need a Plan* by K L Anderson
2021: *Lost River, 1918* by Faith Shearin
        My Sister Lives in the Sea by Faith Shearin
2020: *Amphibians* by Lara Tupper
2019: *Vanishing: Five Stories* by Cai Emmons
2018: *Why No Goodbye?* by Pamela L. Laskin
2017: *Trip Wire: Stories* by Sandra Hunter
2016: *The Quality of Mercy* by Katayoun Medhat
2015: *Report from a Burning Place* by George Looney
2015: *The Solace of Monsters* by Laurie Blauner
2014: *The Lonesome Trials of Johnny Riles* by Gregory Hill
2013: *Going Anywhere* by David Armstrong
2012: *Being Dead in South Carolina* by Jacob White
2012: *Lone Wolves* by John Smelcer
2011: *Dancing at the Gold Monkey* by Allen Learst
2010: *How to Stop Loving Someone* by Joan Connor
2010: *Riding on Duke's Train* by Mick Carlon
2009: *Billie Girl* by Vickie Weaver

These titles can be bought at: https://bookshop.org/
shop/leapfrog

*"It's the end of the world as we know it
(and I feel fine)"*
— *R.E.M.*

Table of Contents

Memories, in which Jack meets Joon, Joon changes gender, there is a Tsunami of garbage, a tech wizard reinvents plastic-eaters, the Chancellor blows up his University, and someone decides to have a baby. In a twist ending hippies inherit the earth. Also, there are Jellyfish.

Chapter 1
ALL ABOUT JACK

"What happened,
What we think happened in distant memory,
is built around a small collection of dominating images."
— E. O. Wilson, Naturalist

— JACK IN THE JELLY TANK

First there is blue. I remember the waves surge and pitch, sloshing, neither cold nor warm. There is no before, no anticipation of after. Now is blue. Blue is soft water, hard walls. The briefest surges of potential buzz past in a yellow blur and fade away in the rhythmic rocking. A second of questioning, then loss of awareness, rise and submerge, cycle around. Be. Dream .... A lash of raw red pain brings consciousness, alongside the black possibility of Not. Soothing blue erases all; rise and fall, slosh and rock, be. Buzz. Pain. Awareness .... Am I dying? Is there anybody out there?

The ending is also blue.

SNAP

— JACK IN THE MARKETPLACE

I wait, like always, scuffing along the boardwalk, spitting in the surf, watching plastic bags swirl like a memory of octopus tentacles in the surge. I've heard rumors and I have questions. So I wait until the thin man shows up at the Trash Café with his larger, squarer companion. Then I wait for them to leave again. It's dull.

The docks are more interesting. I check out the catch as it comes in; buckets and crates full of jellyfish, nets ripped from flotsam, decks scattered with interesting debris. The ocean coughs up jellyfish and plastic rubbish these days. The Fisherfolk are hard men and women from a dozen different races and places, tough survivors of every catastrophe the world has thrown at them. They ignore me or stare hard until I wander on. They're busy enough shifting the catch without getting stung by the odd box jelly; they don't need a Warehouse tramp distracting them, maybe nicking something. But now and again they'll give me or one of the other Warehouse kids a small square of tatty tarpaulin wiggling with seaworms or nematodes, or sometimes a basket of the odder-looking jellies to eat, in exchange for mending nets. They supply improvised gloves of layered plastic and cloth – whatever washes up – to protect from unfired nematocysts tangling in long skeins of tentacles, clinging like nerves to the weave of the nets. But they watch carefully so's we don't run off with the gloves.

The two University men drink in the shade of the café while I parch in the sun and wind. Finally, they finish their business, which seems to have been just chatting with Tao Ownerson and sipping hot algae tea made with water boiled and condensed in a solar still. Nothing could survive in that. Safe water. Tao's the one who told me about their research on the immaturity (*immortality?*) epidemic. I traded a fistful of – mostly – live crickets for the info. I didn't get any tea.

When the University Doctors leave the Café, I follow, drifting from stall to stall behind them as they wind through the jumble of overflowing crates and makeshift shacks that make up the Market. Once it becomes clear they intend to leave the waterfront and climb the hill back up toward the University, I stop trying to blend. It's pointless. No one but Uni folk, or Townies with Uni concerns, use that narrow path up the cliffs. I'm almost on their heels when the big, hairy-faced man turns and asks my business with them. My apologetic *"sumimasen"* clearly irritates that one. But the slender, fair-haired man looks excited when I whisper my reason for intruding. I want information. I know there'll be a price.

They also want something from me. The blond hesitates between taking me immediately up to the University lab for testing or clinching the deal in the Marketplace, where one does deals, after all. I'll squeeze this for what I can get. I tell them I'm hungry; that I need new clothes. The big man looks disgusted but the blond pinches his arm before turning to me with a surprisingly kind smile. He introduces them both (which I ignore) and waves his arm back toward the Market as if offering me the world.

• • •

Time skips forward and slingshots back
Around the planet – why do some memories repeat?
My mind walks through one door,
just to end up where I began.
No exit.

•••

— *THE TRASH CAFÉ*

The Market is a new and exciting place when one has credit. The Uni Docs buy me things. Recycled plasti-weave jeans – remember when jeans didn't crackle and pinch? – a softer, hand-woven flax T-shirt and sarong. Someone salvaged a container full of antique coats made of real milled cotton and is flogging them in the Market. I wear my new/old coat with tails sharp as a tern's wing – extinct seabirds skimming long-ago waves. The coat overhangs crackly jeans and remaindered combat boots; even in the gritty wind they make me sweat. But I don't care. I'm making memories. I imagine swooping out over the surf. In my fancy clothes, I feel like the Luck-in-the-Leftovers. The two well-dressed men who are paying for it all stop to help admire me in every surface that reflects.

The Trash Café is the only place left on the boardwalk that's protected by walls and windows where folks with credits can sit out of the wind and watch rubbish swirling in the surf. I get to be a customer today.

"Charlie." The biggest man talks while waving us to a table, continuing a conversation I've been ignoring for a while. "You didn't give your full proposal. The University could withhold research approval – but you've definitely piqued their interest at least." He chuckles, a deep note that can be felt through the bones.

"What proposal?" I ask. A hot current of air gusts through the funnel of the open door and retreats again, sucking the words away, leaving me breathless.

"We're running out of time," the big man mutters. He seems to understand I won't have remembered his name. He re-introduces himself as Leopold Vassily, "Call me Leo," professor of something unknowable called … socio-biology? The thin man, Charlie, seems safer, and his research (on immortality? I hope) should have the answers I want. No one else matters – not yet.

"We have questions." Leo seats himself at the rickety table. I sit opposite, gingerly. Tao raises an eyebrow and greets me with the name I gave him earlier, along with the crickets.

"Jack."

Now the researchers know that name too. Charlie fills our mugs and, ignoring the public cistern, heads for the solar still with an empty water pitcher.

"How old are you, Jack?" Leo asks. "And where from?"

Those are questions I avoid. I examine my cup carefully but there's no maker's mark. There's none on me either. "Dunno," I say. "Born inland – in old Chicago." I'm a good liar. Chicago was once buried in the massive snows and winds that fragmented the Midwest. No records to prove or disprove. There are refugees from all over wandering through, looking for a place to be – like this semi-arid northeast coast. Wasn't this temperate rainforest once? It's nothing new.

All things repeat.

I pick up my cup to avoid Leo's gaze.

"You sexually active, Jack?" the man asks abruptly.

A jolt of adrenaline shakes my hand and the clay cup sloshes. Him using that name is worse than his question. I tell myself I'm just not used to hearing it anymore.

"Why? You interested?" Jack. The name is comfortable as an old hat, but feels too intimate for strangers to use. I've had lots of names, but Jack is the one I use when change is coming, or I need a bit of luck. *Jack be nimble, Jack be quick, Jack jumps over the candlestick*. I manage a stiff smile. Leo is hard to read; brown eyes camouflaged in bushy hair and whiskers. They seem like kind eyes, but Jack-the-Survivor has learned to distrust even his own first impressions.

"I'm curious whether *you* are," the man says. "How's your libido?"

"Don't have much to compare to," I mutter. I decide not to wait for the distilled water Charlie's paying for and tilt my cup (Jack's cup) to taste the silty-gray cistern water. "Don't feel up to populating the world if that's what you mean." Tao told me earlier that Charlie's research has to do with why so many humans and animals can't breed. But he's also some big brain in genetics. That's what interests me most. What makes us what we are? (*What am I?*)

Leo chuckles deeply, the light table vibrating with the sound. "Where do you live, Jack?" My hand quivers along with the table.

"Oi," I say. "Why don't you tell me where *you* live – *Leo*?"

"With him," Leo says calmly, pointing to the blond lecturer who wafts back toward us on another gust from the door. "Dr. McCauley – Charlie. I know his work intimately."

Charlie thumps down the newly filled jug with a "*Hmph*." Our poor table may not survive this meal.

"You should pay him properly, Charlie," Leo says. "Food and clothes are fine, but the lad doesn't have a place to be."

I stare. Why would he know that?

"What say, Jack? Want to room with us while Charlie tests his pet theory?"

"Don't decide that on your own!" Charlie's eyes are pale blue with white lashes and brows, his chin hairless. He looks like he'd disappear if he stepped into a sunbeam. The bright ponytail whips around angrily.

I half-listen to the men argue. The food arrives. With a muttered *"Itadakimasu,"* I eat pickled jellyfish with my fingers from the common bowl while they talk. As usual, it's the only thing on the menu. Jellyfish is what the Fisherfolk catch, and for so long now no one seems to remember when it was different. But I know – as much as I know anything, my memories a mix of half-forgotten stories, bought information, flashes of insight, and great yawning gaps; especially when the memory pertains to me. I think I remember how Japanese became part of the *lingua franca*. Maybe even how I got here – sometimes. But what feels like my memory is also told on the Town docks as an old Fisher's tale – and there are even older tales layered over that.

It's the story of the 7,000 islands of the legendary *Nihon-koku* archipelago sinking beneath The Great Wave. Back in a time so long ago the snows hadn't yet made the middle-country impassable; humans still had it in them to feel generous to hungry strangers who washed ashore, especially strangers with survival skills to share. The Jellyfish Masters came by sea, along with a wave of hungry immigrants, and taught the people how to catch and prepare Jellies. The Fisherfolk even made a harvest festival of it, though no one celebrates it anymore. Thanksgiving, it was called, *Kinro kansha no hi*, though it used to be *Niname-sai*, the celebration of rice, the origins of which not even I recall (though, gods, how I do miss rice).

So here we are eating pickled jellyfish today, dried-shredded jellyfish tomorrow and, on good days, jellyfish stir-fried with kelp, jellyfish sashimi with vinegar, jellyfish burgers, jellyfish satay, jellyfish tempura, candied jellyfish. When was the last meal I've had sans jellyfish? If it really has anti-aging proteins – I may live forever.

We are what we eat.

I push the bowl away and the men stop talking abruptly. I wipe my fingers politely on the table and stand. "I'll have my credit voucher now, *kudasaimasu*." I bow, hoping the blond will pay in advance. I want the information those credits can be traded for. The Doc has also promised answers after doing his lab tests. I'll get what I need – though I'm almost afraid of knowing. Suddenly I just need to leave.

"Where will you go?" Leo's voice is gentle.

I grab my cup of cloudy water, draining it quickly. Water is life.

"Gotta go," I plead. "*Oitoma*! I can … I'll come tomorrow …."

Charlie reaches for his satchel, but Leo puts a restraining hand on his arm.

"Jack." Leo's voice is so deep and resonant it hurts the heart. "We'll pay you to help with Charlie's research. But come with us. You'll have a warm place to sleep, food, and no one will harass you. Promise." There's kindness in this voice.

I can only turn away – just in time to spot Joon outside, making his way toward us up the littered boardwalk. My face flushes hot. Joon is in his usual shabby black-on-black and looks thin and dangerous. Hazel eyes are narrowed under the thick coils of his dreadlocks and his hands are hidden in deep pockets. I scan for a knife, but Joon isn't stupid. He won't show arms near the Market Guard. He stops at our table and nods to me alone.

"Jae. Forget to check in?"

"Couldn't." I say miserably, sitting again quickly to hide my new boots under the wobbly table. "Been ... busy. We was just ...." How do I explain my new finery and all this food?

"You a friend of Jack's?" Leo asks, deep voice rumbling. "Won't you join us?"

Joon ignores him. "Time to go, J-boy." I look away. I don't want to go anywhere with Joon in this mood.

"Leo ...." Charlie has collar insignia identifying him as a Uni Doc. I can see Joon calculating whether he's the one in charge just as Charlie gives Leo a push and the bigger man stands, looming over Joon, dark eyes deep and impossible to read. I imagine Leo as a bear – but I have animal metaphors in my head that no one else gets. I also know Joon will just get stubborn if challenged.

"Jun, is it?" Leo's deep voice is soothing. "We'd like to talk to you too – about a business transaction."

"Might have a minute for business." Joon's uncomfortable. He *seems* to be backing down. Wow. One up for the big guy. But I notice Joon watching Leo closely and I feel the first cramp of what might be jealousy, might be my jellyfish refluxing. Joon slides gracefully into one of the rickety chairs.

"And it's Joo-oon," he adds, nodding for Leo to slide over the food bowl. Like me, he doesn't hold back when someone else buys. "Jae and Joon. We come as a set." He smirks, but I know the anger is still there under the tight smile. It always is.

Leo picks up the sweating clay pitcher Charlie brought and refills our mugs with real filtered water, the clearest I've seen. It tastes delicious. It tastes like clean dirt.

Once Joon settles, Charlie starts. "We're paying Jack – Jae? – to help with our research. Perhaps you could as well?" Big Leo clears his throat but Charlie ignores him. He's in lecture mode. I watch Joon's face, waiting for the storm.

"Can I assume that you're also ...." Charlie stops suddenly, wincing. It's obvious Leo kicked him under the table. "Ow. *Ah*. Perhaps I should just tell you about our project." Charlie glares at Leo, who grins, showing big white bear teeth.

Charlie talks about the rubbish in the water and food and how everyone's bodies are messed up, so there aren't any new births.

"... but recently, among the street kids, we've discovered true hermaphrodites, or intersex adolescents, able to choose their own gender – and other surprising adaptations."

I know! Ask me .... Hermaphroditus, son of Hermes and Aphrodite, so pretty some tramp water sprite got herself welded to him. But was it consensual? I mean, who invited her onboard anyway?

"This isn't remarkable in an era of human-generated hormone mimics created, to put it bluntly, by our own garbage."

Poisonous rubbish creates hermaphroditic superheroes maybe? That's an old one.

"These changes are obvious results of plastics, pesticides, industrial pollutants, and other endocrine disruptors – hormone mimics – flooding our environment. Indicator species like frogs – before they died out – exhibited feminization of males and females with occlusions, cancers, and reproductive difficulties. Humans were similarly affected. The horrifying extinction of our marine mammals, seals, whales, dolphins – along with the entire class of Amphibia – was just the beginning of a massive loss of species diversity."

I miss the trilling of frogs. I picture them in another memory, hopping, eating flies. Being used to poison arrows – or maybe that was in a film.

"Now almost every species on our planet is in decline. We don't normally see reproductive possibilities in any species besides jellyfishes, some insects, and bacteria – yet here's the possibility of an advantageous mutation in humans."

He sure is long-winded. I watch Joon. Charlie finally gets to the point, about how he believes some of the most messed-up *can* still have kids, once they grow up.

(*I never will. Never.*)

Joon eats and maybe listens. When the food is gone, he pushes away the bowl, leans back, and says, "*Ge.* So, what you *hetchi* pervs want is to – what? Fuck my freaky boy Jae and create a race of superherms?"

I can't help giggling. I figure Joon's gonna blow now. Why doesn't he?

"What I'm offering," Charlie says sharply, "is hard credits to Jack *and* you – for help with laboratory research –"

"Charlie thinks the street-kids are humanity's last hope," Leo cuts in abruptly. "Despite the reality that even if a sub-species emerges that can breed, it will have no plants or animals with which to share a very lonely existence."

Charlie glares. "Unless we discover a regulating hormone or … gene …."

Leo just smiles fondly at his partner.

Joon's mouth turns down. "So what am I, then?" he asks. "Some kinda control? Like, to compare my boy Jae to, *neh*?"

"No." Charlie says. No one speaks. Joon stands, shoving back his chair, which clatters to the floor. He glares at me and stalks away.

"But I never said anything!" I wail – Jack is abandoned again. "I never said!"

Charlie's eyes are hound-dog sad (*no more dogs, dogsgone*). "You didn't. There are visual indicators ... sometimes. Slim build, no body hair ...."

I want to go – but where? Joon is beyond angry. I can't go there.

"Jack," Leo says. "Can you take us to others like you two?" The words tip me into panic. With no destination in mind, I knock back my chair and run. It's what Jack does.

Jack be nimble, Jack be quick, Jack had better run like shit.

• • •

Jack is cold. Jack is alone.
I've eaten too much and feel ill. Why didn't I get the credit voucher?
Why did that Leo make me feel so .... Frack! I hide in an alley and consider what to do next, how I will survive for the next little while.
Jack is cold and alone ....

• • •

NonK: Language Diffusion

(archived from Universität Wein, Dynamics of Condensed Systems)

"Languages are an important part of culture, yet many languages in the world are undergoing changes due to globalization … simulations show that interaction with other speakers in the village and neighborhood is the most important factor influencing changing language dynamics."

—University of Vienna, Faculty of Physics. Circa 2019

"In the field of linguistics, internet may be more important that geography in the spread of languages"

—Dr Barbara Partee, Distinguished Professor
Emerita of Linguistics & Philosophy,
University of Massachusetts Amherst. Circa 2022

• • •

— IN BETWEEN

The Market Guard don't find me until after the other Warehouse kids do. By talking to the scientists, I've become a traitor. They don't hold back. The guards find me curled up as small as I can make myself, cradling one hand, covered in bruises. They carry me up the hill to Charlie. I drift awake from a long, hot nightmare. *Dreams within dreams.*

Charlie is asleep nearby, long hair loose about his face.

"Mother?" Charlie wakes with a start. Not Mother.

"How old are you, Jack?" he asks, soothing my bruises with a cool cloth.

I have no answer.

• • •

21

"Time to wake up …."
But if I do, it will hurt.
"Jack?"
Ah. Grounded by a name.

• • •

The Market Guard made it clear they expected Charlie to "take responsibility," meaning the Uni is answerable for my good behavior now. The Uni and Townies police their own turf, Uni up, Town down near the water.

The University rises like a fort on the cliff above the harbor. Just outside its walls is a still-used faculty dorm, an early, experimental, storm-proof building meant to sway like a tree in high winds. Other areas of what was once a sizeable city aren't in as good repair. The Town below the cliff is reduced to clusters of buildings and shacks around the port and a few ruins radiating outward – with the Uni overlooking from above. I've heard there are a few dorms inside the Uni walls where Townies working there can also live. But kids like me live in the rusting warehouses to the south of the port Town, a little lower than the Uni Windmill farm, where the cliff has a milder slope to the south. Most Townies and Fisherfolk congregate near the eastern port and the Marketplace, which traffics in sea wrack, ocean salvage, and jellyfish. The University trades power from its wind farm, access to its library, and leftover millet and wild rye from its experiments with starvation grasses. Supposed transients like me, scavengers sheltering in the rotting warehouses, are considered parasites.

"Do you need to tell anyone where you are?" Charlie asks, and I shake my head glumly. Better the others don't know.

In Jack's new room there's a thick porthole window overlooking windy gray streets. The building sways slightly on friction plates when big gusts roll past. Weak electric lights are powered by roof turbines. There's a soft hemp futon on the floor. It's stunningly luxurious. There is nothing to do in this room.

It's well into morning. I wander out and find Charlie talking on a vid phone. I haven't seen a working one in a long time. He slaps it blank and smiles. I'm used to social smiles that mean nothing. Charlie has a lot of things. Charlie must be good at this surviving game.

(Smile back, Jack.)

"You'll need more than clothes," Charlie says and drops a handful of Uni credits on me, just like that. I pocket them fast. He's given me enough to trade in the Market for anything I might need for a month! The Uni will honor its credits with power, battery charges, light, heat, and sometimes even wheat and vegetables. And, of course, they honor credits with information.

Charlie gets it.

"I'm paying for your help with my research. We will conduct regular tests and you can access all results as we go." Charlie smiles a lot. "Come on. Leo's going to show you around Uni before we head to the lab."

"You two're … together?" Asking feels meddlesome and a little mean.

Charlie's eyes narrow a little. "Leo and I have a committed, monogamous relationship – if that makes you feel safer."

I can't help asking, "how can you stand that beard?" And Charlie laughs.

"He can shave every morning and have a beard by noon." His tone is mournful.

But the Leo who meets us inside the big doors of the Uni is recently clean-shaven, though easily recognized by his size. The man is huge, well over five feet. His deep brown eyes stand out, almost matching his messy chestnut hair. He's probably good looking – I think? Charlie's pale face blushes pink and his long blond ponytail twitches out of the way as he reaches up to peck Leo on the lips. But Leo's eyes are on me.

"Ya'okay?"

I shrug and turn away, but keep sneaking looks. I feel shabby and small, not quite sure how I fit in. When have I ever?

• • •

Crack. Snap.

• • •

— UNI

I stay with Charlie and Leo. We don't talk about Joon – or why I got beat up – and Charlie drops the mask of Lecturer when we're alone, but I know he wants to know how many others like Jack and Joon are out there. (I need to know too – so badly. Is there any one of them like me?) But I can't pull my multiple lives together into any kind of explanation. Charlie never once mentions an overly long lifespan as a side-effect of toxic garbage. His research seems focused only on our possible baby-making superpowers. (Eat your heart out, Spider-Man, plastic hormone mimics are the new radiation – now in pink!). And I never mention how very long I've been alone. I'm in Charlie's world now – out of the wind – with daily walks through a quiet maze of halls, branching off to the bio lab with its acrid smells, and the psych lab with its carefully neutral colors and huge two-way mirror – a fragment of which would be worth mega-credits in the alleyways of the Market.

I become familiar with the guards at the entrance, the servers in the cafeteria, the few lab and hydroponic workers. No one questions my presence and I slowly start to lose the feeling of being a bug on a pin. Charlie gives me (free!) access to the University's online databases to answer my questions – but what should I ask? This after multiple warnings about cross-checking information. The warning are unnecessary. I've understood for a very long time that nothing is ever what it seems.

This is the first time I've had easy access to the University's fragmented – and contradictory – collection of databases. In the Market it's referred to as Noncomp's Word Bank, or NonK. NonK is my digital alter ego. We both have trouble remembering things. My head keeps just so much in it and no more. But then an image, a knowing, will pop out of nowhere. This can complicate day-to-day existence. But Charlie's research and NonK's databases, however flawed, are my hope for answers if I'm ever to understand *what* I am.

• • •

NonK: From noncomp. (adj) idiot, moron, stupid (Eng.); 'baka' (Japanese). Derived from the Latin 'non compos mentis'. IE: "Dude, you're such a noncomp." (Archived by NonK from The Urban dictionary.com, New Millennium circa 2010).

• • •

— ON THE SLAB IN THE LAB

It's finally payback time – for the food and shelter, but mainly for the information I hope to get with those credits. I follow Charlie to his lab. He takes blood and saliva samples, strips me down, runs tests, and, in a confusion of excited chatter, little of which I can follow in the bewildering rush, calls his colleagues into a huge amphitheater-style auditorium. We're on a spot-lit stage surrounded by empty seats rising up into dimness. High in the gods, shadowed figures ring the auditorium, looking down at us from the dark. Invisible voices murmur from above. Welcome to University, little guinea pig. Isn't this what I wanted? To know?

From Charlie's first words the gender-neutral pronoun is tiring. I'm not an 'It.' I am myself – caught in a nightmare, on the slab in a lab. This is *not* the information I'm here for.

"Demonstrably ...." Charlie's whole personality has flipped to stone-cold lecture mode – hardly human. He points toward my junk as if I'm nothing more than a prize specimen. "... it has two functional reproductive systems ...." Charlie has something to prove, something he wants from the invisible faculty watching from the dark. He's donned authority like a mask.

I close my eyes. Here we go. I'm lying on a table wearing nothing but a hospital gown – like the dream of arriving late to an exam in one's underwear. I imagine a dream-self observing me observing myself, telescoping back until it's impossible to tell who is watching who is watching ....

"Note the lack of body hair and a slim build. The outer structures are almost completely androgynous ...," the thin man drones.

My thoughts are free to swell and ebb, sloshing back and forth through time. Androgyny: Seeming neither male nor female – even if one is both? *That's me all over*, as the Scarecrow said ....

"... yet here we have the possibility of an advantageous mutation. Though once intersex beings were thought to be less fertile, in our current sterile environment, once these youth mature they may well be the only ones able to breed at all. Theoretically we could have – as epitomized by this specimen – the future of the human race." Say *what*?!

There is a mutter of outrage from the invisible audience.

"So, unlike the rest of us, this specimen has a future?" An angry voice shrills, followed by sudden silence. Then voices start to whisper from above, "The Chancellor has a point ...!"

A deep bass suddenly dominates. "The writings of the great E. O. Wilson make the point that, while we might 'save' a species – in a zoo for example ...."

My flanks twitch. My daydream crumbles.

"... we haven't saved a thing if we don't have an environment to put it back into. *Ergo*, no matter what we do, whatever 'superpeople' may develop –"

"Hermaphroman!" a voice yells out, to canned laughter.

"Quite. The point is, in this poisoned environment, we – and the species we share this planet with – are heading toward extinction."

There is silence. Dreams of silence. The audience looming above the pit theater is a mass of dark, restless movement.

"But perhaps hormone Zed ...." Does it have to sound like an old comic strip? *Hermaphroman! Biff, Bang, Boom!* I raise a subtle middle finger to the crowd, my hand hanging off the table, knowing no one will get the gesture.

"… is transferable to other individuals or even species?" Charlie-the-Lecturer says. But even he doesn't sound convinced, his professional voice cracking with uncertainty. "Perhaps we've found, in our mess of estrogenic garbage, something that can increase humanity's chances of survival by even a fraction?"

Is he making that up? A sop for his audience? I feel used. What is Charlie thinking?

"But Gentlepeople, either way, isn't this specimen an example of evolutionary theory in practice? We know that most mutations die, and those that survive pass on their genes …."

"Are you saying that *we* are failed mutants?" the angry voice shrills out again. In response, the whispers swirl once more around the shadowy figures seated in the gods. "Listen to the Chancellor …!"

"Or are you suggesting we might control our own evolution?" The deepest voice rumbles, cutting across the rising sounds of anger. Deflecting. Challenging. I know this voice. "Doesn't that smack of Lamarckism – that antique theory of acquired adaptation?"

"It worked with rats," a thin voice wavers. "One early experiment indicated that the offspring of adult rats who had learned a maze learned it faster with each generation …." The voice fades uncertainly. Derisive laughter scatters throughout the dark hall. Silly, there are no more rats. They left this sinking ship long ago.

"What I'm saying" – Charlie's lecture is done – "is that more research is indicated." The audience lets out a collective sigh at this, the accepted cop-out line.

Time to move. I slide off the table and yank my trousers on (finally!) as figures in lab coats climb down out of the shadows and crowd around the speaker. The voices from the dark diminish and become frail and human as they step down under the spotlight. There are no students. The faculty talk all at once, like schoolchildren on a field trip. (I remember children.)

A massive hand takes my elbow and I look up into the stubbled face of bear-like Leo.

"Let's get out of here, Jack." His deep voice resonates through all the cycles of time and memory.

• • •

NonK: Hermaphroditus, son of Aphrodite and Hermes.
Ancient Greek: Έρμαφρόδιτος.

Ovid wrote that while exploring the woods of Caria, the handsome – but very young – boy found a pool inhabited by the naiad Salmacis. She tried to seduce him, but when she was rejected, Salmacis wrapped herself around the boy and forcibly kissed him. He struggled while she called out to the gods that they should never part. Bizarrely, the capricious gods answered by blending their bodies into a creature of both sexes.

In some Eastern religions the union in one being of both creation and conception denotes abundant fertility.

(Taken from fragments of: Wiki free/Hermaphroditus circa 2022)

• • •

— TIME SURGES

I see Joon several times during brief visits to the Market. Joon keeps his distance, but I know he means for me to see. I'm left breathless and disoriented. On bad days – the Joon days – I dive into Charlie's virtual library. I choose histories and lose myself in time until my eyes weep – from the backlighting, or so I tell myself. I avoid fiction. I could lose myself in story. My brain is already so full, so disorganized, it's become difficult to keep my memories separate from stories and dreams. Even with eyes wide and staring at the here and now, the wail of older winds haunts every empty room.

I eat well from the hydroponic tanks and greenhouses; avoid jellyfish when possible. My body feels good. One hunger's satisfied, at least. Jack-the-Survivor thrives. Jae pines. What would make us both happy?

Then Charlie mentions that I've grown a centimeter and gained three kilos already. I stop eating. My hands are shaking when the researchers meet me in the lab to draw blood.

"What's going on, lad?" Leo's resonant voice is out of place in a lab, filling the space as if it will shake apart the hand-blown glass vials and pipettes. "You're sugar-crashing. And if you get dehydrated too, you're frack-all useless to us – and yourself. You in love or something?"

"*Frack* no!" I flinch. Lies don't flow smoothly these days. Life is too easy. "You want consistency for the tests, *na*? If I don't eat, I don't grow. So I stay the same, *ne*?"

Charlie frowns. "You're at that post-pubescent stage when you're supposed to have growth spurts, Jack. You've heard of anorexia?"

"Is he *post*?" Leo says thoughtfully.

I feel ill.

"Jack, you will not run away this time." Leo's voice is stern. "I won't have you disrupting Charlie's research. What's so upsetting to you about the idea of growing the hell up?"

"He's *pre*-pubescent? Ha? Leo – that could explain so much."

I do *not* want to have this conversation.

Charlie hands me a cup of sugar-beet water. "No blood-draw today. But ... Jack, how old are you really?"

I wince. Wrong question/misdirection.

"You asked about the others." I stop, ashamed.

"You're safe here, Jack," Leo says and Charlie grips my shoulder firmly.

"There are lots of us," I say finally, heart pounding, willing it true, willing them all like me (don't leave me alone!). "Dunno how many. We come and go. But no one tells!" I feel like crying (like lying).

I know what Charlie's most interested in right now, and it's not longevity (yet). "I've seen someone go through that – change. It was awful. She got huge, strange. She couldn't walk past one of you lot," I say, gesturing at the adult men, "without getting harassed. She almost caused a riot in the Market. We barely got her away. One Townie-bastard, who followed us, he said she smelled uber sexy. Said he couldn't stop himself, the jerk. None of us reacted. So she hid, never went outside. Ever. Being shut up sent her mad. She became this awful, quaking lump that just ... *ah*! I don't want that happening to me!" My eyes feel hot. Charlie squeezes my shoulder but the terrible image stays; loss of freedom, loss of body. Loss of self.

"What about the others?" Leo asks.

"There was another guy who started getting soft, like her. He starved himself. But it didn't really work. While he didn't trigger *that* change, he got thin and sad – lost hope. Lost himself. Maybe he couldn't accept any changes? I don't know what happened to him. One day he was gone."

"This is why we need to know more, Jack," Charlie says. "You have this hormone mimic in your system complicating things." (Some comic book deus ex machina.) "Your friend may have expressed some kind of pheromone that some jackasses with no brains or awareness decided was an invitation. When we understand, we can help. All of you."

"That's why I said I'd be in your study," I say miserably. What am I? Will I always be alone? "I need to know. But that's why Joon is angry. Why I can't go back." I've been giving up their secrets to protect my own.

Joon. My heart may crumble to dust.

"Would Joon come here?" Charlie asks eagerly.

But Leo growls. "Was it Joon who hurt you?"

I shake my head. "Ah, no. And no. *Gomennasai* …. Sorry."

So we're all surprised when Joon arrives that night, face dripping blood.

• • •

— JACK & JAE

Jae has Joon in his bed for the first time in months. Joon is sleeping, a line of drool stringing down from sculpted lips. His brown face is so lovely in sleep – mouth relaxed, fierce eyes lidded. I'm worried about the others, and why Joon is hurt, but it's peaceful watching him sleep. Joon rolls onto the bandage that covers a gash along one cheekbone. He hisses and the hazel eyes half-open. I stroke the smooth forehead and Joon's eyes close again.

I want to know what the men are saying. As Jack, I often wander at night. I hear things. Jack is braver than Jae, has been around longer. It's Jack who pads barefoot to the cistern for a drink. The moon is full, so when I enter the living space I can clearly see people outside on the balcony overhanging the inner courtyard. My scalp prickles and I think *intruders*, but I know it's really Charlie and Leo.

I slip closer – don't want to consider whether I ought. I've been watching the two men at home, at work, testing my feelings when I see them touch. When Leo pushes Charlie's hair back from his face, I feel pain. I tease the feeling like a loose tooth.

It makes Jack a lonely boy.

I creep across the room. Charlie's breathless whispers alternate with Leo's bass rumble. Two bodies tangle with the moonlight, shifting and sliding, bright skin and dark shadows. A hand, massive and square in the darkness, twists into silvery hair; a breathy voice gasps as the hand tightens and draws a shining, moonlit body down. A furred giant – a demigod or satyr – erupts from below, swinging the smooth tree-nymph body underneath; muscled chest and thighs heave in the dark. I'm unable to move. My heart thunders wildly with conflict: fear, loneliness – longing. I can't look away. Then the great shaggy head turns and dark eyes stare directly into mine, slitted with what looks like fury. Jack runs.

• • •

It's Jae who curls next to Joon, watching him sleep (though Jack's heart races). I remember Jae and Joon's many nights tangled together, usually under a filthy tarp in an abandoned warehouse. We cuddled for warmth, for companionship. Joon would lay his head on my shoulder, legs layered. Never was there a hint of the … thing I've just witnessed. Surely I'd know if Joon felt that way. What's wrong with me? With us all?

I love Joon. I believe Joon loves me. I run a fingertip along the side of his face. Joon murmurs in his sleep; the beautiful lips curl and fingers close around the hand I slip into his. I lay my head next to the darker one on the futon and drift into memories of dreams, chastely holding the hand of my lovely, dangerous Joon – while the world ocean shrinks to a rocking swell, soothing us to sleep. We drift and dream, flying out over dark waves.

• • •

"Are you sleeping?
Are you dreaming, Jack?"

• • •

— JAE & JOON

Without fuss or explanation, Joon stays. It's several days before he turns on me – on Jae – and asks abruptly, "Why didn't you come back? Why did you leave me?"

(*Back off, Jack, don't need you now.*)

I hold up two damaged fingers, still lightly strapped – from my run-in with the Warehouse kids when I was first taken to Charlie. They're healing faster than the timeline Charlie thought likely, but still twinge occasionally.

"You know why. We have to know more. I had to change something. You wouldn't come with me, and that was hard. It was so hard. But, Joon, I had to do this!"

Joon grabs my splinted fingers and squeezes. I wince.

"I heard. I took care of those *gaki* punks. They won't touch you again, *ne*? I let 'em stew. Let 'em know I'd come for them in my own time. Were they in a panic by the time I jumped 'em!" His face is bright and fierce. "I was slower than usual, though." And Joon fingers his bandaged cheek thoughtfully. "Guess I was distracted. That's your fault!"

"Joon!" I start, but he stalks over to where Leo is working and ignores me. We're in the lab. Joon isn't exactly taking part, but he's been watching. Charlie often asks whether he'd like to participate, but he simply ignores all of Charlie's requests. The only person he smiles for is Leo, and it's starting to get on my nerves. No doubt as Joon intends.

— MOSTLY JOON

I know Joon's mad at me, so I eavesdrop while he's being grilled by Charlie and Leo. (*I can hear Joon wherever he is.*) The researchers are in the blood lab discussing the merits of citronella versus methyl salicylate – wintergreen – to mask human scent should Joon or I "exhibit a disruptive pheromone event." Charlie argues for his pet theory that the "events" I described happening to the Warehouse kids are probably "non-adaptive traits" that don't promote survival in otherwise fit individuals, "suggesting that the excessive pheromone production might simply be an artifact of maturing bodies." A trait that could put us in danger, rather than help us survive.

"Assuming that Jae and Joon's development even fits the biological imperative of procreation." Charlie is really holding forth. I can see Joon's confused expression through the open door of the lab. (Charlie's saying most living things want to make babies, make copies of themselves, I want to explain. But what does this world have to offer any new life?)

Charlie keys a question into NonK's erratic database and the ancient computer's relentlessly utilitarian voice echoes through the lab:

• • •

NonK: "Effects of Pheromones on Humans"

"The possibility of sex-specific pheromones affecting human mating behavior was once regarded as improbable, since humans lack an obvious olfactory bulb for decoding odors.

"However, in the New Millennium, magnetic resonance imaging (MRI), showed that parts of the brain respond to airborne human sweat.

"Further experimentation showed that hetero women smelling androgen-like compounds – like testosterone in male sweat – activate the hypothalamus, which coordinates hormonal and behavioral rhythms in the brain. This increases cortisol, which increases blood sugar. Hetero men, in contrast, activate the hypothalamus when smelling estrogen-like substances found in female sweat.

"Later studies indicated that for homosexual humans the response is toward the same sex, with homosexual men

responding to androgens (like testosterone) in the same
way as heterosexual women. And homosexual women
responding to estrogen similarly to heterosexual males.

"These responses suggested a role for human
pheromones in mating behavior and a biological basis for
sexual orientation.

(This entry has been summarized
from fragmented archives titled:
Wiki Free Encyclopedia, Circa 2011.)

• • •

The computer makes a lonely whine as the lab terminal finishes and powers down.

"It's saying sometimes we give off a smell that makes people horny, *ne*?" Joon looks at Charlie accusingly. "*Bakayaro.*" Joon knows that much already. "How you gonna stop it's what I wanna know."

"Masking the 'scent' may help you and your friends go out in public, Joon," Charlie warns, "but it doesn't change the fact that this pheromone seems to be a result of physical changes your Warehouse friends go through, not the cause – though there could be a feed-back loop …."

"However!" Charlie adds quickly. "We'll figure out how to control it. You'll feel less panicked when you have more control over your body. We can all improve control with conscious awareness."

"*When* I do?" Joon sounds frustrated. "Doesn't matter," he says roughly. "What good is any of this? I have to take Jae back to the Warehouse."

My shoulders tense. First I've heard of this.

"Why?" Leo steps closer to Charlie. He's been hovering nearby. Joon eyes the bigger man like a threat.

"Mother wants him," Joon mutters unwillingly. "She knows he's been ratting us out."

"Will they take him against his will?" Leo asks carefully.

Joon glares at him resentfully. "No. But he'll go anyway. An' she won't go easy on him."

"But … why?"

Joon sighs. There's no easy way to explain our relationship to Mother. There just aren't enough words. But he tries. "Eh, it's just, if your mum wanted you, you'd go, *ne?*"

Charlie and Leo look dumbfounded. "Wait. This is his actual mother?"

"Mine too."

I've never seen Joon look so helpless. I clench my fists as if I can channel his anger back to him. Joon is better angry.

"Joon." Charlie's frowning. "You and Jae aren't even close to the same phenotype." Joon looks blank.

"Your skin is different," Leo says bluntly, "your hair is different, your eyes are differ– actually, Charlie, they have very similar eye color, come to think of it, though the lashes and shapes are different. Jae's got my epicanthal folds and Joon's a round eye like you."

Charlie peers at Joon. "Does Jae have eyes the same shade of green as yours?"

I raise my hand to my eyes. I'd noticed right away. It was my badge of belonging when Joon first brought me to the Warehouse.

"*Hai!*" Joon laughs as if Charlie's being stupid. "Everybody does," he shrugs. "No biggie."

"I don't, Joon," Charlie says. "Mine are blue and Leo's are brown."

Joon frowns.

Of course he'd have noticed, as I did. Why hadn't we thought it strange before? Leo's deep, warm eyes sometimes darken to black, seeming to be all pupil. And Charlie's are blue as the sky. Cold, in a way, but also not. Like Mother's ....

Joon picks up a metal tube on the lab bench and peers at his warped reflection.

"We've all got 'em green," he says. "Except *her*, I guess. All of us at Warehouse."

Charlie shrugs. "Maybe a gene linked to intersexuality?"

And he dismisses the most obvious trait linking me to my adopted family as if it's nothing. We share our eye color and our male/femaleness, our "intersexuality," as Charlie calls it. And even with all that I *still* seem to be something new and strange. Why?!

Charlie'd like to keep us around, he tells Joon, for as long as it won't put us in danger at the Warehouse. Charlie believes the important thing to do now is gather information (at which Leo rolls his eyes). Joon, to whom beatings don't classify as "danger," agrees.

I know Joon's priority will be to eat as much as he can, as often as he can, as long as he can. Joon is afraid of nothing (yet). He'll answer their questions, he'll take their food, then he'll take me, and we'll go back to the way we were. And that will have to be enough. *Frack*! Why did I think anything could change?

"The trick," Charlie says, pulling out an ancient recording device, "is to ask the right questions." I come out of my gloom enough to be surprised he knows this.

●●●

Once I told Joon that the stories I read – back when I allowed myself fiction – helped me imagine our lives. Joon can't read, so I told him the story of *Oliver Twist*. Joon was fascinated by Sykes' dog. He never understood my excitement in comparing us-at-the-Warehouse to Fagin's boys, but Charlie, who has a collection of ancient digital entertainments, seems to get it.

"But that's just how things is done, *yeh*?" Joon argues. "We get credits or trade, we bring some back to *her*. We stick together and Mother keeps us out of the big winds – and hides any of us going through ... the change." He whispers the last word.

The pitiful Fagin bears no other resemblance to *her*, as far as Joon's concerned. Mother never leaves the Warehouse, but hides in the dim interior, managing her "boys." I think (*I hope*) they've all been living this way for a very long time. Days drift by, filled with enough hardship that there's no time to consider alternatives. Survival is all. The Warehouse kids come and go. It's usually the bigger kids, especially ones fighting the change, who seem to drift away. No one asks where the new ones come from. Sometimes they wander in bloody, usually scared, always hungry. Older than they look, I have to believe. But how much older? (Is there anyone out there like me?)

When Joon found me, hiding in a rusted culvert, he'd gone from being alone in a big volatile group to having a friend to protect, scrap with, sleep with, roam the Town with. I belong to Joon. I can't remember anymore who beat me to a rag and left me to crawl into the slimy water of that culvert, where I lay in a fever, hidden – until Joon came.

Joon is my miracle. Another like myself? Resetting instead of aging? Can I hope my long loneliness is over? Charlie will figure it out, no? Yes? Please ….

"How old was Jae?" Charlie asks, but Joon just stares at him. Not the right question.

Joon brought me home to *her*. He wrapped me in a ragged tarp and held me while I shivered, gave me water when I heated up, and carried me to the long-drop when I had to go. Joon even fought my fights until I was big enough to fight for myself.

Joon takes credit for teaching me that too.

Charlie listens with a frown. "How big was Jae when you found him?" he finally asks. This is a question Joon can answer. He holds his hand about a little over a meter off the floor.

"The size of maybe a ten-year-old?" Charlie mutters. "I could have sworn you two were the same age, or that Jae was older …."

Joon snorts. "What's age matter? Bet I'm older'n you. We grow when we eat, *ne*? I gave him mine lots of times. Fed him up so he could fight like me." He's proud of his foster parenting. Joon likes fighting. He's good at it.

"Are there any girls at the warehouse?" Leo asks.

Joon just stares, finally saying, "Well, *duh*." Leo grimaces in apology.

"I think what Leo means is," Charlie says, "are there any of you who identify as female? Who choose to be feminine."

Joon's face pales to ash. It takes a minute for the men to realize he's blushing. One hand covers his nose and mouth, muffling the words he mutters behind his palm.

"I do."

• • •

"What pronouns? Why? I'm a boy and a girl.
I'm nothing. I'm no one."
Strangely familiar words, resonating down through time.

Snap.

• • •

— PAYBACK

It's the second week A.J. (After Joon) when the sky falls
in earnest. Charlie and I are returning from the greenhouse, baskets loaded with fresh vegetables, their smell
a heady earthiness that makes me bounce happily on
my toes. I'm ahead of Charlie when I step through the
main door into the solar kitchen. I stop abruptly. Joon is
draped against Leo, who has a very strange expression
on his face. Joon leers at me as I continue slowly into the
room, feeling like I'm struggling against a tide. Something that both burns and freezes sloshes in my stomach. It hurts bad.

"Isn't Leo a sweetie," Joon purrs, watching me
intently. "He's showing me all kinds of things to do in
a kitchen ...." Eyes locked on mine, Joon runs his hands
slowly down Leo's back, then startles when Leo growls
deep in his throat. Suddenly he shoves Joon backward
onto the counter, scattering cooking pans. Joon's expression shifts almost comically from studied seduction to
surprise – then fear.

I hardly realize I'm moving until I find myself pushing and pummeling Leo, yelling at him to get off, and
Leo's eyes are all wrong, blind and glassy; the only sound
coming from him a snarling growl. His forearm catches
me sharply across the nose and I stagger back, hearing

noises from the door as Charlie comes in and drops his baskets, the vegetables' earthy scent lightening the pungent atmosphere briefly as they scatter across the floor. Joon is wailing shrilly. I scramble up, grab the water bucket from the cistern and empty it over Leo's head. I swing hard and smack the bucket right across Leo's face. The kitchen quiets. Leo shakes himself and stands straighter, eyes blank. There is a moment of awful silence. With a low moan, Joon scrambles from the room. The washroom door slams and locks. I look over at Charlie, who's still by the door, face expressionless, but I see his nostrils twitch and eyes dilate. Charlie steps forward and grabs Leo by the forearm.

"Out!" He rasps, voice thin and stretched, "*Out* right now, you big bastard. Do it! *Go.*" He pulls and pushes Leo out the front door and slams it shut.

"Open the windows," he says to me. "No. Keep them shut. We don't want more pests. Hand me the sprayer and some citron, quick! I can't stay here long either." He stares hard at me.

"You okay? Feel weird at all?"

"Ahh." I don't know what to say. There's nothing about the last few minutes that hasn't been weird.

"Wait! There's no citron left. Frack!" Charlie rarely swears. "Try vinegar. Here, pour lots of this in with water and spray like hell. Cover the whole flat. I gotta get out of here!" Charlie covers his mouth and nose, leaving me holding the pump-sprayer, confused. "*Spray!*" Charlie shrieks, and slams the door shut behind him.

I spray. I have no idea what else to do. I spray the kitchen. I spray the outer room. I spray toward the ceiling and around the windows. I listen for Joon. From the hallway I hear a muffled keening and follow the sound, leaning my cheek on the cool washroom door.

"Joon," I whisper through the door. "It's okay. They're gone. Lemme in, Joonie, it's okay."

There's silence for a long moment, then a rustle and the bolt shoots free on the door. I open it carefully, but Joon scrambles back into the farthest corner, jamming himself behind the dry-compost toilet. He's biting on a cloth stuffed in his mouth. His eyes go wide when I reach for him. I gather him in my arms and sit, hugging him hard, wrapped as far around my friend as I can get. After a while the soft keening fades and Joon starts to relax against me. I stand him up and half carry him into our room, carefully shutting the door.

"Joon," I say sadly, "when did it start?"

"You left me," Joon is weeping exhaustedly, body limp on the futon, "you left and didn't come back. How could you leave me alone?" I scan Joon's body; it's still as painfully slender as ever. I touch my fingertips to his chest; there's no obvious swelling, but Joon shivers at my touch, so I pull back quickly. Joon stares up at me, head limp on the bed, eyes swimming with tears.

"I don't want it!" he weeps, fear palpable.

"That's why we need their help!" I say fiercely. I show Joon the sprayer. "Look. Charlie didn't react. He told me to spray the apartment. It must be to hide your scent. I'm sure they can help us, but you have to stop fucking around, *Baka* Joon! They're good guys. I like them. Don't mess with Leo again!"

"As if," Joon whispers. A boneless hand reaches for the sprayer and Joon sprays his own head without lifting it from the futon. I can't help laughing a little, despite everything.

"I don't like you messing with Leo," I mutter. Joon's eyes widen.

"Not you!"

"No. Not me. Just don't like it." I lay my face on Joon's wet cheek and hold him again until I feel him finally relax into a restless doze. I slip from the room. After another thorough spraying of the apartment, I open a window just enough to let the wind whistle in. No human pests swarm the balcony. I grab my jacket and go to see if Charlie needs help with Leo. Damn Leo! He's been the calm one up until now, an adult we could count on. What the *frack*?

I find them in the overgrown weeds beside the street. Leo is sitting on a rusted bench, head bowed, hands gripping his tousled hair, rocking slightly. Charlie is leaning on a broken starlight pole, just watching the big man. I can't interpret the odd look on his face. Just as I reach them, Charlie straightens and walks around the bench to stand in front of his distressed partner.

"Leo," he says. Leo stops rocking, but doesn't lift his head.

"Leo, if you don't look at me now, you never will." Charlie reaches out as if to touch Leo's hair, then drops his hand by his side.

Leo looks up at Charlie, his expression pitiful.

"Gods, Charlie," the man groans. He grabs Charlie and pulls him close, burying his face in his partner's midriff.

"Shit, Leo" – Charlie grabs Leo's hair with both fists – "I don't know whether to hit you or hold you." Leo groans. "You were caught by surprise. I get that. But really, Leo? I'm so *mad* at you. You're better than this."

Leo leans back, pulling Charlie with him so the slender man is across his lap. He wraps his arms around his lover, but won't lift his head.

"Did you feel it?" he asks, deep voice muffled.

"Only just. I left Jae spraying the apartment with vinegar. I don't know if it will help."

"I don't want to go back." The big man sounds like he's weeping. "I'm not that person, Charlie," he whispers.

I can't stand it anymore. I step forward. "Charlie? Is there anything I can do? Joon's sleeping. I think the apartment is clear, but …."

"This is going to be tricky," Charlie says grimly. "We don't know what set Joon's pheromones off, and I'm not comfortable even taking clothes from there right now. They might have his scent on them." Charlie shivers. "The two of us will stay inside the Uni tonight – *if* …," and he glares at me, "if you will promise to hang tight with Joon. Don't leave. Keep him safe. We have to find a way to help Joon, and to isolate and negate that insidious … smell."

"Actually, Leo." Charlie pulls Leo's head up so his partner has to look at him. "Will you go to the lab with me right now? We might be able to get what we need from you – I want a cheek swab and blood samples to see what's going on with your hormones – but I won't risk bringing the boy there yet. I … also have a theory that should increase your self-control."

"Yes," Leo whispers. "I'll do anything."

"Yes, you will." Charlie shakes Leo's head by the hair again, roughly but with affection. "And you will pay for your sins. But first we have work to do."

• • •

It takes a while. Charlie can't get a full picture of what's happening from just Leo, so he returns to the flat the next day in full protective gear, drawing curious questions from the other building residents. Joon refuses to cooperate. Even so, Charlie decides to bring Leo back to the flat and try to recreate the "event." Charlie turns the flat into a sterile field lab, sealing doors and windows, and dividing several areas with walls of plastic, each on a separate ventilation system. "It wouldn't do to release this into the neighborhood," Charlie mutters.

Finally, a nervous Leo is ushered back into the flat, sans protective gear. Charlie stays kitted up, and we all sit in the plastic-draped outer room, acting as if we aren't trying to hold normal conversation inside a giant condom, as Leo jokes shakily. He's made Charlie bring sedative patches and a tranquilizer gun, just in case.

Joon looks like a human dishrag. His short dreads are clumped, his skin ashy. He clearly wants nothing to do with the experiment, but I insist. He sits next to me, our shoulders touching, as far from Leo as he can get. Leo does his best.

"Joon," he says, soothingly, though I've an idea how hard it is for him to be there at all. "I cannot apologize enough. I should have been in better control. It's a terrible thing not to have control of your own body," he adds sympathetically. "I ... I'm so very sorry, lad." His deep voice cracks like a teenager's.

Joon must hear Leo's sincerity, but my friend is in survival mode. If he can't run away, he's going to get mean. I see his eyes narrow and try to forestall him.

"We all know why we're here," I say, then giggle. I can't help it. But now Joon's glaring at me.

"Oh come on, Joonie!" I say impatiently. "Let's just do this thing and get it over with, *ne*?" But silence descends with no pheromones forthcoming. We eat lunch. We watch an old black-and-white Charlie's fond of: *Days of Wine and Roses*. Charlie and Leo discuss the moral choices of the main character – the man who saves himself at the expense of his lover. I hope Charlie isn't making a point. I'm most interested in the lost landscapes, full of living rooms, roads, and cars. Joon is focused on all the fantastic clothing and stuff. I feel him relax a bit as we watch. But Leo remains unscathed.

"I hate to say this," Charlie finally says, "but maybe you should sit beside him?" Charlie's clearly sick of the hot gear he's wearing. It must be awkward talking through that mask. He's ready to measure pheromones. "Joon?" But Joon just glares. Leo clears his throat.

"Why not let Jae try something?" he suggests. "Maybe you don't need me?"

"You know we do," Charlie says sharply. "We need a high-testosterone male to set it off. ... Probably."

"What if I'm just in the vicinity?" Leo asks, and Charlie nods grudgingly.

"Worth a try."

The two men look from me to Joon.

"What about it, Joon?" Leo finally says. "Mind if Jae gropes you a bit while I stand by and emit testosterone?" He grimaces apologetically.

"*Frackin'* pervs," Joon snarls, "*hetchi!*" But he reaches over and grabs my arm, dragging me across his lap. I stare up at my friend in surprise.

"What if this sets Jae off ...?" Charlie starts, but Leo interrupts.

"Too late."

Joon brings his face down to mine and clasps my head in both hands. I watch the light green eyes quietly. What's this look? And then I'm being kissed; Joon's soft, full lips moving on mine. It feels good. Joon's eyes half-close and the kisses become intense, harder. His tongue slides between my lips. I taste Joon shyly, his mouth salty and wild as the ocean. His fingers roam through my hair.

It all feels so – good. But Joon's breathing is changing and his heart thuds loudly. I hear Leo's voice rasping, "Now! Give it to me now!" I twist in Joon's grasp to see Charlie slapping a ton of sedative patches onto Leo's neck. Leo is sweating, hands clutching the chair arms, eyes on Joon. Then he goes limp, and Charlie is bustling around the room with his collection gear, ignoring his unconscious partner.

Joon grabs my hair and pulls my face back for another deep kiss. I feel I'd enjoy it more, except for Charlie being so busy around us, once even sticking a swab into Joon's mouth while we're kissing. Joon absolutely ignores Charlie, groping me in places I've no memory of having ever been groped before, finally pushing me down on the couch and climbing on top. Joon is tugging at my trousers when I clasp the insistent fingers in my own.

"Joon?" I say quietly. He stops, but pulls his hands free and wrings them anxiously, as if in prayer, looking so pleading that I laugh up at him.

"Please, please don't stop me," Joon pants. "Oh gods!" And then Charlie slaps a patch onto his neck too and Joon slumps on top of me.

"Wow. Was that necessary?"

"*Hmph*. Sorry to stop your fun, but I'm done and Leo just twitched. I don't think you want him waking up. I wasn't sure how much sedative to use. Didn't want to overdo it."

I struggle out from under Joon and help Charlie drag Leo into one of the other sealed rooms. We leave him snoring on Charlie's futon, a sudden growl making us both jump and laugh breathlessly. Charlie locks the door.

"Whew." Charlie steers me into a third room and takes off his mask with obvious relief. "The good news is that Leo clearly has more control when he's conscious of the pheromone effects. We can increase that with feedback tools. But listen, Jae, while I won't stop you from going back to Joon, there's always a chance of this triggering changes in you. And frankly, Joon could be maturing enough to become pregnant one day." I gape. "I admit it's unlikely right now, but it will be, eventually, if my theories are correct." Charlie smiles wryly. "You're not ready to be a father yet, are you, lad?"

I flinch. "I think I might, *ah*, hold out for a more romantic moment, *ne*?"

• • •

NonK: On the Chemical Basis of Love
(Fragments archived from Wiki Free, Love, circa 2011)

LOVE can be considered as an evolution of the survival instinct, used to facilitate cooperation and the continuation of the species through reproduction, but primarily to allow human beings to collaborate against threats.

BIOLOGICAL MODELS tend to divide love into overlapping phases of Lust, Attraction, and Attachment:

> *LUST implies a focus on mating, a short-term passionate desire that involves increased testosterone and estrogen.*

> *ATTRACTION encourages obsession and ongoing exposure to a specific mate. The brain releases pheromones, dopamine, norepinephrine, and serotonin at this stage, which act similarly to amphetamines, stimulating the brain's pleasure center.*

This leads to effects such as increased heart rate, loss of appetite and sleep, and excitement. This stage may last for years.

ATTACHMENT involves longer-term bonding that allows for decades of toleration of others for childrearing, survival, and joint creation of complex structures and ideas. Attachment is generally based on commitments, mutual friendship, or shared interests. It has been linked to high levels of the chemicals oxytocin and vasopressin.

However, because of its abstract nature, "conversations about love are commonly reduced to thought-terminating cliché and vulgar proverbs, ranging from Virgil's 'Love Conquers All' to The Beatles' 'All You Need Is Love.'"

• • •

— IN THE HALLOWED HALLS

Joon and I hike through the echoing halls of the University. The way is empty and well lit. Abandoned treasures gather dust in otherwise empty rooms. The students Charlie described as once crowding the halls have dwindled to nothing. At a wide intersection, glass cases display specimens of extinct species. We inspect colorful preserved frogs and stuffed seabirds. Joon stands for a long time in front of two small, toothed whales, smiles curving painted mouths.

"There were some long as the hall," I point upward to a giant skeleton hanging from the ceiling. A great bowed bone shows where the jaw must have been.

"Good that one's dead, *ne*?"

"Stupid. That one ate critters the size of millet grains. You never heard the old stories?" Sometimes I forget and talk as if I've seen these alive and in the world. Joon does not.

"And this one?" Joon says, fingers splayed on the glass where a dolphin's laughing eye is frozen in time.

"There are stories of drowning sailors being saved by those," I lower my voice as we all do when speaking of the lost ones. "Charlie thinks they died out around the time *these* took over the oceans." I point to three huge aquarium tanks set in one wall. Each swirls with a different kind of jellyfish, rising and dropping in artificial currents like lovely little plastic bags. The first tank holds numerous tiny creatures. The next contains just two jellies, each the size of a 30-inch church bell. Joon stares hungrily.

I point toward the first tank. "Charlie calls the tiny ones *hydrozoans*. They aren't edible like the jellies the Fishers harvest, the *scyphozoans*." I'm showing off. I like using the right names for things (except for myself). "Charlie says *hydrozoans* are incredibly adaptive survivors. He says they remind him of … us."

But Joon looks only at the giant jellies. "Do we eat these?"

"Dried, shredded, pickled, marinated. They're the same kind we ate last night, stir-fried with crickets and salt-kelp. They can grow bigger. Charlie says more than 500 pounds."

Joon presses against the glass, staring at the enormous animals.

I want Joon to notice the *hydrozoans*. They have high bells the size of my pinkie nail and opaque pulsating sides that expose bright red stomachs.

"I like these best." That gets his attention.

"Charlie says most jellies are short-lived, but this one, *Turritopsis*, can stop being an adult and return to its immature stage if it's under stress. He says it's pretty much immortal." I watch Joon carefully. "Of course, that only helps the individual creature. It doesn't add diversity or anything to the gene pool." Joon says nothing.

"But Charlie says when it does mature it can choose its gender – choose to be a male or female and repro-duce sexually – you know – make babies from several parents. It's only when the pollution's toxic or weather's bad or there's nothing to eat that it kinda turns inside-out and goes back to the beginning again. Then it roots in a new place and starts over. Like you and me …?"

We contemplate the tiny parachutes, small surviv-alists rising and falling in the current. A disturbingly successful species – going nowhere.

"Maybe like you. Not me. You remember birds, ya freak," Joon finally says. "And frogs. But I can choose who I am. Can *you* do that?"

He gives me a look that tells me he has more to say, but then flashes a bright grin that doesn't reach his eyes and stalks away down the corridor, dreads bouncing in mimicry of the thick, deadly tentacles of the sea wasps in the very last tank.

I lean my forehead against the glass. (*Snap. I float with the tide, letting the currents take me …. Crack.*)

My skin shivers and I push off the aquarium glass. For a brief moment I imagine cracks spider-webbing through it. Then the glass is clear and whole again.

I turn and hurry after Joon – as I always must.

• • •

The Trash Café is starting to empty. Joon seems well protected with his heavy-on-the-garlic diet and citron-based cologne. "No musk perfumes!" Charlie had been careful to emphasize. Those perfumes are rare, but valued, and still available in the Market, at a cost. "No animal- or gland-based anything." He wants to be sure we don't create more problems with animal pheromones in the mix until he can come up with a more stable mask for Joon's scent. Joon seems fine to me. No one around us is reacting. Though I do notice one old Townie woman watching us. Her hair and face are pale and soft, her eyes so washed out they seem almost colorless. She's been staring at us for a while. Probably an old-time bigot, I reckon, and, with a tingle of glee, I fix her with my eyes while I lean across the table to kiss Joon on the lips. But I quickly discover I should have been paying attention to Joon, whose hand swings up and cuffs me a stinging slap across the face. I stare at him, eyes watering, hand to my cheek. Joon is almost speechless with fury.

"*Yoseyo*! What're you thinking!" he hisses. "What if I …? *Do Aho*!" And he shoves back his chair and stomps down the pier.

I'm horrified. What was I thinking? What if I'd set Joon off?! I steal a glance at the old woman, who gives me such a warm, sympathetic smile that I plop my head down on the table. Stupid-head *baka*. I'm so dumb about people! I never get it right. No one is ever – ever – what they seem to be.

A hand touches my arm lightly; the elderly lady has come over to my table.

"*Sumimasen*, so sorry to intrude," the light voice warbles. "But I believe we know someone in common, and she'd like to talk to you." And then she says a name that changes everything: *Kumo Onna* – Spider Woman – also known as *Mother*.

• • •

NonK Keywords: Spider-Woman (USA) / Kumo Onna (Japan)/ Anansi (Ghana)
(Mixed and matched from Wiki/Anansi, circa 2011 & 2022):

Anansi (Ah-nahn-see), the cunning spider, is a Trickster deity like the Nez Perce Coyote and Uncle Remus' Brer Rabbit (Tricksters often change the rules of nature, sometimes maliciously). Anansi tales originated with the Ashanti peoples of Ghana. The spider is also known as Ananse, Kwaku Ananse, and Aunt Nancy.

> Anansesem stories traditionally began with: "We do not really mean that what we are about to say is true. Let the story come, let it go," and ended with: "This is the story. If it be sweet, or if it be sour, take it somewhere, but let a little come back again."
>
> Western alternatives include: "Once upon a time" or "Everything I tell you is a lie."

Kumo Onna (ク モ 女), Spider Woman, is the result of the new lifeform fusing itself with an innocent bystander. Thought to be taken from the myth of Jorōgumo (Japanese 'woman-spider'), a yōkai from Japanese folklore that shapeshifts from a giant spider into a lovely woman.

Spider-Woman (USA) *is a fictional character appearing in American comic books circa 1977. She's often isolated, later killed, resurrected, then discontinued despite – or because of – being a powerful female hero.*

• • •

Chapter 2
OTHER PEOPLE'S MEMORIES

— JOON & JAE

Joon returns to the café feeling a bit calmer but ready to get Jae back, and good. But the table has been cleared and there is no sign of Jae. (*And yet this is my memory too. Am I Joon now? So many people live here in my head.*) The tabletop has something drawn on it in a greasy finger painting: three triangles inside a smeared circle, the safety symbol that marks the bolt-holes leading to the Warehouse. (*I remember drawing that. We drew that!*) Joon hurries back toward the University to tell Leo and Charlie that Mother has taken Jae.

• • •

— MOSTLY CHARLIE

Charlie, Leo, and Joon leave before dawn to make the long trek south across the cliffs before descending toward the outskirts of Town and the plundered, rotting warehouses that clutter the coast. Joon takes them even farther, to where the land starts to rise again. They're coming to my rescue. I make an awkward damsel in distress.

Charlie and Leo are more familiar with the high ground behind the warehouses that leads to the aging wind farm powering the University and most of the Town. Below the first rise, Joon approaches a massive building, farther inland than the rest, with a giant rip in the rusting metal for a door. At the entrance, Charlie stops.

"I'm going in alone," he says. "I want the two of you to wait out here. Come after me if I'm not back in an hour. It's foolish not to have a backup and I don't want to risk losing Joon while retrieving Jae."

Joon rides over Leo's instant protest. "He's right, *Onisan*. You won't do well in there. Charlie's the type *she* tolerates. She doesn't like change, *ne*? If we all go in at once ...."

Leo is not pleased. "This is incredibly stupid." He sighs. "Joon, is this building one space or broken into separate rooms?"

"The building itself is just one space." Joon looks uncomfortable. Charlie stares hard at him. They've already agreed privately to keep Leo out of this.

"So, I should be able to get to you quickly," Leo mutters. "I brought a battery torch," he tells Charlie, "but I'd like to keep it, so I can find you if needed."

"He won't need it," Joon assures them eagerly. "Better not to light the main space anyway."

"Main space?" Leo asks. But Charlie's already pecking him on the cheek and stepping carefully through the rusted doorway. Leo watches his partner being swallowed by the darkness inside and moves forward as if to follow.

"One hour!" he bellows into the dark. Joon claps a surprisingly strong hand over Leo's mouth and they stare at each other, Leo's face darkening with rising suspicion.

•••

I watch. I'm there – and not there.
They are the voices in my head. The stories in my heart.
The loves that create a life.
Ghosts, players on a stage, yet real to the touch.
They are part of me.
Who knows how anyone remembers anything?

•••

— CHARLIE MEETS A GIRL

Charlie stands in the middle of a large, dark space. For a few moments he's blind, waiting for his eyes to adapt from bright sunlight to the dark. Even blind, the space feels huge, echoing, yet too quiet – as if it's listening. Then, out of the dark, invisible hands touch his arms and back, too many hands, pushing and pulling him.

Joon warned him that hands would guide him. It was Joon's idea to leave Leo outside. His reasons seemed valid at the time. Leo is too defensive. Charlie is one she'll be able to talk to. And he'd warned Charlie about what lay ahead. But knowing doesn't help in the moment, in the dark, with too many silent hands touching him. Charlie is led across the giant open space, and then they're shuffling downward, through the tunnels Joon didn't mention to Leo. It's dark at first, then increasingly lighter. Charlie and his shadowy guides come to a cool, hollow space deep underground. He's prepared for the mob of silent children leading him through the twilight tunnels. But that's before he sees *her*. Nothing could have prepared him for that.

• • •

She is half-lying on the far side of a dim room, propped on a mushroom-shaped dais growing out of the packed dirt floor. She's naked, massive pale breasts and stomach billowing under a tumble of matted black hair. She's like some monstrous queen bee. The room even smells oddly sweet. *Ah*, but she's not completely naked, after all. There's a brown loincloth draped across her lap, half covering the ivory-pillar legs. As Charlie steps closer he notices a man kneeling, forehead touching the ground before the dais, as if in supplication to a bizarre goddess. He isn't moving, and Charlie wonders briefly if he's dead. Already Charlie's trying to find words to describe her to Leo. An image of a puppet from one of his old movies, *Jabba da Hut*, comes to mind, and he almost laughs out loud. But she's far more attractive than that, he realizes. Something about her … perhaps she's more like the Venus of Willendorf with those motherly rolls of flesh and her obvious allure … *huh*? Charlie hasn't been attracted to women for years, not since well before his divorce. Leo is his ideal, in the flesh and in his fantasies. Can he actually find this quivering mountain attractive? It's true her pale skin almost glows in the dim light. Her ebony hair tumbles softly around a face that's almost completely hidden. The long hair curls in masses around pendulous breasts. Charlie takes a small bundle from his pack. Joon warned him not to approach *her* without a gift. He places the packet of candied jellyfish at the base of the dais, where he sees another similar bundle.

The man kneeling prone at her feet finally moves, turning just his head to grin at Charlie. Charlie recognizes him as one of the Townies, a rough-salvage man from the docks. The man's grin could be mistaken for a rictus of fear. Charlie turns away, fighting down a sudden urge to shove the man, kick him away from *her*, then sink his fingers into those soft rolls of white flesh. What's the matter with him? He hears a tinkling laugh from the goddess on the dais, and it's as if he's never before heard such a lovely sound. Her voice! How can anything compete with Leo's marvelous deep tones … but!

Without knowing how he got there, Charlie finds himself on the dais, leaning against the billowing stomach. He feels like a small child and a randy teenager, all at once. Time seems to have passed. The Townie has disappeared, and Charlie has no idea when he climbed up beside *her*. Her eyes are still shadowed by coiling hair. She's talking to him, saying something he seems to receive through his groin rather than his ears. He feels wonderfully horny and alive. He wants to keep listening to her voice forever. What it says is less important; he knows he'll remember when necessary – *she* tells him so. Her tinkling laugh chimes through his bones, and he nestles against her side, reaching up to take her hand, like a child with its mother.

Something in his head is panicking though, in the back of his mind, even while her touch sends a deep serenity washing over him in persistent waves. What is it? Isn't there something he has to remember? Something he needs to do? *No*, the tinkling laugh says to him, as the warm hand envelops his, *there is only me. Only this.*

The tide washes over him again and his mind fogs with a desire for … a mother? But his mother hadn't been this. Not soft and – smothering.

No need for effort, the silvery laugh teases him. *Give your thoughts to me, give me your deepest self* …. And, sinking into the insistent tide, Charlie does.

• • •

Leo! He can't tell Leo. He can't! What the hell happened to him? Why did he …? Where is he? Charlie is cold. Bereft. Time has skipped forward again like a damaged copy of an old film. He finds himself stumbling through the chill and dark of the Warehouse, feeling ill, following some faceless boy to meet with the others; his people. He hasn't found Jae, he didn't resist *her*, it's all a disaster. What will he tell Leo? Gods! What did she do to him? How? His skin feels feverish; it's shivering of its own accord, in patches, like a horse shaking off a biting fly. He feels dirty – exposed.

Charlie staggers out through the ripped and rotting door of the Warehouse, from cold and dark to the unbearable spotlight of the dry sun and desiccating wind. He falls right into the arms of Leo. His Leo. Jae is there too, standing near Joon, watching Charlie glumly. Joon looks relieved. Leo is frowning.

"Charlie! Where the *frack* have you been? You look like hell, love. What happened in there?"

Charlie's eyes water. He's short of breath; how could he have thought anything was more beautiful than Leo's beloved bass rumble? He drops his head against Leo's chest, gasping with an effort not to weep. Leo wraps his strong arms around Charlie.

"Let's get you home. We have Jae. You must have convinced her to give him up, right? You can tell us about it at home. Let's get out of here."

But Charlie knows he won't be able to tell Leo anything. What could he ever say that Leo would understand? It's as if she's already driven a wedge between them. He shivers. He doesn't want to think too hard about *her*.

Charlie looks up to see Jae watching him with troubled eyes. The boy nods. He *knows* ....

• • •

"It's ti-ime."

• • •

— CHARLIE EXPLAINS IT ALL

In the end, Charlie can't tell Leo all of it. He gives Leo his image of *her* as the Venus, and that makes Leo laugh. He can't explain why she let Jae go – or took him in the first place *(and I ain't sayin')*. Even now Charlie has no idea if he did anything or told her anything to make her think they wanted Jae at all. Yet here he is. Mission accomplished. Leo praises Charlie to the skies and Charlie feels horrible. He feels like a newly made addict, one who shouldn't think too hard about that one temptation, the one that makes his gut burn with shame. He clings to Leo when they are alone, and stares dry-eyed at the ceiling after Leo falls asleep, sated by Charlie's desperate lovemaking. If Leo is aware of Charlie's tension, he lets it go; gives him time to find his center again.

Jae is the one Charlie feels most relaxed with over the following days. Jae knows, so there's no need to talk about what happened at the Warehouse at all. Joon likely knows too, Charlie realizes, but it isn't important to Joon. It seems to Charlie that only Jae matters to Joon these days, as they explore their developing relationship. Jae is still physically immature, but Joon is clearly blooming. It's easier for Charlie to focus on the boys. Possibly because of Joon's interest in Jae, Joon's own control is stronger now. He wears the masking scents, but Charlie's exercises and feedback devices also help Joon practice turning his pheromone allure off – and on – though both take self-discipline and, most of all, awareness. Joon is clearly motivated.

Even Charlie has to smile when he catches Joon, who was leery of even stepping outside after the kitchen incident – now testing his hard-won control by practically bombarding Jae with pheromones at odd moments. When Joon stares hard at Jae with an odd toddler-before-a-tantrum look of concentration on his face, Charlie doesn't stand too close. But he believes it's significant that Jae doesn't react, other than to ask Joon once if he needs to visit the long-drop.

Charlie's pretty sure Jae is in for a surprise from Joon one day soon. Watching them is amusing and keeps Charlie from thinking too hard – about anything really. When he does let himself think about it, about the Warehouse, or even about his data collection from the boys, Charlie's thoughts veer away until he's sick of his own inability to face his problems. While observing the boys, Charlie starts to wonder if he's seeing the same avoidance behavior in Jae. Is it really likely that Jae, who's so attuned to Joon they seem to move in tandem, never notices Joon's intent stares even when they're so laughably obvious? What exactly is Jae avoiding? These thoughts are so much more interesting to consider than the dismal shadows lurking in Charlie's own head.

Charlie becomes certain Jae is hiding something. It's a pleasant mental puzzle to ponder. But the puzzle isn't compelling enough to make Charlie look for any implications from his own data, which he still veers away from thinking about too much. He goes through the motions, works in his lab, runs tests on his growing collection of DNA samples and records his results mechanically. But he doesn't let himself analyze or think deeply about what the results mean. This is very un-Charlie-like behavior. Charlie is not himself.

It's weeks before Charlie admits he's off-track, that everything he's been working toward could easily be left behind if he doesn't deal with the thing at the Warehouse that both attracts and repulses him. But when he tries to imagine going back there, he finds himself kneeling in the bathroom, vomiting into the dry-comp toilet.

Leo finds him there, wiping his mouth. He hoists Charlie up, helps him to bed, tucks him in, ladles him a drink of water from the cistern, and settles beside him with an expectant look.

"You gotta talk to me sometime," Leo rumbles.

He waits for a moment, but Charlie doesn't answer.

"You don't have to tell me what happened at the Warehouse unless you want to, Charlie. I can tell it was bad. Some days I want to level the place." Charlie feels a protest rising, but Leo keeps talking, voice grim.

"But that damned place holds something for us. It's the thing that gave us Jae and Joon." His eyes soften, but his voice does not. "And it seems it can take them away again too."

Charlie's head snaps up to look directly at Leo. "What? No!"

"There's a mystery there," Leo says. "Solving it may help us understand some of the other mysteries in your research – or it may not. But we have to do what we can to protect our ... growing family?" He pauses and takes a deep breath. "Maybe even our world."

"Charlie," his voice drops even further, "have you been noticing the increasing ... entropy ... here at the University? Forget students; there are fewer researchers left. Even George Salsbury is gone. Said a while back that he was going to try sailing to Europe since it was the only way to find out if his colleagues' experiments on plastic-eaters are still ongoing over there. No one's heard from that sector for a year. I mentioned the dangers of sailing through all that free-floating trash, but he said he'd got hold of an old solar airfoil with no submerged propeller to foul ...." Leo sighs. "I doubt he'll be back. Not that he won't make it!" he adds quickly. "But if they are still working over there on that plastic-digesting microbe he's been cultivating ... I suppose it's to his advantage to stay there." The men are silent for a few moments.

"Even the Town is dying, Charlie," Leo whispers. "Despite the power we send them, the food. It's subtle, but every day there are more empty buildings, fewer people on the streets. The transit system is long gone, of course; no one has the resources to fix anything anymore. Maybe no one can. The Town just feels empty and decaying. Or was it always like this?" Leo's voice turns almost petulant. "We've been sheltered up here in the University. We have our own power plant and greenhouses, our own population and concerns. We just hide and pretend that nothing is happening out there. And nothing is! We're just ...."

"'Not with a bang but a whimper …,'" Charlie quotes softly.

"What?"

"This is the way the world ends," he recites. "'We are the Hollow Men ….'"

"Charlie …."

"No, listen!" Charlie says, suddenly fierce. "Every year there have been more floods or storms that take out yet another part of the Town. And how long has it been since we've heard from anyone outside? I know what you're saying. There are no resources – or motivation – to rebuild anything. People just … leave. And we're losing communication with the rest of the world. It just keeps getting smaller. If you think about it, the very things our predecessors feared have also solved at least some of the problems they wrote about. Epidemic sterility has sure kept our birthrate low!" Charlie clasps a hand over his own mouth.

Leo squeezes his partner's shoulder in sympathy. (*Poor Charlie, who will never have children. Charlie, who wants them more than anyone.*) But Charlie straightens up and continues. "Climate shift gives us constant wind for power – and constant wind damage. In my lifetime we've developed algae-based foods – but there's little else in the oceans humans can eat other than jellyfish. Jellyfish were here first and they'll outlive us all.

"In fact, forget *hydrozoans* and our little theory about their immortality maybe being an intersex gene link. It's only the edible *scyphozoans* that keep us alive at all. The *cubazoids* are poisonous. The corals are probably long gone. The environmental tipping point has long passed. From a stable ecology we've shifted to a wildly variable one, like a seesaw out of control. You and I barely remember when it was otherwise. What will our children remember?"

"Children?" Leo says, frowning.

"Our descendants," Charlie says firmly. "You said it yourself. Jae and Joon are family, and if I'm an observer of any kind, I think it's clear they're at least somewhat fertile and could potentially have a child of their own. Our family is growing, Leo." Charlie's voice becomes more animated than it has for weeks. "But it's time for a changing of the guards. The world is shifting into something fiercer and more dangerous than ever before, at least for our species. It will take new organisms with different survival skills to continue on. And maybe we have a chance to help one along, to help the intersex street kids. To continue something of our human legacy.

"Listen, Leo." And as he says it, Charlie feels it to be true. Why has it taken him so long to articulate this? "Mother Earth has incubated us for a long time, but now it's time for us to grow up. Maybe even move on." His tone becomes wondering, understanding coming with the words. "Mothers have a tendency to want to protect, to shelter, don't they? Maybe *her* purpose is …. Maybe *she's* keeping them in a kind of stasis?" And Leo knows Charlie isn't talking about Mother Earth anymore, but *Kumo Onna*.

"Maybe *she* doesn't know anything else to do but to keep them hidden, keep them safe, until …. But it's been so long. And – hidden away in that dark maze – she knows even less about what's going on outside in the world than we do. Maybe she's been waiting so long that now it's all she *can* do."

Charlie is clearly thinking out loud. Leo waits for an explanation. Instead, Charlie stands and pulls on Leo's arm.

"Come. There's something I want to show you in the lab."

Charlie leads the way through the long halls of the Uni, saying only, "I believe I have evidence to support one of our theories, though I think we should keep it quiet for now."

Leo follows silently. He's sure they've already talked through every aspect of Charlie's research over the last months. In many ways Leo-the-Sociologist has been the theoretical engine behind much of Charlie's experimentation, so Leo isn't expecting anything too surprising. But he's curious. It's always interesting, and alarming, the way Charlie can take an ephemeral theory and find concrete ways to examine, to prove or disprove, to test something as airy and insubstantial as an idea – sometimes extrapolating conclusions Leo could never have imagined.

Charlie pulls a sheaf of papers from under a bench, pushing aside a palette of gels. There are stuttered lines across the gels that mean a little bit to Leo. He knows the theory behind comparative DNA analysis: that fragments of DNA strands pushed across a gel via electrophoresis – an electrical current that separates molecules by their size and electrical charge – can be compared to like or unlike strands. But Charlie has also been researching something he calls "messenger" or mRNA and analyzing gene expression – a characteristic or effect attributed to a particular gene – but most of that is outside of Leo's training. He does know Charlie is somehow measuring the expression patterns of thousands of genes simultaneously, to determine which genes are active in different tissues or at different stages of cellular development. For this Charlie needs NonK's records and data. With DNA fragments from Jae and Joon, Charlie wants to isolate a few specific genes' biological expressions. Ultimately, he hopes to figure out which gene switches on which physical attribute, or even behavior. NonK provides the sequencing software, the research papers and database that Charlie has been building on. Charlie is NonK's biggest fan.

"These publications are the current body of human knowledge," he's fond of saying, often after the heartbreak of not finding a particular experiment referred to briefly in other papers. Charlie knows better than anyone what NonK's limitations really are. Before the Warehouse trip, Charlie had been so very excited about a hint he found that there might be an alternative method of analyzing gene expression by directly measuring protein levels. But sadly, the method wasn't to be found in NonK's databases. Some days Charlie calls NonK's missing data his "Lost Alexandria" and grieves over these key gaps in his "scientific body of knowledge." On better days, he sets out to reinvent them.

Charlie used to remind Leo that all science relies on the backs of others that have gone before, theories and research building one from another. Even as a social scientist himself, Leo is gobsmacked by Charlie's work ethic; his focus, his ability to understand, create tests, and infer results otherwise opaque to Leo; his sheer, glowing brilliance in that sterile room full of neutral glassware and blank countertops, scattered gels, and inscrutable X-rays. Leo loves to watch Charlie at work. Even now, scrabbling through the papers he's sorting for Leo, his energy glows.

Charlie flicks on a screen that pulses with un-keyed colors. He pushes a printout under Leo's nose, already turning away to the wall safe that holds his lab journals. The door hangs open, per usual. There is no way to shut it on the bulging mass of books and papers stuffed inside. Leo imagines that it hasn't been closed in decades.

"Look at this. Look here. This genome sequence clearly shows that almost all the Warehouse samples are expressing the immortality gene – to varying degrees – very similar to those we isolated in Jae – and in the *Turritopsis* hydrozoan, our eternally self-replicating little jellyfish. That same switch in the Warehouse kids' DNA has been turned on somehow." Talking through his research with Leo is getting Charlie fired up again. Able to see the big picture. Think things through.

"When – where did you get ... never mind." Charlie's data sampling can be remarkably subtle. Leo knows he has a jacket with a texture like a burr that can passively collect hair and skin samples just by brushing up against unsuspecting passersby. When Leo questions the ethics of this, Charlie just complains that his own hair gets caught the most. Cheek swabs and saliva, or other bodily fluids, are Charlie's preferred samples when a willing subject is available. Leo wonders if Charlie collected samples from Mother. It doesn't seem the moment to ask. But Charlie said that "almost all" the samples showed switched-on genes of the sequence he was targeting. That means some weren't. Leo has his own theories about the Spider Woman's projected life span.

"Biologically this expression of the immortality gene seems to be paired with – or expressed alongside – intersexuality, and green eyes for that matter. Currently, these androgynous folks don't age like we do. They may not always develop completely into adults either, though. Think about it! If only one in 2,000 true intersex individuals – paired with the immortality gene – were born every year, even if it were only one in 50,000 back when our population was higher, if they didn't die by accident, or disease, they'd just continue on ...."

"Extended childhood implies huge learning potential, but if Mother's kept them mentally under-stimulated?"

"Then they wouldn't realize that potential ... and they might stop growing."

"Physically and mentally. They'd be easier to hide ...."

"Until conditions were right ...."

"Until the environment is ideal for them to emerge, to breed, to realize that potential."

"But what a mistake! If none of the rest of us are left, perhaps a major threat is removed, but if no one is here to teach them, they will lose the opportunity to learn by our mistakes – lose thousands of years of technology, of art – lose those things that still make them part of us!"

"That which makes them our family," Charlie says softly. Leo grasps his shoulders and the two men stare at each other, a sense of urgency motivating them both. "We may not have much time," Charlie continues. "They need more than just their unique bodies to survive what's coming. They need us to teach them. We define ourselves as human by our big brains and ability to learn. But human survival has never been entirely about physical adaptation – and there is also quality of life to consider."

"Perhaps our University can take the place of the Warehouse." Leo is fired up, his mind whirling with ideas. "Instead of Mother hiding them – we can teach them! Maybe ... but we'll have to get the Chancellor on our side first. And *her* ...."

Charlie can't suppress the tremor that shudders through him at the thought of that splendid, terrible woman, squatting in her rusting web.

"'Thoughts of a dry brain in a dry season.'" He quotes a poem that always frightened him with its terrible reflection on the end of times as he returns his papers to the pointless wall safe. But he says it softly, so that Leo won't hear.

• • •

But I hear.
His words are in my head. My heart. Our memory.

SNAP

• • •

NonK Keywords: Seaweed Beer/Recipes
(Mangled from: The Celtnet Guide to Wild Foods, n.d.)

SUGAR KELP *(noun) Southern Kelp (*Laminaria saccharina): *A large brown algae species that can grow to lengths of over six feet. Southern kelp is usually a dark brown color with a rippled appearance and edges resembling a lasagna noodle. When it dries, a sugary white deposit forms on the kelp's surface.*

Japanese kombu 昆布 : *"a Laminaria kelp; sea tangle" is dried and powdered to produce kombu or "kelp tea," also called seaweed tea.*

Kelp Flour Recipe: *3 kg Laminaria digitata (oarweed) or Saccharina latissima (sugar kelp) – or any kombu ….*

Kelp Beer Recipe: *10 kg Laminaria saccharina (sugar kelp), or saccharina kombu. Hops, yeast, blue algae ….*

73

Known as the "poor woman's weather glass," *it's said that if a woman hangs a frond of southern kelp in her doorway, it becomes soft and limp to indicate wet weather ahead. It goes stiff if dry weather is coming.*

Because of this anecdote, *and contrary to what it actually suggests (much like using endangered animal parts for breeding success), seaweed tea is often used as an aphrodisiac by those prone to magical thinking.*

• • •

— CONVERSATIONS IN THE TRASH CAFÉ

Like they did for me, Leo and Charlie try to take Joon clothes shopping in the Marketplace. But Joon is uninterested in anything but the knife vendor, so we eventually end up in the Trash Café, along with everyone else who isn't working in the midmorning heat. It's still too early for food, so we watch the workers decanting a new drink from several huge barrels. After much discussion, Tao Ownerson asks for testers from the loiterers. Leo volunteers our table. The clay mugs Tao sets in front of us hold his latest experiment, taken from a partial description of a recipe he discovered on NonK's public data terminal.

As usual, there seem to be serious gaps in the information NonK provides. If nothing else, the collection of old and damaged databases encourages a healthy skepticism, though the University Chancellor is widely known to be very proud of it.

Tao has tried to ferment a Sugar Kelp beer. But the result is an unexpected bright blue, has well over 40 percent alcohol – he was aiming for 11 percent – and seems to have an unusually energizing effect on his willing, swilling participants, which now include the café's entire clientele and a few hangers-on in the doorway.

Charlie in particular is very animated. By mid-afternoon his pale cheeks are pink and he's sitting in Leo's lap, telling rude biology jokes and candidly answering the increasingly personal questions I can't resist throwing at him. I want to know how Charlie and Leo met and I don't think I'll ever get another chance like this. Joon is more reserved, pushing his chair back from our table, but I lean in and egg Charlie on. Leo wraps his big arms around Charlie's waist and plays counterpoint with his deep voice.

"Leo and I met at a conference ...," Charlie says lightly, leaning against his partner.

"We met on a train." Leo's tone is firm.

"Don't be silly, it was the conference."

"He was straight and in a marriage contract, naughty man." Leo pinches him and Charlie squeaks.

"I was separated!"

"Contracted to a woman?" I notice Joon twitch at that and wonder why. "What was she like?"

"She *is* a very bright, capable woman. We're still friends – and colleagues," Charlie says haughtily.

"She's a vicious, backstabbing bitch who would have eaten her own babies if she'd had any." Leo growls.

"Leo! Mind you, she's not fond of you either."

"My point. How could anyone miss my finer attributes?"

Charlie nuzzles Leo. I make a gagging noise at Joon, who gives a surprised bark of laughter.

"Thank you," Leo says.

"It was love at first sight," Charlie purrs.

"He stalked me," Leo counters.

"Did not!"

"Heckler."

"Well … okay. But my wife and I were separated. Though I had decided it was time to go back and give it another try – before I met Leo." Charlie gulps his beer – I find the blue staining his lips a bit disturbing. "It's his fault really. And it was a conference …. He was so …. I hadn't felt enthusiastic about my work, or anything, for a long time. And there was this big, chestnut-haired Russian with a booming voice speaking so movingly about a topic so close to my own …." Charlie ruffles Leo's hair.

"So he heckled me. He was so rude!"

"I felt … passionate … about his subject. What was it now? Something in social anthro-psychology, of course."

"Oh, very nice. You don't even remember! I was speaking, as it happens, on new trends in blended family structures and how they reflect our societal self-image – and expectations for a future," Leo says, enunciating carefully. He's clearly feeling the blue alcohol too.

"I do remember!"

"I remember this wee scrappy blond with a head of hair like a spotlight, shrieking at me that my definition of the word 'trend' was essentially flawed …."

"I did not shriek. I was at the back of the auditorium. I had to yell to be heard over your big bass drum," Charlie protests.

"You interrupted my lecture!"

"I apologized later!"

"You did. Then you followed me around for the rest of the conference, picking fights …."

"*And* buying you drinks!"

"Yes. To apologize for the fights, evidently. You had me so confused by the end of the session, I didn't know if I had a permanent hangover or if it was just you."

"I was – drawn to you. That felt ... unusual ... to me," Charlie says softly.

"It wasn't a hangover, as it happened; it was just you. I couldn't stop thinking about you afterward. And you were right about my use of the concept 'trend.' You challenged me." Leo cups Charlie's face affectionately with one big hand. I look at Joon but he's staring into his blue drink.

"I went home and ended the contract with my wife."

"And never told me about it!" The two seem to have forgotten their avid audience, which now includes most of the Townies drinking in the café.

"Oh, I'm sure. I can hear it now. Hello, Dr. V., I'm the one who ruined your lecture at the conference in December and, by the way, I'm single now? That would have been elegant."

"We might never have seen each other again. Is that worth worrying about how classy you sound?"

"Then we met on the old commuter train." Charlie faces his audience again, voice animated. "Of course it doesn't run anymore, but it connected this Town to four others until just a few years ago – and back then even more. By then I'd been obsessing about this big Russkie with the bad hair and heavenly voice for about six months."

"And I'd been ogling every blond in academia, trying to figure out what was missing. Got me in trouble a few times too ...." Leo chuckles.

"And then I fell on him."

"He fell on me. This willowy blond fell right in my lap. I was so happy I got lightheaded."

"You wouldn't let me up!"

"Not a chance. I wasn't going to let you go again. Ever."

"I didn't even know if he was interested in me, or men, or anything. All I knew is that suddenly I'm in the lap of this gigantic, gorgeous man who I've been dreaming about for months, and he has me by the waist, and it feels like he's going to do something drastic to me in public …."

"So he jumps up and yanks me off the train!"

"I had no clue where we were." Charlie chuckles.

"He drags me to this skanky flophouse – without even asking if I want to! *Ahem.* But I did want to."

"It was obvious. Trust me."

"Then he leaps on me, but he has absolutely no idea what to do …." Leo laughs helplessly, one hand over his eyes.

"Shut up! So I had no prior perv practice! Sue me."

"You did just fine. Once I took over."

"*Hmph.* You're the perv. Well, anyway. That's how we met." Charlie waves a hand vaguely in the air, adding, "I think it was chemistry. Also luck, love. Nature and nurture. You're the most exciting thing that's ever happened to me." He hugs Leo hard.

"And that's why his ex hates my guts," Leo brags, grinning.

"You could be less rude."

"She'd hate that more. She likes hating me. It's fun."

"Whatever. Now he's stuck with me."

"Yeah …! Come 'ere, I wanna be stuck with you again." Leo squeezes Charlie and leers.

"Eeh, *ii kagen ni shiro!* Knock it off! You two gotta pay for lunch just for making us sit through that!" I'm laughing and notice some of the other patrons laughing with me. With us. It's a good feeling. The Townies don't often give Warehouse folk the time of day, but the Uni Docs seem different, respected, though probably in large part for being generous with power from the windmills and their garden produce. I've never felt this comfortable in Town before. I'm aware there's an almost symbiotic relationship between the Town and the University – but the Warehouse folk aren't any part of that. We're suspect, if we're noticed at all. And I don't think the Warehouse folk are as transient as the Townies like to think. Where else is there to go, once we wander as far as the ocean? There's no turning back. We just didn't get here first. Neither did the Fisherfolk, come to that. They came after the Uni folk. And, as ever, those with the most resources are at the top of the heap ... or cliff, in this case.

"We've got to get directions for making this beer up at Uni," Joon says softly in my ear. I startle in surprise. I thought Joon was put off by the raucous direction of the conversation, but he's smiling at me warmly. His green eyes crinkle at the corners. His full lips are curved and a dimple shows in one cheek. I've never seen Joon look so ... relaxed, happy – sexy.

"Wow." I can't help staring. Joon clinks cups and we lock eyes.

"Shall we leave Big-Headed-San One and Two to their drinking stories and go have a party of our own?"

"Joon!"

Joon laughs, gulps the remainder of his ale, and grabs my hand, pulling me right out of my chair. "*Abayo*, suckers! We got memories of our own to make."

I hear calls of "*Kanpai!*" "*Salud!*" "*Saude!*" "*Sláinte!*" "*À votre!*" from the Townies, and a "*Budem zdorovy!*" from Leo, as Joon tows me out of the café. My head feels decidedly spinny as we hit the wind and sun outside the sheltered café. I wish we'd had something to eat with that blue drink. Even Tao hadn't been able to get it together enough to prepare a noon meal after the morning's ale sampling. Joon's unsteady on his feet as well. He lurches down the boardwalk and staggers up the beach, finally dragging me into a shaded alley between two shuttered stalls. I remember one of the stalls usually sells jellyfish fried with sea salt and kelp and my stomach rumbles. But Joon has other ideas. Once in the alley he pulls me to him before turning us to shove me up against the stall's wall.

"Itadakimasu! Thank you for this meal," Joon says fervently and covers my entire mouth with his full, soft lips, pressing me harder into the wall with his long body.

The heat, the alcohol, and something else explodes in my head. Suddenly there is nothing more important than feeling Joon's bare skin on my own. I pull frantically at his clothing, oblivious to our surroundings. Joon is already lost, raining kisses on my face, licking and biting his way down my neck, as if he'll eat me alive. Vaguely, I notice we're both sweating copiously; the alcohol seems to ooze through our pores, tingeing our skin blue. Both of us are soon shirtless, covered in slick blue sweat, our discarded clothing trampled into the dirt.

A voice disturbs us.

"Ahem."

I feel this isn't the first time it has spoken. I manage to tear my mind away from the awesome vortex that is Joon, looking blurrily out toward the entrance of the alley. The Market Master stands there, bulky body blocking the alleyway, expression grim.

"You're needed at the Café," he says. "Your friends ...."

Joon freezes. I scramble for our shirts, feeling exposed. We're caught like that fox in the old stories, when his tail pops out and gives away his disguise. *Shippo wo dasu.*

Both of us are shaking with emotion as we struggle to get the dusty shirts on over our damp skin. The Market Master just watches, clearing his throat when we lose focus. It's impossible to look directly at Joon without longing overwhelming me. Joon also keeps his face turned away.

I try to push past the Master, my head hanging and face burning with embarrassment, but the bigger man grabs my arm, effectively blocking Joon in the alley too.

"Go quietly," the man says. I'm startled into looking up into his face. His expression is more worried than angry.

"There is trouble starting. You need to take them home quickly," the Market Master says.

"*Hé?*" I start, but the man turns and leads the way back toward the waterfront. He talks as he walks.

"Fisherfolk have always been on good terms with the University," he says tensely. "But there are some who do not react well when their idols show themselves as human. You understand?"

"Ah, no?" I say candidly.

"You seem – not like the usual Warehouse punks." The man stops and turns to me. "Your – association – with the University has given you some standing in Town. Don't waste it. Get them out fast."

"Are they drunk?" I ask, knowing I'm in no shape for a brawl. Joon is following close behind and the very scent of him slows my footsteps. I desperately want to grab him and … uh-oh.

Joon is …!

I stop and try to grab Joon's arm as he passes me, but it's as if he's suddenly grown into a giant. For a brief moment, I think I'm seeing a rooftop-tall, naked, curvaceous woman – one also clearly *not* a woman – a goddess strutting past, dark blue skin scented with everything that has ever smelled warm and good in two centuries of life on the planet.

The Market Master and I both gape as Joon sways voluptuously ahead of us, the very air around him – her? – pulsating with a seductive call that tugs deep in my groin. I have to follow.

Joon glides into the Trash Café.

The café is a raucous mess. Tao Ownerson is standing on a table, cheeks flushed blue, shouting out an atonal drinking song, one arm holding up Charlie, who's waving his mug and one long leg in the air. Charlie's silky hair is loose about his face. On the ground there are four men sitting on a very drunk Leo, who's bellowing: "Gerooff ya barstids!" They're clearly having a fine time. But there's also a group of Townies huddled at the far end of the room who seem to have other thoughts. They're possibly drunk as well, but also angry and uncertain. They surge and fall back like garbage in the surf, undecided about whether to approach the others, or even start a fight. Several clench mugs and even chairs like weapons. But no one is brawling – yet. Maybe we can get Charlie and Leo out before it starts.

But the goddess that is Joon has gusted ahead of us into the room like a dry-season hurricane. The part of my brain still able to observe notes and analyzes Joon's entrance – but even more than usual, there appears to be two of me; one an animal sniffing at Joon's trail, the other cold and aloof, just watching to see what will happen next, ready to do whatever's needed to protect myself.

It takes a heartbeat for the impact of those ferocious pheromones to hit, but then the drunken ones stop in their tracks and faces begin turning toward Joon.

I hear the Market Master whisper, "Oh, *Frack*."

Joon smiles. An audible sigh whispers through the room. Tao drops Charlie in a boneless heap and leaps off the table, sinking adoringly to his knees at Joon's feet. Joon puts his hand on Tao's head and the animal in me growls, even as I coldly notice Joon's triumphant grin, aimed at the bewildered Charlie. The men sitting on Leo rise as one and tentatively step toward Joon, their drunken-laughing eyes going unfocused and strange. Leo staggers to his feet and helps Charlie down from the table. Unlike the others, both of them are clearly aware that something is off. Awareness of Joon's pheromones seems to be the key to resisting them. But the would-be brawlers along the back wall are shuffling over now, as if pulled against their will, still looking angry and confused.

Joon glances up from Tao's admiring eyes to see the wall of strangers staring at him with more predatory looks and the serene smile leaves his face.

It's the Market Master who has it together enough to yell, "Run!" and to block the door the moment I yank Joon outside. Charlie and Leo are still inside, and we hear Leo roar as a brawl starts in earnest around the doorway.

Joon is no longer the blue goddess. He's as frightened as I've ever seen him – and still it's all I can do to keep from dragging him back into that alley. Yet my awareness makes the difference. I know I don't have to respond.

As soon as we have some distance from the café, I grab Joon by the back of the neck and push him to the ground.

"Jae?" Joon pleads, pushing back up on his hands, but I just scoop up handfuls of dust and throw them over him. I start scrubbing at his exposed skin with the dirt, scraping off sweat and dampening his scent. Joon gets the idea and rolls. Then we jump up and run again.

Automatically, I head toward one of the bolt-holes leading to the tunnels under the Warehouse, but Joon stops abruptly and refuses to follow.

"No!" he gasps. "I won't. She'll lock me up. I won't!"

"We have to hide!" I insist, but Joon will have none of it, so we run uphill, toward Uni. Near the gate, we pause for breath. I scan behind us but there's no noise of pursuit.

"Where?" I pant. Joon sinks to the ground.

"Get it off, gotta get it off!" Joon scoops a handful of grit and rubs at his armpits and sides, sanding his skin so hard he draws blood. I stop him with a firm hand on his wrist.

"Charlie's place still has the air scrubbers!"

We stagger up and run again.

It's bad getting into the stormproof building outside the Uni walls. Many of the original residents have been moving into the Uni as library access and communication becomes more difficult; the irreplaceable systems are aging and breaking down. In the short time we've known Charlie and Leo, almost all the faculty have shifted behind Uni walls. Even Joon and I usually stay in the inner dorms now, sharing a suite with the researchers. But Charlie kept his apartment outside, though he doesn't often use it now. There are still a few others living in the building, mostly Townies who work for the University. A door-guard I've never seen before stares at Joon's filthy clothes with stony eyes and refuses us entry.

I show him my ID, but the guard ignores it. His eyes linger on Joon. He's getting that look.

I open the guard's gate without the man reacting at all. He starts to move toward Joon in slow motion, as if he can walk through walls. Joon is the guard's only focus. It's distastefully easy to walk up behind the man and smack the back of his head with his own chair. There's a horrible dull thunk that makes me cringe, but doesn't have much effect on the guard, who stumbles and shakes his head. He seems to become more aware for a brief moment, but then shuffles blindly on toward Joon.

I've run so hard – and perhaps am so pumped with adrenaline – that Joon's glamour is almost lost to me, along with the tipsiness from the blue beer. Then he scares me to death by approaching the guard instead of running away. I feel a zing like static electricity and see – for a bare moment – the blue goddess in a flash, and then the guard is on the ground, unconscious.

Snap!

"What did you do?" I gasp.

"I … I'm not sure. But … I wanna try that again! Maybe I don't have to run." Joon's grin is so feral I scramble back a few steps.

"Joonie, it's me," I say uncomfortably. But Joon just laughs and grabs my hand, and we use the last of our energy to heave ourselves up the stairs to Charlie's place.

"*Frack!*" We both collapse behind the door. The apartment is dusty and cold. Plastic sheets still hang between each room. It's ghostly and cheerless.

"I'll get the scrubbers on," I wheeze, clambering to my feet. But Joon grabs my hand.

"Water first! And see if there is food?" He begs, so I go through to the kitchen.

"Hey! It's stocked!"

Joon lurches up and we pour buckets of water from the cistern over our heads, into each other's mouths, then scrabble frantically through the jars cooling in the cistern, through the cupboards, jamming handfuls of stale algae chips, crumbling goat cheese, and feeding each other olives with oily fingers. We're street kids again, laughing at this sudden luxury of food and shelter.

It feels good.

"What happened back there?" We keep asking each other. "Did you see his face?" "Why didn't the Market Master react? Or Charlie? Or Leo!"

"Do you remember Charlie's zombie film?"

"Yeah! It was like that!"

"What about that nasty blue ale?"

"Yeah. That was some ... strong stuff." Joon isn't laughing anymore.

"It was more than strong. It was like the opposite of all that garlic and junk you've been eating. Like it had the opposite effect!"

"Yeah," Joon says. He grabs the water bucket and leaves the kitchen, water sloshing onto the floor.

"Where you going?" I call.

"Wash. Sleep." I watch him go. I'm still buzzing from our frantic run. In the sudden quiet I can finally think back to how I felt before the run. The alley in the heat. The sensation of Joon's hands on my body. Joon's lips. The seductive blue goddess, like an image from some submerged, ancestral memory. I shiver, dunk my whole head in the cistern, and go turn on the scrubbers.

• • •

A fluttering, ephemeral moment resonates throughout the over-stretched years.
Stuttered heartbeats, anticipation of ... a touch? A kiss?
A movement of air and water that warms and electrifies with hesitant certainty ....
A fragmentary shard of being, so brief, so alive.
So briefly alive.
So warmly wet and curious. So vital.
Not a dry feeling.
Breathless.

• • •

— SELECTION

I'm asleep when Joon slides into bed. I wake enough to cuddle up to Joon's back, and then wake up more when I realize he's naked. This is something new. My whole body tenses. We're lying on the futon, in a sleep pose we've been in a thousand times, spooned up for warmth, but I can hardly breathe. I freeze, not daring to move a muscle, but there's an obvious tension between us. Joon doesn't move either, but it's an unnatural stillness. I can feel a hum between our bodies.

Then, with a sigh, Joon gently, subtly, leans back against me. A zing shoots through me, as painful as it is exciting. My entire body quivers. Joon pushes back a little further, and I put my hands lightly on my friend's hips, then wriggle hastily out of my sleep shirt before pulling him back against me more roughly, skin sticking painfully to skin. I don't want to stop. I'm trembling. I feel Joon's excitement too (*electric blue*). I slide my hands over his back and feel him shiver. I rock him gently, stroking the smooth curves of his chest and sides. Joon is passive at first and I pull away just so I can breathe, but the air between us feels lonely and I lean into him again, skin to skin. Joon gasps. I can feel him shaking slightly. I lower my mouth to the side of his neck and nuzzle. His skin is salty and smooth. I lose myself, nibbling and sucking, sliding my hands over Joon's body until he starts to writhe.

It all feels so *fracking* good, but a far-off alarm bell is banging in my head. I slow down – with an effort. I try to let go, but Joon moans, sounding half-distressed, so I wrap my arms around him, soothing him with my hands, kissing the long ebony neck. I can't let this go too far. Oh, but I want to! It's so exciting I'll lose my mind if we don't stop.

"Holy *frackin'* gods," I moan into Joon's rough hair.

"Is that who's messin' with me?" Joon whispers, and giggles.

I cuddle Joon's warm body and try to calm down. He seems to accept that I'm dampening down the moment and rolls away from me.

I arrange myself by his side, heads together on the pillow, legs entwined, fingers laced.

"*Hai* …? You gonna leave me hanging?" Joon smirks.

"Oh frack, Joon. I'm so sorry. It's just, I don't want to hurt you – ever! Honestly, I just can't risk …." I'm suddenly, deeply horrified by the possibility of a pregnant Joon. But Joon reaches up and smooths the heavy damp hair back from my face.

"You wouldn't hurt me. I'm just teasing. I'm not even sure the girl bits work," he says sadly, craning to see down his length. "But we can still make each other feel good, yeh?

"Jae," he adds wistfully, "do you think of me as a boy or a girl, or …?"

I laugh with relief and let myself be soothed. "Joon is Joon," I say. "You're my best friend and you're so sexy I may die. I love you," I add shyly. Which seems to make it official. Though I notice Joon giving me one of his thoughtful looks. Maybe someday he'll tell me what that's about.

• • •

Several hours later we emerge from the bedroom, sweaty and naked, somewhat shaky in the knees and ravenously hungry. Joon rummages un-self-consciously through the kitchen. Charlie and Leo are back, in the adjoining room, looking hungover and bruised but rather pleased with themselves. Charlie's painting something red over abrasions on Leo's knuckles. I nod but otherwise try to ignore them. They watch us thoughtfully but don't interrupt our single-minded progress through the cupboards. I glance over just in time to see the moment when the ozone-fresh scent of our sweat reaches Leo's nose. He stiffens and sits upright, staring alertly, hungrily. Charlie moves closer, pulling Leo toward him.

"Look at me," Charlie croons, "smell me." Leo buries his face in the loose hair at Charlie's neck. He shudders and sighs, staying very still, face nestled in Charlie's long hair while Joon and I scuttle back toward our room with our spoils: baked algae-chips, a jug of greenhouse salsa, and a quart of goat milk. Charlie croons to Leo the whole time.

"Easy, big guy, it's Charlie here. Think about me. Charlie loves you. It's okay, you're all right, quiet down now. That's my love. That's a baby."

"Charlie, I'm not an idiot," I hear Leo grumble. I tap Joon's shoulder and we linger in the hallway, peeking back to see if it's safe. Clearly it's easier for Leo to resist Joon's pheromones now that he knows what's happening, but he never takes his face from Charlie's neck. Instead he starts kissing and nibbling, while his hands grope lower. Charlie slaps him away.

"*Hmm*, yes, and I've always wanted my partner turned on by drugs rather than me," Charlie says with sudden asperity. "Get stuffed."

"Sure," Leo says with a growl that sounds far too real, then goes for a full-body tackle. We leave them to it.

• • •

I stare wide-eyed at shadows on the ceiling, my love asleep by my side. I'm afraid. Now that I have something to lose I'm afraid of everything: of living, of dying, of change.
I'm no longer the only one I have to protect.
I lay sleepless, dry eyes gazing into dark;
a jellyfish drifting in the currents of time,
in control of nothing at all.

• • •

— MOTHER'S MOUTHPIECE

We avoid the Trash Café for a while. Tao Ownerson sends up a jug of the blue ale along with a note of apology from the Market Master, who writes that he organized the Town to help with repairs to the door and benches. The Town folk who started the fight have been publicly shamed. Everyone is being educated about resisting unexpected pheromones – and that awareness means self-control. The Market Master had noticed this too. No one wants bad feelings between the Town and University.

Eventually Charlie goes down on his own to thank Tao for the gift and give reassurances. Leo sinks the sealed jug of beer in the cistern where we all carefully avoid it. Charlie plans on testing its properties but leaves that for another time. I badly want to try it again but I'm sure Joon won't consider it. The vision of the blue goddess isn't mentioned between Joon and I.

But the day comes back to haunt us, in the form of the pale old woman who approached me once before in the Trash Café. This time she seeks out Joon. We've gone to the Marketplace together for the day; Charlie and Leo want to discuss a problem with the aquaculture tanks with the Fish Master, and Joon and I are along for the outing. I plan to approach Tao to ask about any other alcoholic drinks he might be developing, and Joon is just bored.

This time the old woman doesn't wait until Joon is alone, for which I'm later grateful. I'm determined that Joon won't go anywhere without me. I'm a little surprised that the old lady, with her soft white cheeks and pale, colorless eyes, doesn't seem able to approach Joon openly, the way she once did me. She sidles up in the street, the wind pushing at her wispy hair, and hisses a demand that Joon report to Mother, all without looking him in the face. On impulse, I grab her arm and the pale face turns to mine. I'm startled. She looks far older up close than I remembered, older than anyone I've ever seen in this Town. Her eyes and face are a webwork of crinkles. She seems very keen to avoid Joon, who reaches to pull my hand away from the thin arm – which sends the old woman skittering away like a beetle, shying from Joon's touch.

"It won't be soon!" I yell after the retreating figure, blowing away down the street like a rag. "She'll just have to wait!"

Joon claps a hand over my mouth. "What're you doing, *baka*!"

"You're not going without me!" I'm still hollering as Charlie and Leo emerge from the Fish Master's stall. Joon is standing in the street, hands now at his sides, looking shell-shocked and far more vulnerable than the tough fighter he'd been when we were at Warehouse together. Charlie immediately puts an arm around his shoulders and faces me like I'm the enemy.

"What's going on? This is no place to argue." He glances warningly back at the Fish Master, who's standing in his doorway, watching.

I could care less who hears. "Joon's been called," I say, my voice husky. "Mother wants him." Charlie flinches, and Joon's arm comes up to curve around his waist, returning the comforting touch.

"*Frack*. Not again," Charlie breathes.

"We'll all go," Leo says in his reassuring rumble, stepping in close as if his huge body can buffer us all. "Actually, no. Better Charlie stays here. I'll go with you boys. No one is going to keep Joon there against his will."

We all stare at Leo, who has clearly missed the point.

"We don't even know what she wants," Charlie says tiredly. "It was never clear to me last time why she wanted Jae at all. Was it to you, Jae?" The event seems to have disturbed Charlie's entire existence.

"Mother is in control," I shrug. "She requires us for a lot of things. Food, credits, information." Messing with people's minds – *shut up Jack* – Charlie knows that well enough. "Sometimes she just wants us near. If she doesn't want Joon to leave, he won't want to either."

Charlie looks horrified. Joon hangs his head.

"But, Jae," Joon says suddenly. "Seems like Mother's never made you do anything you didn't want to. Never."

"No," I say softly. "And she won't keep you."

"You can't be sure, *ne*?" Joon wants to believe me.

"I can." I'm firm. "No one else has to go with us. I'll make sure Joon comes back after she gets what she wants from him."

Charlie frowns. "Is that really fair to Joon? Why not just stay away? Didn't you say she kept that one girl locked up, when she went through the change?"

"Char-lie!" I shush him. "Not helping! Nothing's gonna happen to Joon while I'm with him." Joon doesn't seem entirely convinced, but he doesn't look as beaten either.

"I always thought I was the one looking after you," he says forlornly. "But you do have a knack for staying out of Mother's way."

"This is just wrong," Charlie says. "We're all going then. Leo, you'll come with us, yes?"

"I go. You stay." But even Leo doesn't look like he expects Charlie to back down.

"I don't think this is a good idea," I say, but let it drop. After all, how much worse can things get?

• • •

NonK Keywords: Jellyfish, Culinary uses of
(Adapted from: Wikipedia.org/Wiki Free/Jellyfish)

Jellyfish strips in soy sauce, *sesame oil and chili sauce appeal to most palates.*

Only scyphozoan *jellyfish belonging to the order Rhizostomeae are harvested for food;* *with about 12* of the 85 known species commonly used …. Rhopilema esculentum in China (海蜇 hǎizhē, meaning "sea sting") and Stomolophus meleagris (cannonball jellyfish) in the United States, are favored as typically larger and having more rigid bodies than other scyphozoans. Plus their toxins are mostly harmless to humans.

Traditional processing methods, carried out by Jellyfish Masters, involve a 20- to 40-day procedure in which the umbrella and oral arms are treated with a mixture of salt & alum and compressed … reducing liquidation and spoilage, making the jellyfish drier and crunchier.

Prepared Jellyfish retain 7–10% of their original, raw weight, resulting in about 94% water and 6% protein. Freshly processed jellyfish has a white, creamy color that turns yellowish during prolonged storage.

> Pre-New Millennium China, processed jellyfish was desalted by soaking in water overnight and eaten cooked or raw, often served shredded with a dressing of oil, soy sauce, vinegar, and sugar, or in a vegetable salad. In Japan, cured jellyfish were rinsed, cut into strips, and served with vinegar as appetizers.

Fisheries later harvested American cannonball jellyfish, Stomolophus meleagris, along the south Atlantic coast of the United States and in the Gulf of Mexico for export (until the entire ecology of the latter collapsed due to a series of underwater oil spills, circa 2010).

Jellyfish were also harvested for collagen and used for a variety of applications, including the treatment of symptoms associated with aging.

•••

— *LEO'S TURN: SECOND WAREHOUSE VISIT*

('Cause we didn't learn the first time)

Leo leads the four of them *(of us)* to the Warehouse, though he's least familiar with the place. Charlie insists on staying with Leo, and Jae won't let Joon go without him. Leo notices *(and I notice Leo noticing – though Leo is the one relating this particular memory of ours)* that Joon is trembling as they approach the building, which is set apart slightly from the rest of the rotting maze of storage buildings. When Mother calls, her boys go, but with Joon already into the change, proximity to *her* is clearly frightening. He and Jae have already told Leo how Mother treats that one kid everyone calls Madgirl.

The four of them step easily enough through the rotten hole in the metal that serves as a doorway, careful of the rusty edges. Everyone but Leo knows the huge dim space beyond. The darkness rustles with sleepers or those who can't sleep. There's always someone sheltering from the burning sun outside. It smells of dust and ancient cloth. Leo is surprised it doesn't smell like other rough shelters he's been in; it lacks the sour reek of garbage and urine. Somehow the space is dry and stale, but not dank. They walk into the darkness, Leo expecting to trip over something, or someone, with every step.

Leo knows from Charlie now about the underground tunnels starting on the far side of the big room, but the darkness is its own maze, and after only a moment he has no idea where the entrance is. He turns full circle, expecting to see light from the ripped doorway, but there is nothing. He reaches out and catches Charlie's sleeve – he hopes.

"Everyone stop!" Leo's voice booms out in the empty space and is lost, no echo returning. The air is muffled and still.

The almost subliminal rustling at the edges of the emptiness also stops. The darkness is listening to them now.

Leo takes Charlie's hand and grips it firmly. He reaches out with his other hand toward Jae and Joon, but finds only empty air.

"Joon?" He says quietly. There is no answer. *(He doesn't call out to me – to Jae. Does he know it's pointless?)* The rustling begins again.

Leo stands very still. He hears footsteps coming, lots of footsteps.

"*Dawn of the Dead,*" Charlie mutters and Leo feels Charlie's hand grip his own more tightly. That's reassuring. He'd had a brief moment of doubt, wondering if that *was* Charlie's hand.

"How'd you get a guide last time?" Leo whispers. He's sure they're surrounded by invisible people. His eyes have adjusted enough that he can distinguish empty darkness from moving darkness now, and most of it is moving. It seems a long moment before he hears Charlie's voice call out, strained and shrill.

"We're here to see *her*. We have a proposition for her. Please …."

Leo always thought of himself as a tough guy. He can reason himself out of most fears and has little patience with people who thrive on crises or are prone to panic over small things. But he feels the first flutters of fear as invisible hands reach out from the dark and latch on to his arms, shoulders, even his legs. Too many hands pull him and push and seem to have no bodies attached that he can clearly see. When Charlie's sweating hand is pulled from his, he cries out and starts to resist in earnest. It's like struggling against a tide, or a dream in which he can't make headway. But Charlie's voice calls out, this time without fear, just Leo's name and "it's okay," from the direction in which the hands are pulling him, so Leo lets the tide sweep him along until the darkness gives way to a pale battery-light and he can finally see.

What Leo sees are dozens of young people – boys? Girls? Most could be either or both – crowding dim corridors that can't be part of the Warehouse they saw from outside. It smells of damp cement. Are they underground now? He thinks he sees Charlie's pale hair up ahead and calls out again. This time the sound is muffled and constrained, damped down by the close walls and bodies that surround them. It's enough like the between-classes rush at University – as it used to be – that he manages to take a deep breath and regain his center somewhat, calm his racing pulse. They're only kids, the lost ones Charlie and he have come to save. But who will save us from them?

Leo goes with the flow, seeing mostly the backs of young heads; knotted hair, brushed hair, ragged clothes, few clothes, even some fancy suit jackets like the one they'd bought Jae. It's difficult to distinguish particulars; there's such a visual cacophony of textures. Dim dome lights flicker from recessed alcoves. But it's enough so Leo can see the shining eyes of the youngsters moving next to him. No faces are turned toward him, though hands still gently push and guide. No voices murmur. There's only the sound of feet shuffling and swishing cloth. All eyes are forward, shining, moving toward the end of the corridor and whatever waits beyond.

• • •

NonK Keyword: Intersex
(Quoted from Wiki Free /Intersex, n.d.)

*"**INTERSEXUALITY** as a term was adopted during the 20th century and applied to humans whose biological sex cannot be classified as clearly male or female. The term 'Intersex' was initially adopted by activists who criticized traditional medical approaches to sex assignment.*

*"**Research in the late 20th century** led to a growing medical consensus that diverse intersex physicalities are normal, though relatively rare, forms of human biology.*

*"**In some cultures, intersex people were included in larger 'third gender'** or gender-blending social roles along with other individuals. However, in later Westernized societies, intersex people have been expected to conform to either a female or a male gender role. Whether or not they were socially tolerated or accepted by any particular culture, the existence of intersexuality was known to many ancient and pre-modern cultures."*

NOTE: *Intersex references can be found in the Sumerian creation myths – specifically those surrounding the goddess Ishtar – from well over 4,000 years ago.*

DEFINITION: *"During the Victorian era, medical authors introduced the terms 'true hermaphrodite' for an individual who has both ovarian and testicular tissue,* *'male pseudo-hermaphrodite' for a person with testicular tissue, but either female or ambiguous sexual anatomy, and 'female pseudo-hermaphrodite' for a person with ovarian tissue, but either male or ambiguous sexual anatomy. The first call to replace the term 'hermaphrodite' with 'intersex' came from the British, circa 1940s."*

• • •

— THE UNDERGROUND

Leo flattens himself against the nearest wall as soon as the corridor empties into a larger space. It's dim, but feels big, echoing. The hands leave him as people scatter into the room. He scans the space for Charlie's light hair, thinks he sees him, and is about to push off the wall when he sees another head of blond hair in a different direction. He squints, waiting for some distinctive movement to give away Charlie's lithe form. People are still pouring in from the doorway, and perhaps from other hallways. The huge room is beginning to feel crowded. They seem to be deep below the hot surface. The air is cooler here, and Leo can detect motion in the air, a slight breeze blowing through.

He scans for Charlie impatiently. He barely registers that most of the people have stopped walking forward and are dropping to sit on the floor. All that matters is that he can finally see over the milling crowd. He spots half a dozen blond heads, though none as brilliant as Charlie's, and is about to edge along the wall for a new perspective, when he sees dreadlocks he's sure he recognizes as Joon's. Jae is nowhere in sight.

Leo fixes his eyes on the back of Joon's head and wades forward, stepping over and around bodies, eyes fixed so he won't lose Joon in the shifting mass. There are no complaints as he pushes past. Hands stroke and pat his legs, but no one restrains him. He can see something happening on the periphery of his vision. Arms are waving, seated figures rock side to side, and there is a pressure in his head that he impatiently brushes aside. He's determined not to lose Joon and almost cries out when another body blocks his view, moving away to reveal – no Joon. So Leo fixes his gaze on the spot where Joon was, and keeps moving forward. It's lighter now, as his eyes adjust. There's constant rustling and a humming begins, as annoying as a mosquito. The hum rises in pitch and intensity from all around the room, vibrating through his body, so startling he almost loses his focus ... instead he widens his eyes until they water and plows on.

When he reaches the spot where he saw Joon, Leo allows himself to stop and really look around.

The room is a sea of bodies. What must be hundreds of people are cross-legged or kneeling on the floor, facing what he assumes is the middle of the room. There are more young people in this place than he ever imagined. They're rocking and humming, the sound filling the room with a vibration that intensifies by the moment.

All Leo wants, all he can think about, is finding Charlie. His lover must be out there somewhere. But the humming distracts and fills his head. The rocking children seem ecstatic, moving together in rhythm, but the hum irritates him when he's already feeling frantic. Even the air of the place smells wrong, a sickly sugary smell. Leo has never liked sweets. He tries to brush the hum away from his thoughts, though he notes that there seems to be a locus, a place where the rocking bodies and the humming intensifies, toward the middle of the hall – if there can be a middle in a space so large he's lost any sense of where the walls are, or the exit.

Leo moves toward the locus and spots Joon again. Unlike the others, he's on his back, dark head resting in the lap of a pale boy who's certainly not Jae. His eyes are closed and his face utterly calm – even disengaged. Leo wades in and grabs Joon by the armpits, lifting him bodily away from the boy, and keeps walking for several strides before standing him upright, hands still firmly under his arms. Joon's eyes open and he looks at Leo with only mild interest.

Leo risks a glance back, but the pale boy is rocking and humming with the others. There's no complaint or pursuit.

"What's going on, Joon!" Leo growls, but Joon's arms are twining around his neck and the boy is pressing his body against Leo's. Leo holds him away and shakes him a little, then lets go with one hand and smacks Joon's face, hard.

Joon's head rocks and tears start from his eyes, but there's little comprehension in his expression. Again he pushes against Leo. Leo pulls him away by his hair and roars, "What. Is. Going. *On!*"

Joon slumps seductively onto his shoulder; the full lips caress Leo's ear.

"Mother wants us. Mother wants you," Joon says softly. Leo stands rigid while Joon's full mouth finds his. There are no pheromones forthcoming. As the soft lips move on his own, Leo knows he's completely in control, but it's still a little hard to push Joon away. He yanks the unresisting boy (*a "boy" who may be older than Leo*) up into a fireman's hold, slings him across his shoulders, and wades forward once again. Joon is unexpectedly light.

He giggles and strokes his free hand down Leo's back. Leo ignores him – with an effort.

Leo follows the hum. He keeps his eyes down to avoid stepping on bodies and lets his ears guide him. The hum intensifies when he moves in the direction the kneelers are facing; he can feel it in his bones and teeth. As he steps through and around the rocking bodies, he can't help seeing Charlie everywhere when he does look up. A jolt of adrenaline cramps his stomach every time he spots blond hair. Once he puts Joon down to yank a blond boy upright, but it's another blank-eyed kid with clinging hands, and he almost loses Joon to him before he gets them disentangled.

Leo wades on through the sea of bodies until he finally staggers out of the crowd and into a less busy central space.

The most intense hum is coming from a huge pale being reclining at its center – Charlie's Venus of Willendorf – and he's found Charlie.

Charlie is draped over the dais at the feet of the pale figure, his long bony frame in awkward contrast to all that billowing flesh. He isn't moving. Leo feels a surge of red-hot anger and suddenly it's as if he's standing in a tunnel of wind pushing against him. He staggers back. The hum is not meant for him. A wave of nause-ating anxiety washes over him; fear, rejection. It takes him a moment to understand these aren't his emotions. He steps forward again, Joon still draped across his shoulders, and the pressure goes up, shoving him back, accompanied by more waves of fear. The contented rocking and humming from the many bodies behind and around them falters.

Leo shivers and leans forward, struggling to take a step. Joon seems a heavier weight now and he's trying to get down. Leo swings him to his feet and sees comprehension in Joon's eyes. They turn together, and Leo can somehow feel Joon radiating unspoken waves of love and reassurance as the boy spreads his arms and steps forward, toward *her*. Leo takes a deep breath and tries to calm his own breathing and thoughts as he matches Joon, step for step. The wind and pressure subside; the hum starts up again, first from the bulky body and then from the others as they join the hum again. Leo is beside *her* now. Joon reaches out a hand to stroke Mother's obscuring black hair while Leo picks up Charlie's wrist, feeling for a pulse.

Charlie's arm falls bonelessly to the ground and Leo can't help another surge of anger, which is instantly answered by the quivering being beside him. He's beaten to his knees by an unseen weight. Joon takes up the hum, continues petting Mother, and the pressure subsides again. Charlie moves – he's alive! Leo pulls him into his lap and hugs him close, rocking silently with relief.

Minutes, or hours, pass while Leo rocks Charlie, loving him. Without realizing, he matches the rhythmic rocking throughout the hall. He finds he's leaning against *her* soft side. Joon also shifts closer, cuddling *her* like an overlarge infant. The anger and fear are gone; there is only the hum of Joon singing to Mother – and Mother singing to her brood, who respond by intensifying the hum. Leo feels amazingly calm and focused, despite the hive-like threat underlying the hum. He slides gently out from under Charlie and stands at *her* side opposite Joon. He reaches his hand up to brush the black, coiled hair away from her face. He looks into her strange, pale eyes, the same color as his beloved Charlie's – and yet so different. The eyes suddenly shift, looking directly into Leo's, and he recoils violently.

• • •

Snap

• • •

— VISIONS & REVISIONS

Leo feels happy. Just … happy. They are free, they are home, and nothing matters to him more than that. Everything is just *fine*.

Home is Charlie, who is soaking in an ancient cast-iron tub. When did they get that? It's brimming with steaming, scented water. The scent is something Leo can't quite place – antiseptic? Lilac? Charlie is humming. Leo loves everything about Charlie. But the humming bothers him, makes his head spin. In the steam his chest feels tight; breathless. But he's happy. Calm. Home. *Hummm.*

Charlie asks him something he doesn't quite hear. Then the words build shapes distinct from the buzzing, silhouettes of language appearing in his head.

"You looked into her eyes."

Leo has to think hard. Yes. *Her eyes* ….

"*Hmmm.* Describe her …?"

Leo catches at his thoughts as if they are chips of rock, no longer whole, but busted up pieces whirling in a windstorm. "Charlie. I'm … I'm almost sure she is, ah, male pseudo-hermaphrodite. She's … very female-looking, but ….

"She is beautiful, *hmmm?*"

"Not … quite. But her eyes …." Charlie's eyes, made wide and strange. Frightening. No. Frightened …?

"She *feels* beautiful," Charlie hums sorrowfully, but he beams at Leo. Leo is so happy that Charlie can finally talk to him about this.

"She looked ...," Leo pauses. It's very hard to keep the image of her face clear. "Her eyes were ... protuberant ... like that bulgy-eyed animal – from your movie – a rabbit?"

"*Hmmm?*"

"I think ... your goddess is ... afraid? She's ... different from our boys." As he talks, grabbing his fragmented thoughts, slotting them together into something more solid, Leo feels clearer, the fog less stifling. "She controls them, limits them. Maybe not with evil intent. But ... Charlie, perhaps she's not that intelligent? Perhaps she ...."

"Wrong." Charlie's voice, tuned to an uncomfortably high register. "She has an extraordinary mind; different, powerful." The hum increases in pitch until Leo bats it away, irritated. Doesn't Charlie know he can't *think* with all this noise?

"I'll tell her ...."

"*Hmmm.* You wish to talk?" Charlie surges up out of the tub, steam running off him like water, and Leo finds himself facing the soap-slick body of the man of his dreams. It's so beautiful and appropriate – after that descent into hell – he laughs with the sheer joy of being this man's lover.

"Charlie, you better get back in there or come out and face the consequences." Leo knows he's leering.

Charlie sits back down quickly. Oddly, the water doesn't slosh. The steam rolling off it hides him completely. Leo is offended.

"Oi!"

"Talk first, *hmmm?*" The steam hums in Charlie's voice. "What will you say to her?"

"I'll tell her we can help. That we'd welcome her at Uni. That we can teach the kids how to survive better ...."

Encouraging humming from Charlie's direction.

"And if she comes to us, the others will follow, no?" Leo's smug. This is a good plan. "All our problems solved. If you can help control her pheromones – which seem much stronger, more selective, than Joon's – then maybe we can get to the bottom of that setup at the Warehouse."

"You would question her mysteries, little man?"

"This from the foremost geneticist at the University," Leo laughs. He's so happy. "What's wrong with exploding a few myths? Do you want us to live in caves, dancing around a fire and hitting the ground with clubs?"

"*Hmmm.*" Leo hears his beloved's voice echoing as though down a long tunnel. "There are worse ways to exist."

"Charlie, I don't think she's as threatening as we feared. The theory that she may be a member of a short-lived sub-species that caretakes a longer-lived one makes sense. Think about it; male pseudo-hermaphrodites don't tend toward longevity. The internalized male gonadal tissue tends to go cancerous around the fourth decade ...."

"Enough!" Charlie's voice is sharp, and still irritatingly un-Charlie-like. "What makes you think there could be anyone like *her?*"

Leo is surprised. "What do you mean? She's from a long line of women just like her. She's the last. She said .... *Umh.* I don't remember, but ... didn't Jae tell us that? The one who should have replaced her is that Madgirl. Remember? But the girl is dysfunctional. I'm not sure

106

what our people can do for her, but your Venus doesn't have much hope ...."

"How do you know all this!" Someone is shouting and Leo is confused. Why does that sound like his own voice? He wants to say, Charlie! Calm down. What's the matter? But he's getting angry.

"You get the answers to everything that easily? Exactly the answers you expect? How do you know she's telling the truth? How is she talking to you? How do you know *any* of this?"

Why is Leo the one yelling these words? His head hurts. Humming fills the steamy room like angry bees.

"What the hell?"

But Charlie, his beloved Charlie, is out of the tub, his body as insubstantial as the steam, yet he's shoving Leo, pushing him out of the room. A door slams in Leo's face and he hears something scrabbling behind it. Someone is blocking him out. Not Charlie?

"Charlie! What the *frack* are you doing?" Leo pounds on the door, and the more he pounds, the angrier he gets. From euphoric, his mood flicks over to total fury. A pulse in his head begins to throb and he sees everything through a white fog. It doesn't occur to him that he's acting unusually, or that he isn't standing in their apartment, as he should have been. From a cool hallway deep underground, Leo attacks a too-solid wall with his fists and feet, growling and spitting, thudding into the wall again and again. He's sure he hears someone, his beloved Charlie, crouched on the other side of a door, weeping.

— WHAT JOON SAW

Joon has been observing Leo for a while now. He watches him crouch in a hewn rock tunnel, rougher and deeper than the smoother maze adjacent to the Warehouse. Joon's been sent, of course. *She* wants this violent man as far from her as possible. Joon is relieved Mother has mostly ignored him in the pulsing chaos of Leo's anger. In some strange way he knows he's being protected by the rage Leo projects.

Leo crouches by the tunnel wall, rocking back and forth, sucking on his knuckles, which are torn and bleeding. His eyes are as vague and strange as that time in the kitchen and Joon approaches with caution, Charlie's trank gun in hand.

"Leo?" he says softly, and Leo looks up at him; his eyes widen and he grins happily. "Charlie!" he cries, and grabs Joon, hugging him close, pinning Joon's gun arm to his side. But Leo only sits down hard on the stone floor and cuddles Joon in his lap, swaying and crooning and petting his hair. After a tense moment, Joon relaxes and goes with the flow.

• • •

Joon is certain he can't drag an unconscious Leo from the tunnels, so he takes a chance and – trank gun ready – coaxes Leo into moving forward. He goes along with Leo's fantasy – pretends he's Charlie – and uses a combination of endearments, "come on, love," and taunts, "Hey, idiot, get those feet moving!" It seems to work. Leo beams and follows wherever Joon leads. The hard part is keeping far enough ahead so Leo's groping hands can't slow them down, but not so far that Leo squats on the floor with a hurt look and starts rocking again. It's slow and exhausting, but once they reach the higher levels, it gets easier. Joon notices Leo's expression becoming less vacuous, and he grabs at Joon less often. As they emerge into the dim lights of the upper tunnels, Leo starts to stride in earnest. Joon has to sprint to keep up when the ripped opening becomes visible and Leo suddenly dashes for the light.

Once outside, Leo whirls around to face Joon. His face is pale and shocked. There are black circles under his eyes and gritty stubble already showing on his chin and cheeks.

"But ... where's Charlie?!" he shouts, grabbing Joon by his upper arms. Joon can only stare. The gentle Leo is gone again and rage is building behind the dark brown eyes. It's Jae, stepping out through the ripped doorway into the bright glare of the sun, who takes the gun from Joon's hand and shoots, thunking a trank into Leo's upper arm. Together the two boys catch and help the heavier man down onto the hot ground.

• • •

It's empowering to look at the world from behind Leo's eyes.
However upset or disturbed,
his thoughts are firmly well intentioned,
not like my own malicious, insecure self-questioning
(of which I tire).
Charlie's point of view is more motherly, anxious,
but sexy too, when his thoughts turn to Leo.
Joon's mind is my own, violent, yet sweeter,
and seemingly unaware of me.
I could chase Joon's inner thoughts like butterflies
and never catch them, never know him deeply.
But he is beautiful ....

• • •

Charlie tells me privately that we probably ought to have woken Leo for the trip back, so he could feel the transition for himself, a tie-in to something real. It's taken him days to believe he's truly back at the University. But we were all so tired, and it was easier not to fight anymore, but to just slog along with the unconscious man dragging behind on a homemade litter of scavenged rubbish. Easier to pull that massive body along than to wake the man and deal with the emotional upset that *she* evidently caused.

Everyone is back safely, but it hardly feels like a step forward. It's Charlie who finally convinces us we brought back something important.

"Tell me again," he keeps saying to Leo, who's pinching himself and glaring at Charlie suspiciously. "What exactly did you and the – your dream Charlie – say to each other? Do you think she was communicating to us through this ... *ah* ... vision?"

It's tough on Leo, but he tries. He doesn't leave out his feeling of joy when he thought Charlie was talking to him again, or his candid pleasure in his lover's naked (if hallucinatory) body. Charlie allows him to sidetrack into that, but not for long.

"Okay, so let's shelve the idea that Mother may be a short-lived caretaker of a longer-lived group of individuals. That may be true, but we've no way of proving it yet. For now let's try to sort out which parts of this 'memory' are hallucination, her input, or just your preconceived expectations. You say you went into the caverns with a crowd of Warehouse kids, but Leo, after the entrance I saw no one but my guide on the way to Mother's chambers, and later I saw only you …." Charlie's voice trails off at the tragic expression on Leo's face.

"So – when I saw you with Mother?"

"Leo," Charlie whispers, "I wanted to tell you. The same thing happened last time …. She gets in my head so fast, and so … deep. I'm sorry. I just couldn't talk about it …."

Leo tries to laugh. His eyes are red-rimmed. "Well, you always were more bi than me …." Charlie smacks his arm. "*Ow*! No, I mean it, Charlie. You've always liked women – except for me. I've never been interested in women that way at all. Ever. So it's not surprising that something about me put her off. Call it testosterone poisoning. I'm a little outside of her experience, I guess."

"Bit of an extreme reaction?" Charlie wants to lighten the mood. "Hey! You saying you're more manly than me?"

"Come on, love. Who has to shave three times a day? *Ah*. And you don't know how scared and angry I was. I was searching for you everywhere. She even threw Joon at me." Leo looks apologetically at me. I shrug. Mother is a force of nature. Like an earthquake – or the wind.

"But I was totally focused on finding you. Then when I finally saw you …*frack*! I thought you were dead, Charlie. I thought she'd killed you. I was ready to tear her apart."

Charlie touches Leo's arm. "If she's as empathic as I think she is, having you come at her that full of rage …."

"I probably scared her into creating that hallucination … but Charlie, there was a moment. I calmed down when I realized you were alive. I think I really did look into her eyes."

"I was never able to," Charlie says, shuddering.

"So that whole conversation I imagined having with you … was something I got from her?"

"Well, that's the theory," Charlie says. "But it sure is hard to separate the millet from the weevils."

"The what from the who?" Joon comes into the room, looking exhausted. He shoots me a look that means he's going to make me give up secrets. "How's our maniac?"

"Beaten," Leo says, leaning back against the rolled futon. "It's abundantly clear I'm nothing but a liability in that setting. Joon, I can't thank you enough …."

"Just did," Joon says firmly. "Besides, *Onisan*, it was fun leading you by the nose for a change!"

"Sure it was," Leo says tiredly. Then to the room in general, "So, what now?"

"You need to hear what Jae found," Joon says, looking over his shoulder at me. I've been listening to the men hash through their Warehouse experience without comment, but Joon has been insistent that I tell them where I was when all this was going on. It feels wrong. Or maybe just weird. I'm going to have to do something, take action on something I'm not certain of yet. Give up secrets to get answers. But more than anything, I need to know *(who I am, what I am)*. So I've agreed to tell. Some things.

"A complication." Joon adds, "Or maybe one of Charlie's chances for change, *ne*?"

"The dual opportunities and disasters of Yin and Yang," Leo sighs. "Bring it on. But, Charlie?" He adds, "We will discuss this later, yes?"

"*Hai*," Charlie says, hesitantly sitting on the floor next to Leo, who scoops the fairer man to his side with one arm and holds him there tightly. Charlie's face and body visibly relax.

• • •

— *WHAT JAE SAW*

I'd gone along to the Warehouse willingly enough when Mother called Joon. We always do. I thought the summons might be a chance to see Madgirl again; hoping she – or what she's become – can help explain what's happening to the others, and help Charlie make them less vulnerable. The first time I'd tried to talk to her – just after I met Charlie and Leo – I'd seen enough to know I had to try again. So, after the second call from Mother, I broke away as soon as we all entered the Warehouse, with the same destination in mind. I knew my way around; I wasn't afraid of Mother. I was careful never to be a threat. She knew this and tended to let me come and go at will. *(Must I tell it all?)*

I felt bad for what happened to Charlie – what was probably happening again – but didn't think I could explain it without making Charlie feel worse. One's interactions with Mother have a lot to do with one's own mindset. I wasn't afraid for Joon; I knew he could look after himself and no one was going to lock Joon away while I was around. The others weren't in any real danger, I felt, not yet, and they could keep Mother distracted while I visited Madgirl again. I wasn't even afraid for myself, really, unless I thought about turning into something like Madgirl. She repelled me, but I was also intrigued, revolted. I dunno. But there was something important to be learned from her. I was sure of it.

I stood outside Madgirl's room. I'd been inside only once. It was a cave really, the door a miniature version of the front entrance to the Warehouse, a giant rip, torn through rusted metal. It seemed open to the hallway, but I knew she couldn't leave, because Mother wouldn't let her. Mother had let us believe Madgirl was flawed, a danger to herself and others – and couldn't be let free. I'd seen for myself the quaking thing she'd become and the aggression her presence was met with outside. I'd be hiding too, if it were me. But I was starting to understand that none of this was Madgirl's fault, and to believe I never would be like her. Charlie and his knowledge of the culture of the outside world, and our inner DNA, were making me more secure – and more curious. Sometimes I felt like I'd known all this before and just had to relearn it; but then couldn't define what "it" was. Maybe Madgirl had some answers.

I ran a hand along the edge of the ripped metal and cut myself immediately. I popped the bleeding finger into my mouth and heard a low laugh from inside. The short hairs on my neck prickled and I had to remind myself that any strong emotion like fear, in this place, was likely to draw Mother's attention. I calmed my breathing and started to hum. It was a bouncy little tune: "Here we go 'round the mulberry bush ...." I hoped Madgirl was listening. I stepped through the rip. Mother's restrictions evidently didn't extend to anyone going in. I just hoped I'd be able to get out again.

It was too dark. I stood inside the doorway, waiting for my eyes to adjust. No one should have to be closed in this dimness for long. I was just beginning to adjust to the low light when a shape leaped at me from the shadows. I jerked back violently.

"POP! GOES THE WEASEL!" Madgirl shouted in my face and then she was gone, back into the shadows.

I laughed uneasily and she laughed back at me from the darkness.

"Do you need anything?" I asked, at a loss, wondering who took care of her. Her home didn't smell like an animal's cave, but what I could see was untidy, with a plastic tarp shredded across the floor and clothing strewn about. There were no obvious tables or chairs. I could see a clay pot on its side, and a water skin. So she was being fed at least.

"Whatchu got?" The voice was mocking. She sounded sane enough. Mostly.

I pulled some candy from my pocket and it was snatched away as soon as I opened my hand. Madgirl crouched on the floor, sucking on the sweet millet-paper wrapper around the candied cannonball jellyfish I'd scored. I got a chance to look at her. She'd changed.

There was no sign of the gigantic breasts or hips she'd had after the change hit, nor was she the violent animal that she'd seemed on my first visit. She was a waif dressed in a rag. Visibly female, from the few curves that protruded, but she was pale and dirty, with long matted hair and some kind of markings on her skin – possibly acne or fungus. She moved well, and her eyes didn't look mad, if that meant anything. She crouched on the floor and sucked and chewed on the candy with an expression of sheer bliss. It made me want to give her more, but my pockets were empty now.

"Know you," she said unexpectedly, when the candy was gone and the millet paper too.

"Do you?" I said. "I remember you too." I sat on the ground and we were silent for a few moments.

"Mother didn't send you," she said. A statement.

"No. I want …." What did I want? "Do you want out?"

"I'd do anything," she said simply, scooching over to sit beside me. She looked straight into my eyes. "Anything."

"What are you?" I managed, swallowing hard, thinking of Joon and where he might be right now. When Madgirl had first been brought to this cave – through

115

the riot of scary, unmindful Townies outside – she clearly hadn't had the self-control Joon now did over his phero-mones. Though even then neither I nor the other Ware-house residents had been affected.

The girl made a disgusted face. "Ain't it obvious? I'm Mother's replacement." She looked down and picked at her rag of a tunic. "But she don't want me." Her voice was a whisper. When she looked up I could see the shine of tears in her eyes.

"Why does she need a replacement?" I asked, startled.

The girl wrinkled her nose. "It's her time. She's old."

I couldn't fathom what she meant. Mother had been around longer than I'd been at Warehouse, but it never occurred to me that she'd be ending any time soon. "I don't understand."

"No," and the girl looked – patronizing? Sympathetic? What was that look? "You wouldn't."

"Are you like me?" I almost whispered. It was always so hard to know what the right questions were.

"There is NO ONE like MEEEEEEE!" Madgirl shouted, jumping up and spinning around and off into the darkness.

"Wait. Can I come see you again? Can we talk again?"

Her voice issued from every corner of the cave. "A' course. You gonna get me out. I wanna see the light again," her voice whispered softly, next to my ear, then harshly, from farther off, "but you'll have to take care of Mother ...."

• • •

It was Madgirl who broke my fingers, I finally tell Char-lie and Leo; it happened just before I'd started living with them. That's one of the reasons I hadn't been in a

116

hurry to go back to Warehouse later. That time I'd been lurking outside her room, trying to decide how to talk to her, when I was jumped by two Warehouse kids after me for outing Joon in the Trash Café. They'd punched me a good one and I'd fallen back into Madgirl's den. Like a shark – another long-lost species – aggravated by the scent of blood, she'd gone for me when I was down. In the end, it was the other two who'd pulled me out, half-conscious and bleeding. They were shocked by what they'd started and afraid of what Mother would do. So they got me out of there and took me to the dock-side clinic where the Market Guard picked me up. Later on Joon beat up the two who'd saved me, I tell Charlie and Leo wryly, while Joon grins nastily.

"*Na*, but I'm not scared of Madgirl anymore," I say candidly. "And I'm not really worried about being like her either. She said it herself, there's no one quite like her. And I'm thinking – really – that no one should be shut up like that, especially someone like her, even if she's a bit ... mad. I think maybe we should go get her out, *eh*?"

The three of them (*my family*) stare at me in shock.

"Come on! The Warehouse kids might even follow her back here to Uni – she's mother's replacement! Anyone up for another trip to hell?" Finally. *The conduct of a thousand years to be determined in an hour*. What have I been so afraid of all this time?

• • •

I remember it all. All but what I imagine to be so.
The difference is inconsequential.

• • •

Chapter 3
RESCUING MADGIRL & THE GREENHOUSE

"Leo, you'll stay here and look after Joon. Jae comes with me." Charlie throws me a bag, which I stack in the corner with the other supplies we're gathering from Uni stores. Leo grabs his partner by the arm and yanks him around.

"Are you nuts? I don't want you anywhere near that evil … spider!"

"We will avoid Mother. Believe me. I need Jae since he has the connection to Madgirl. We'll be fine. You … just check in with Joon now and then so he won't feel abandoned. You don't have to babysit him. Just make sure he doesn't decide to follow us to the Warehouse or something stupid."

"Avoid!" Leo seems at a loss for words. He changes tactics. "Charlie, you know I can't be alone with Joon," he starts, but Charlie stops him with a tired wave of his hand. His shoulders slump, and the lines of his face show his exhaustion.

"You're a liability, and Joon is afraid. Find a way to deal with it, Leo. You're a big boy; you haven't had a bad reaction to him in months. You can handle it. Just be smart." And Charlie glares at him.

"Smart is to run screaming, not babysit a man-eater," Leo grumbles. "Or go looking for one …." But he's already given in – to that argument at least. It's true he hasn't lost self-control since the first time, when Joon had him pinned in the kitchen. He didn't even twitch during the brawl in the Trash Café, but then he was pumped up with adrenaline and totally focused on Charlie. But he's consciously aware of his reactions now; surely he can protect himself – protect them both.

I'm pretty sure Leo is more concerned about Charlie and *her*. But I keep my thoughts to myself.

"How do we keep in touch with you?"

"Don't know," Charlie says curtly. "The University's server is still functioning – just. So we might be able to post on NonK."

"Oh, yes. That's helpful. I'm sure NonK will tell me where to dig up your moldering remains if Mother deep-sixes you." Leo frowns at me. He's made it clear he thinks freeing Madgirl is a bad idea. But he hasn't come up with another way to lure the Warehouse kids to Uni, and nothing is more important to him than that.

Well. Charlie is more important.

"*Frack*, Leo, thanks for that image. It's your theory that Mother's dying anyway."

"We're all dying," Leo says irritably and leaves the room. I follow.

We find Joon in the kitchen.

Leo stomps in, ready for an argument, but Joon looks so desolate it's impossible for Leo to pick a fight. I start grabbing supplies from the cupboards. I want plenty to eat on this trip since we won't be coming back right away.

"So ... I guess we're being abandoned for an unspecified amount of time." Leo gives me a dirty look but addresses Joon. "Anything you've been wanting to do?"

Joon brightens. "I'd like to see the big greenhouses?"

"Really? *Um*, okay. So let's pack a picnic or ... hey, why don't we camp in the habitat tonight? I've gone with Charlie a few times, and it's just magic. Sometimes you can see the stars at night. If we're near the scrubbers, maybe we could build a fire .... I'll check with maintenance."

I leave Leo and Joon discussing their plan and go help Charlie load our gear into a small solar tractor. It'll carry our stuff, but is dependent on the sun to recharge. Cloud cover is never predictable, so I've loaded an extra battery. After we free Madgirl, Charlie wants to keep going to the wind farm as a neutral place to assess and figure out our next steps, hence all the food.

Back outside, Leo sneaks up behind Charlie and wraps his arms around him. "You sure about this? You look tired, love."

"I'm sure," Charlie snaps. But he does look on the verge of tears. Leo kisses his neck and steps back. Charlie doesn't turn his head. He keeps loading gear, face turned away.

"Three days," Leo says. "If I don't hear from you by then, I'm coming after you."

"Stoopid," Charlie whispers. "We'll be fine."

The camp-out idea seems to have lost its appeal. Leo and Joon watch us as we do a last check of the tractor. But I have no doubt Leo will follow through, if only to keep his mind off Charlie.

"Come on, lad," he says gruffly to Joon. "Let's see if we can survive without them." He gives Charlie's back a long look, nods to me, then puts his arm across Joon's shoulders and steers him back toward the building. "Let's raid the kitchen."

I run after them and silently hand Leo a fresh packet of millet cakes and salted jellyfish wrapped in nori. I add a flask of *ume* wine with whole rare plums floating in it like yellow sea creatures. I nicked that from the Uni kitchens weeks ago. I slip a second, squashy packet into Joon's hands. It holds his favorite candied cannonball jellies. I really hate those things, but Joon adores them. Then they turn away, walk back through the main Uni doors, and are gone.

$$• • •$$

It's time.

$$• • •$$

— THIRD TIME LUCKY

Charlie goes over the plan in his head. Grab Madgirl; bring her to the tractor, which he and Jae will hide near the Warehouse; then head away from Town. He's not keen on bringing a potential empath that can manipulate others' emotions – and who also has powerfully unstable pheromones – back to the University. So he's decided to take her farther south of Town and inland up to the University's windmill farm. He and Jae will hang there for a couple days until they decide whether it's safe to bring her in or better to cut her free. If she wants out, then they'll try to give her that. Afterward, she might have to survive on her own. Charlie plans to provide her with the pheromone blocker he's been developing for

Joon. For safety, he and Jae will each carry a small spray bottle of blocker hidden in their pockets. Charlie also has the trank gun. He knows they might not be able to work with her. Charlie hasn't discussed this with Leo. It was so hard to leave him behind, but Leo is just too susceptible.

If things go well, and she's willing to cooperate – and not too strong – Charlie intends to bring her in. He sincerely hopes she can help attract the Warehouse kids to Uni.

Charlie and Leo have already spoken to the aging Chancellor (*though it's clear they'll go through with this anyway*). Leo talked with him about how the student body had slowly disappeared, along with many of his faculty. Charlie even reminded him what losing his own son had meant to the Chancellor. Together they convinced their reluctant senior, at least for now, that the University needed young people and had to become more inclusive to survive.

Charlie firmly believes that while the Chancellor may have quailed inwardly at the idea of hordes of uneducated, unwashed Warehouse kids infiltrating his hallowed halls, he is also an intelligent man who has seen his share of change in seven decades of life. During his tenure the University often worked with the Town in times of crisis. It currently provides the Town's power and much of the Market's fresh produce in return for fish – jellyfish now – and labor. Charlie and Leo somehow convinced the Chancellor that while the Warehouse kids aren't skilled Townies, they have the ability to learn. At this point, the Uni has very little to lose. New life could bring fresh hope. After that it was a matter of a single meeting to get the Deans onboard, with Leo politicking among them. None but the most bitter wanted the University to turn into a dead museum.

Charlie left a letter for Leo with the Chancellor, a plan for the future – just in case he and Jae don't return.

The sky is darkening, so Charlie looks for a spot to hide the tractor, so they can camp overnight. The Warehouse isn't far now, but the tractor is slow, and Charlie wants to face the Warehouse in the early light, when he's fresh. Jae's made it clear he doesn't want to go in after dark either since Mother's curfew is strict, and it would be pointless to get a beating when they don't have to.

Jae builds a fire and they warm up a stir-fry of kelp and jellyfish to have with several carafes of millet beer. Charlie figured they might as well bring luxuries since they don't have to carry it themselves. He's exhausted, as much from his own trepidation as the killer schedule he's been on for months now. He feels driven to find answers, as if time is running out. He can feel time slipping away, yet there's no pending crisis that he can anticipate enough to guard against. He just has an insubstantial feeling that he needs to hurry.

"Hope Joon and Leo are okay," he mutters, only vaguely aware he's worried about them. There is so much to worry about; he hardly knows what to choose first. His mind feels overfull.

"Why?" Jae sounds startled.

Charlie speaks without thinking, a worry he's barely acknowledged bubbling up. "Jae ... what would you do if Joon didn't have *your* child? I mean, assuming he can get pregnant?"

Jae looks surprised and doesn't answer at once.

"But ... it would be Joon's child."

"Would you be able to love it?"

"I love Joon. How could I not love Joon's child?"

124

"Would you be jealous?"

"Why? If I want a child, I'll have one too!" And Jae beams delightedly, as if he's just discovered something new and fun. But for an instant Charlie sees something else, something tired and old and sad, peering out through the happy mask.

"What if you're not his kid's father?" Charlie asks abruptly.

Jae just stares as if he's never heard the word "father" before.

Wrong question. Maybe. But if so, then why does Jae look like he's rehearsed his expressions? Something's off. Charlie feels sad. Some days it's clear that Jae's just so full of shit. Charlie decides to focus on the task ahead of them.

• • •

Time swirls, beating against the tides.
I watch from somewhere up among the bones of the ceiling.
I can't be here, can't have seen what happens next,
but I remember it, like an old story told too often,
or maybe like a movie about poison dart frogs ....

• • •

— IN THE GREENHOUSE

Leo watches Joon as they step into the habitat and sees his expression change to something very un-Joonish. Joon is too cool for surprise, too jaded for newness. But Leo observes a look of such vulnerability and awe that he looks around the place with new eyes himself. It's green. It's damp and lush. The unceasing wind is quieted. There's water everywhere; condensed on the leaves, dripping from the dome. Water rushes by next to their feet in open rivulets and streams. The air smells of damp leaves and clean dirt. There are sweet fragrances too, overhung by rich loam. The place holds a luscious promise of fresh food and air and clean water. There are no barren horizons here, just leafy jungle. No derelict buildings, no decay except for plants growing back into rich soil. No broken and eternally waiting human-made ruins. Everything is alive. Joon's face runs with sweat like tears, eyes wide, lips parted. Leo is deeply moved. He takes Joon's hand in his and leads him deeper into the garden. They pretend this is the real world.

There is a freshwater pond, lost in the green. It's emerald with algae where collection chutes exit, but the center is clear. Real fish, with fins and bones and brains, dart in tiny schools in the shallows. Joon is half-naked already, poised over the shallows, entranced by the fish. There's a gigantic splash, soaking him, and he startles back. Leo erupts from the middle of the pond, his unkempt hair gone seal-slick to his head, the huge brown eyes wild as a sea creature. They stare at one another. Joon continues to strip down. He walks slowly into the water. He can't swim. It doesn't occur to him to care.

Water laps at Joon's toes like cool tongues, rising quickly to his thighs. The chill line continues up his body to his chest. He shivers at the contact. Underneath, his limbs are cool and not quite his own. He is less weighty here. With the hot, ever-present wind shut out, the leafy world is stillness and anticipation. His mind feels lighter, dizzy. He keeps going.

Joon is underwater, eyes wide and staring, tentacle-dreads floating wide. A huge blurry shape shoots toward him, another pair of eyes, another water being. Hands slide up his body to his armpits and heave. Both bodies rush to the surface, billowing and light in the water's embrace. Joon is reborn, head emerging, gasping. Leo holds his face up out of the water, laughing. Joon's body drifts against Leo and the contact is so soft and silky Joon pulls Leo close for a moment, chest to chest – a moment of weightless skin on skin – before Leo sets him on his feet in the shallows and dives away with another huge splash. Joon is left alone, damp and just a little chilly in the tropical air, craving that incredible lightness once more.

When Leo finally swims back, Joon is sitting in the muddy edge of the pond, hands deep in the silt, bottom and legs in the water. He beckons to Leo, then grabs his face between muddy fingers and pulls him close. The seal head is in his hands, almond-brown eyes wide. Joon presses his lips to the colder ones.

"I love Charlie. I always will." Leo pulls away, mud streaking his face like scars, but Joon catches his arm. Leo floats. Joon sits in the mud.

"I love Jae," he says. "I hate him too, sometimes."

"That's probably about right," Leo mutters.

"Charlie likes women." Joon is searching for the right words. "Mother knows …."

Leo is still. This is something he can't talk about. Something Charlie can't talk to him about.

"I'm old," Leo says instead. "You're just …. There's so much I don't understand about you. You look …."

Joon snorts. "You *know* this! I've been young for a *very* long time. Longer than you've been old. But not … like Jae." His expression becomes terribly sad.

"How old …?" Leo starts, but Joon puts a hand over his mouth.

"I can make a child," Joon whispers. "Charlie would like that. He wants to look after children, yes?"

"He can't ...," Leo says, pulling Joon's hand away but keeping hold of his wrist.

"Neither can Mother. Neither one. Both sterile now."

Leo mentally files that away for later.

"You and Jae ...."

"Jae doesn't want another Jae in the world!" Joon explodes. "He says if he did, he'd have one with himself."

"Can he do that?" Leo's tone is bemused.

"Shove it up his own twat? Probably. If anyone can."

"You sound bitter."

"Jae will make a great father – because he doesn't want to be alone. But he won't make a baby with me." Joon *is* bitter. "But he'll love it for my sake. Just in case there's no me around in his future." And this time Joon's eyes look so very old.

"I don't understand."

Joon sighs. "You always say children are a kind of immortality. I can offer you that. It's what Charlie wants. Do you?"

"I don't .... Gods. Yes. I do. I really do."

"You don't like women. Well lucky you. I'm the compromise, *ne*? A man with a womb."

"For *frack* sakes, Joon," Leo pulls away, into deeper water. Joon follows, floundering. The bigger man reaches out to hold him at the surface. Their bodies float together. Joon's eyes half-close from the sensation of Leo's warm body sliding against him in the cool arms of the water.

"I want you," Joon murmurs, winding his legs around the big torso, arms clinging close. Silky skin on skin. Weightless. "Do you want to live forever?"

Finally. The right question.

— EMPTY WAREHOUSE

In the end, we decide to sacrifice Charlie to Mother after all, as a distraction, while I sneak Madgirl out of the Warehouse. Charlie isn't happy about it, though I point out Madgirl is unlikely to leave with anyone but me. We both know it could backfire, with Charlie's presence announcing our intent rather than masking it.

But a revolted kind of fascination seems to draw Charlie. He keeps asking whether it's possible to just hold a simple conversation with Mother, as if that might keep him from being caught in her vortex. I think he knows he's lying to himself, but having a plan seems to be the only thing that lets him walk across the warehouse and down that long tunnel. But in the end, all our plans are dust. Mother's not there. The tunnels are empty. The entire Warehouse is apparently devoid of life.

I run, feet thudding in the strange silence, Charlie close behind. The ripped door to Madgirl's prison stands as seemingly open as ever, but the inside smells rank and stale this time. I'm so sure it's been long empty that I'm already turning back when I hear a shuffling in the corner. Then Madgirl is on me, suddenly and with force. Her eyes are staring and her sweat stinks. She hits me hard in the chest and slaps at my face with half-closed fists. Her breath stinks of bile and worse. She's weak. I throw her off easily and she crouches on the floor, snarling. She's nothing like the lucid woman from before. Her eyes are shadowed and she looks half-starved. She tenses to spring again, but then Charlie's there with the trank gun.

• • •

"Was it just a dream? Was any of it real?" Charlie's having trouble with this latest turn of events. We're walking beside the tractor, using the remote to steer. We're almost to the Wind Station. The girl is asleep in the cab, her hands and feet bound. Even in sleep she twitches and growls. She hardly seems human.

"Where could they all have gone? There were at least a hundred people living there. Weren't there?" Charlie seems anxious.

"We got Madgirl. Let's keep to the plan," I mutter. But I'm also confused, my stomach queasy with unease.

We stop the tractor at the base of Windy Hill. Windmills stretch out for miles across the rolling hilltops, some moving, some broken and crumbling, a few laid out on the ground like fallen trees. The tall blades are lovely, sweeping through a cloudless sky otherwise devoid of life. The station itself is out of sight over the crest.

"Jae, just tell me that Mother exists and I'll take your word for it. Right now it feels like she's just a dream."

(Isn't everything?)

"She must have sensed something happening; probably dug in deeper somewhere. She's all about hiding, about waiting; remember?"

"Yes, but ... what'll we do if we can't find the kids?"

"They have to eat," I say grimly. I'm bone tired. I have that weird feeling this has all happened before somehow. Déjà vu.

"I don't think this one has eaten in a while." Charlie bends over the unconscious figure. Madgirl's eyes are moving like crazy behind her lids. "Odd. Subjects aren't supposed to go into REM sleep when they're tranked with this mix," he says, and puts his hand to the pulse in her neck. The girl's eyes fly open, huge and blue. Like Mother's. Her teeth snap and he withdraws his hand quickly.

"Whoa! Easy, girl. I was only saying we'll feed you when we reach the station." He looks at me, but I ignore them both, trudging forward, facing the windmills, looking for the shelter of the station. Then food, the universal common denominator. That should be a good place to start.

• • •

— BACK AT THE GREENHOUSE

Nothing's working. What started out as intensely sensual has become a comedy of errors. Joon is tense, and nothing feels right. Even their wet skin sticks together painfully.

"*Shimatta*, Leo, STOP." Joon's getting mad, even though he knows it isn't helping.

"Look, Joon, clearly this just wasn't meant to be." Leo tries to pull Joon in for a comforting hug, but Joon smacks his hand away.

Leo starts to laugh. Joon is offended.

"Joon, this is just wrong," Leo says. "No! I don't mean that way. We've burned that bridge, gods help us. Let's try something else. I remember, long ago, one of the crèche parents telling us kids that, once upon a time, when a fertile woman was ready, a fertile man could practically look at her and she'd get pregnant. What I mean is, it might not be necessary to go all the way."

Joon brightens a bit.

"Come on," Leo rumbles up at him. "Let's just have a bit of a play and see how things go. She also said it worked best when both partners were satisfied …."

Leo pulls Joon down beside him and they face each other, giggling nervously. Leo strokes Joon's face, and then reaches lower. Soon the breathless giggles turn to sighs and moans. Neither of them notice when the hot wind blows in.

•••

— TILTING WINDMILLS

I shut the tractor down in front of the wind farm station, a square shack just over a crest with a spectacular view of ongoing rolling hills studded with white towers and fallen giants. The door is ajar, so I call out to see if the Station Master is in, but there's no response. Those of the great windmills that are working hum dramatically overhead, though a number are motionless. The few still functioning are more than enough for the needs of the University and the Town. Once the farm served a much larger population.

"Let's get her some water." I turn around in time to see Charlie fumbling with Madgirl's restraints.

"What're you doing?" I leap toward the wagon, grabbing Charlie's hand. Madgirl's eyes are wide and feral. She looks like she'll really bite if released.

"How do we feed her if she's all tied up?" Charlie says calmly, pushing my hand away.

"No! You don't know what she'll do! We gotta go slow."

"She already doesn't trust us," Charlie says. He looks down at Madgirl and must have been startled enough by her expression that he stops untying her. Her eyes are wide and shocked, glued to his.

"Just give her water for now," I tell him. But when I put the goatskin bag of water to her lips, the liquid dribbles out of her mouth as she stares, unblinking, into Charlie's face. Charlie steps back.

"*Shimatta!*" I swear. "That was good water too. Aren't you thirsty then?"

Madgirl's eyes shift to my face and she lunges toward the water bag, clamping on to the end and sucking hard. "That's it," I say. "And there's food when you're ready."

Madgirl nods her head violently, still sucking on the bottle.

"Okay then. If I untie your hands, will you be good and just eat your food?"

Madgirl nods once, less enthusiastically.

"Here." Charlie hands me some kelp-flour bread with crushed, sautéed roaches and lentils baked in. "Journey-bread. It's a whole meal in itself."

I untie Madgirl's hands but leave her feet bound. She's wary but subdued. She keeps staring at Charlie's blue eyes.

"He's a looker, our Charlie, isn't he?" I chuckle. Madgirl *humphs* irritably, but when he hands her a chunk of the loaf, she snatches it from his hand and stuffs more than half in her mouth, groaning.

"Poor thing …," Charlie starts, but I ignore him and sit right in front of Madgirl, blocking her view of him.

"First off, we aren't keeping you prisoner."

Madgirl snorts and stuffs more bread in her mouth.

"We aren't. We're keeping you tied to protect us from you."

Madgirl grins around an enormous mouthful.

"We came to get you out of there. We will let you go, if you promise to stay calm."

She nods.

"Also!" I hold up my hand. "You need to choose. You can come back to the University with us, or you can go your own way. If you do join us, we hope the other Warehouse kids will come too."

Madgirl stops chewing. She seemed to curl in on herself.

"You can lead them," Charlie offers softy, stepping forward to join the conversation. I shoot him an anxious glance. This could go wrong so easily.

"They need you," Charlie continues. "It's your place to be leader now, yes?"

Madgirl swallows hard. "Mother has – finished?"

Charlie frowns.

Why does this feel dangerous?

"This isn't about Mother," he says carefully. "It's about you, and your siblings from the Warehouse, coming to University to work with us, to share our resources. To learn."

Madgirl picks at her bread. "Mother is – dead?"

"No! At least, not that we know of."

Madgirl starts chewing again, her eyes on Charlie. Her fawning expression makes my skin shiver.

"Mother is in control. She keeps them safe."

"It's time for everyone to come out from underground. No one is safe anymore. You all need to learn things that can help you survive. We can help. But it's time to stop hiding."

"*Hmm.*" Madgirl chews her bread. Charlie shoots me a look that says we should back off for a bit and let that sink in.

"I'll answer any questions you care to ask," Charlie says, turning away. "When you're ready."

I start unloading our overnight gear. I watch but don't interfere when Charlie releases Madgirl's legs. She's subdued around him, though she continues to watch his every move as we use the remaining daylight setting up for another night out.

• • •

It's the dark of early morning when I hear something moving in the cabin. We're sleeping on the Station floor, leaving the bed free for the Station Master, in case he returns. I left the tractor, with its University insignia, in plain sight out front, so no one will be startled by our presence.

At first I think the Station Master has come back. But something's creeping across the floor toward Charlie. The hair prickles on my neck. It's the girl.

"That's my friend you're stalking." I say quietly, getting my feet under me in case I have to move fast. Madgirl freezes. Neither of us says anything for a long moment.

"Move away from him," I say firmly, and Madgirl sits up. She giggles breathlessly. "What do you want?" Maybe we should have asked her that sooner. I'm relieved to hear Charlie stirring.

"His eyes …." Madgirl hisses, scooching back quickly as Charlie sits up.

"What's up?"

"I think she's disturbed by your eyes," I say to Charlie without taking my own eyes off the girl. "He isn't Mother, you know," I tell the girl, "even if his eyes look like hers."

"Do they?" Charlie's startled.

The first light of dawn glows just over the hills. The windows frame the highest windmills speeding up as the upper air heats. The hum of the huge blades rises to a slightly shriller pitch. The noise adds to the tension building in the room.

"No wonder the Station Master doesn't stay here," Charlie mutters and gets up. He shuffles to the window.

"They look like how I'd imagine bird wings," he says dreamily, "beautiful."

Madgirl's eyes track his every move.

"Birds didn't twirl their wings like that," I say grumpily. "They flapped them like ... well, like roaches do when they fly."

"Roaches hum when they fly," Charlie protests. "Or more of a whirr, really."

Madgirl is staring at me now.

"You knew birds?" she hisses furiously.

I don't answer. Charlie turns from the window and she cringes back.

"Oh, for ...." Her cowering submission is irritating. "Now look. Why don't you give us a real name to call you by, and let's talk about what we can do for you at Uni. I don't know where your Warehouse folk have gone, but there was no one there when we rescued you. Do you know?"

Madgirl slowly shakes her head.

"Well, if we're lucky, maybe they'll make their way to Uni on their own."

"Hungry," Madgirl says.

"You're hungry? We have some more bread, and I think Jae brought some of that candy you like."

"They're hungry. Mother's failing."

Charlie looks at her sympathetically. "I thought Mother might be approaching senescence." Madgirl looks confused. "Aging, coming to the end of her life."

"It's her time," the girl says fiercely. "But she doesn't want me." She clenches her hands.

"To take her place?" Charlie says softly. "I don't think she'll have much to say about that at Uni. We want you. We need you. We'd like you to lead the others."

For a bare moment Madgirl's face blazes with excitement, then just as quickly her expression blanks to neutral.

"Who controls? You?" She stares into Charlie's eyes again, a moth to flame. She can't seem to look away when they make eye contact.

"Stupid girl." I'm sick of this whole performance. "How many times do I have to say it? He's not Mother! He can't control your feelings. He can't read your mind. He just has blue eyes!"

That's my second mistake. I should have known it was too late for Madgirl. She'd been neglected, shut up in the dark, and left alone for far too long. She reacts to my confession of our powerlessness like a praying mantis going for the kill, one minute motionless, the next whirling into action. She scoops a chair from the table and throws it at my head. I duck and the chair smashes into the wall, but she's already going for Charlie. He yells as she comes at him. She flinches, but in a moment has the bedclothes over his head, hiding the disturbing blue eyes. I scramble toward them as she thuds Charlie's head against the windowsill once and he goes down. By then I'm on her, but somehow, from somewhere, she pulls out Charlie's trank gun and shoots me straight in the chest. I drop like a rock beside Charlie. Madgirl bolts for the door as the world goes dark.

— *THE WAREHOUSE KIDS*

Leo's skin is all gooseflesh. Joon's body is a warm damp lump cuddled up along one side. They seem to be lying on wet moss, but there is a persistent breeze drying his back. He wonders sleepily if his clothes are nearby, but the wind keeps at him until he wakes up more fully. There's something wrong. There shouldn't be a dry wind in here, not in the greenhouse habitat. Joon stirs and Leo sits up quickly. The abrupt motion must have set off Joon's internal alarm because he's suddenly alert and crouching beside Leo. The greenery around them sways and sighs, shifting side to side. With each sweep it exposes, then covers, staring pairs of green eyes. The children from the Warehouse have found food.

•••

— *DULL HEADS AMONG WINDY SPACES*

When I open my aching eyes, the morning light outside has already faded to twilight. The industrious hum of the windmills competes with a buzzing in my head. If I'd realized this is how it felt, I never would have tranked Leo that time ….

Ah! I struggle into a sitting position, stomach roiling with nausea, and see Charlie against the wall by the window, watching me. There's blood in the fair hair, and Charlie doesn't seem in any hurry to get up.

"Y'okay?" I rasp.

"Yeah. Don't wanna move. Headache."

"*Hai*. Dun matter anyway. Take your time."

"*Hmm*. She took the tractor."

"*Shimatta*."

"Yeah."

We're silent for a while. Everything hurts. I eventually struggle to my feet, but my heart pounds and I feel dizzy and sick.

"Any water left?"

"Pack. By the food safe."

"She leave food?"

"Dunno."

The pack is gone and I swear again. I stagger to the door and fling it open. On the ground where the tractor used to be are scattered boxes and bags. She threw them all off the seats before driving off. I hope she crashes.

There's no food, but the first aid kit is there. Why would she throw that away? I scoop it up and carry it to Charlie. I rummage and find some of his precious store of aspirin. So many medicines are long gone, but the Uni once had plenty of aspirin and doled it out sparingly. Charlie told me once that it's probably all placebos now, but I don't remind him of that and he licks up the powder I pour from the packet into his hand. I think he hurts too much to even grimace at the sour taste. I find a cabbage in the Station Master's food safe and cut it in half, using it as a cool compress for Charlie's head. The other half I cut up into a pot with some wizened onions and brackish water I find in the cistern.

"He wasn't living too well out here, I guess," I mutter. From the relative crispness of the cabbage though, the Station Master can't have been gone too long.

At least there's plenty of power. The oven battery is in good condition, and I use the stored wind power to heat my makeshift soup. Hopefully the heat will kill any bugs in that questionable-looking water.

I feed it to Charlie slowly, and after a while his color seems better, less pale – if possible.

"Better," he sighs. "What do we do now?"

"Go back. Nothing else to do."

"Guess so. But sleep first. It's a long walk."

"Yeah." I'm worried about Charlie. I can't tell if the man is most hurt by the blow to the head or his disappointment in our failure. "We'll find another way," I say, for comfort, but without conviction. I feel pretty bad too. "We don't need her."

"Maybe not," Charlie says. "But doesn't it always feel like … no matter what we do … it's always too little, too late?"

"I've felt that way for very a long time," I tell him. "But then I met you and Leo, and no matter what, you keep trying. So many things I wouldn't have thought of, so many new ways of looking at the world and our place in it. You give me hope. And I needed hope so badly, Charlie."

"Ah." Charlie smiles at me. "Well, then. Let's hope we can find something more to eat tomorrow, because this soup tastes like crap."

I laugh weakly. "Okay." And we rest for the night, leaving the next day to fend for itself.

•••

The Empath's thoughts demand attention.
She is not in my head. I do not see through her eyes,
nor would I wish to.
She is … too much and too many for any long lifetime
of memories.

But a moment so personal, so linked to who we are,
broadcast in brief fragments, is laid down in this body's memory.
There for us all to access.
Just a shadow of a memory of the end of a goddess.

• • •

— MOTHER ABOVE GROUND

Perhaps it's normal for children to grow up and leave home, but when they take her child, the one she's hidden away to keep safe, she follows. As any mother would. That's how Mother finds the windmills. She's been outside so seldom since her youth, her temperament and training gearing her toward hiding and safety. Toward the dark. But she dares the outdoors for her girl. The sun scorches and blinds her and the wind bruises her pale skin. Her bare feet blister and her heavy body screams from fear and the labor of walking in the open. She keeps her eyes down, scenting the trail. When the wheel tracks lead her to the white towers, she stumbles inside the first one she comes to and hides in the dark until she stops shaking. Her big quivering body takes too long to recover, she hides too long, and the girl is gone when she emerges. She can smell it. But she steps outside just as the morning light crests the hills. The wind comes with the light, turning the great white blades so that when she finally looks up into the sky it's full of whirling, sparkling wings – angel wings – the moving air vibrating with a hum of happiness she hasn't felt in her four decades of life underground. She broadcasts her joy out into the world.

— UNIFICATION

Of course Madgirl beat us back; she had the tractor. Charlie and I must have been a day or even two behind her since we were hurting for a while and then on foot. Why didn't Leo come find us? First thing, we grab food in the cafeteria, which is where we hear the news. When we burst into the main lecture hall, I wonder for an instant whether we got turned around somehow and ended up back at the Warehouse. Warehouse folk fill the hall, sitting on tables, chairs, the floor. But there is also the Chancellor standing on the dais with Leo and Joon (*my Joon!*), and there's Madgirl, facing off with them, hands on hips, as if she's the head of an army. I look around and judge that the army is at ease, however. They look more entertained than threatening. Charlie and I make our way to the dais.

Leo's talking excitedly at Madgirl while the Chancellor looks on benevolently. Madgirl seems to be ignoring Leo and watching Joon.

I bound up to the dais first, only partly to put myself between Madgirl and Joon. Being near Madgirl feels dangerous – but I can't resist grabbing Joon around the waist and pulling him close. Joon's face lights up and he kisses me enthusiastically. Leo and Charlie meet more sedately, but after letting Charlie greet the Chancellor, Leo envelops Charlie in a hug. Madgirl watches it all, a few steps removed from the group, her expression sardonic.

Charlie and I finally face her, with some caution, and she nods her head mockingly.

"My kidnappers! Plans for your strange new world are ... progressing."

My eyes widen. Madgirl is far more articulate than even the first day we met. All outward signs of the snarling demon from the wind farm have vanished. I hope.

"You seem … well," Charlie says carefully.

"And you seem deceived." Madgirl's shark grin shows all her teeth. She jerks her head toward Joon.

Charlie looks from Leo to Joon, swallows hard, and ignores her. He turns to the Chancellor. "I take it you have met the new leader of the Warehouse students."

The Chancellor seems surprised enough it's clear he's not yet made that connection to the ragged female in front of him.

Leo takes Charlie's lead. "Our hope is that, *ah* …."

"Madgirl," the girl says, grinning even wider.

"Madgirl … will help our new students adjust and be their go-between." Leo stares meaningfully at the Chancellor. "She has the most influence over the Warehouse group. We need her goodwill and abilities."

The Chancellor *harrumphs*, but nods his head slightly to Madgirl.

"We welcome all who promote learning," the Chancellor says, but I detect a touch of distaste to his mouth when he addresses Madgirl. She isn't likely to miss that.

"I'll be a part of what's to come," Madgirl says, "but you'll want to look to your own house first," and she jerks her chin again at Joon, then steps off the dais, and is immediately surrounded by the Warehouse kids, all wanting to touch her hair and pet her hands. They crowd around her like ants on a sugar beet. The Chancellor watches with even more evident distaste.

"I don't suppose we could manage without …," he starts.

"No," Leo says firmly. Charlie clutches at his arm, staring after Madgirl. The Chancellor *harrumphs* again before turning to address the hall.

"Gentlemen," he says loudly, cutting across the buzz of voices. Charlie flinches at the unusual, exclusively male, form of address, and glances up at Leo, but his partner is avidly watching the crowd.

"Again, welcome to the University. We are delighted to have everyone here, and are looking forward to a unique and productive collaboration. I trust everyone has settled into their dorms now, and shortly there will be refreshments in the cafeteria. After that, I'll ask you all to report to the main hall again, where we'll break into small groups for placement testing. This is not difficult. It's merely to help us measure your potential in the various fields of study which we cover here.

"We will also be sorting everyone into work shifts for the cafeteria, labs, hydroponic gardens, and aquaculture farm. Each shift will be assigned a faculty member who'll be in charge of helping organize schedules, and who can answer questions. Until orientation is complete, I ask that no one access the library or NonK, and the labs are out of bounds unless a faculty member is present. Thank you for your attention, and again, welcome to this exciting new collaboration. I look forward to your progress."

Leo claps, which starts Joon clapping, and then a more hesitant Charlie. But the rest of the young people just turn toward Madgirl, who doesn't move for an uncomfortably long moment. When she does put her hands together, just once, staring directly at the Chancellor, there is an explosion of sound from the Warehouse kids. It's clear that a challenge has been given. A sign of more conflict to come, no doubt. I sigh. For now,

I want my own people somewhere private so we can talk – and rest. Charlie is still looking white and drawn, even for him.

Leo and Charlie are very quiet as we leave the hall, all heading toward Charlie's outside apartment, or so I hope. But Leo stops before the Uni's big front entrance and suggests food at the cafeteria before leaving the building, so we end up there instead. Charlie mutters that he doesn't think he can ever catch up after days of eating nothing but cabbage. The others ask for our story, and he asks me to describe the conflict at the wind farm. But despite Charlie's injury, Leo just doesn't want to believe that Madgirl could be a problem. In the end we agree to wait and see. There isn't much else we can do, as Leo points out.

Joon and I sit together, Joon half in my lap. But Charlie remains quiet and reserved. I catch him watching Leo with a lost expression on his face, and Leo seems to be avoiding direct eye contact with him.

I pick up some pickled jellyfish from the common platter and feed some to Joon. Joon sucks on my finger for a moment, holding my wrist and grinning. I can't wait to get home.

Leo coughs, and says, lightly, "Get a room, boys," before turning his attention to Charlie, who has his head down, studying his food.

"I was so worried when Madgirl showed up alone. But it seems like she'll work with the Chancellor. Thank goodness you two are back safe."

"Why don't you tell us what's been going on here?" Charlie says.

The big man flushes red.

"Guys?" I say. "What's up?"

"What's up is that Madgirl is possibly psychic, or at least highly empathic. So what did she mean about looking to our own house, Leo?" Charlie says stonily.

Leo doesn't say anything.

"Joon, I want you to come to the lab for a pregnancy test," Charlie says sharply, still watching Leo.

Joon's eyes widen. "Charlie," he says breathlessly, and no one could miss the hopeful excitement in his voice. Even Charlie's expression softens somewhat. I lean back hard against the bench seat, feeling like someone dropped a rock into my stomach.

"Charlie, let's go now!" Joon says, grabbing my suddenly limp hand. The usually cool and taciturn Joon is babbling into the grim silence around the table. It's so unlike Joon we all watch him, fascinated.

"If I am, you will all have to help me with it! Charlie, you can be Mom too, *neh*? Or whatever you call it. Godmom? Grandmom? Megamom?" Joon giggles breathlessly. "Jae will make a great Dad, won't you Jae? – Jae?" Joon looks at me so anxiously that I force a smile, and tuck my arm around him again. But it's Charlie he's mainly watching, and his smile soon fades. The fair man looks ill.

"Creating life. *Frack*, Joon. Making a new life now, in this ...." My voice fades. "But I love you, Joonie, of course I'll help any way I can – you might just have to be a bit patient with me." I rub my eyes. I feel so tired.

I raise my head to see an expression on Leo's face I can't really interpret. It's sympathetic, but also – triumphant? Leo obviously shares Joon's feelings about a new life.

"And you?" I ask Leo, my voice husky.

"I want this for Charlie and me as much as anything," Leo replies. "It would validate Charlie's theories, and make all of this," and he waves his hand, encompassing the whole University, "worthwhile. Even now, even in these frightening times. New life brings hope." And Leo's deep voice rings like a bell.

I stare at him in amazement. There is an answering excitement in Joon's face, and something close to resignation in Charlie's, though the man's eyes are tense and pained.

"All right." I draw a trembling breath. "Let's see if we can make a life worth living then." And I find I can laugh a little, if a bit breathlessly, through the flutter of panic in my chest. I put my hand on Charlie's across the table and Joon takes Leo's to create a circle. Leo puts his arm around an unresponsive Charlie and hauls him close. "Guess we're in this together." I feel sick and hypocritical. Charlie nods, but he looks bad. "A family?" My voice cracks.

"*Stoopid*," Joon squeezes my hand softly, but I can't take in my lover's happy excitement, and I avert my eyes.

• • •

— MOTHER MEETS THE EARTH PEOPLE

Mother stays. She's found her patch of heaven. It's clear to her now that her daughter left under her own control, so there is no imperative to follow. She sits out under the sky, face turned upward, watching the wings of angels, until the sun scorches her and she retreats into the shade of the tower, breasts pressed to the stone, her body vibrating with the hum of the blades. She carried no food or water with her, and feels no need to fetch any. Mother is dying, and she's happy.

When the small, earth-colored people approach her with gifts of food, Mother ignores them. She's done protecting children. But when they bring water so clear it seems like a piece of the sky itself, she lets them bathe her face and wet her lips. When they put ants and small beetles into her mouth, she lets them, because it makes the wizened faces smile. The flavors are sharp and acid and she rolls them on her tongue, then accepts a drink. The sky-water tastes of copper and iron and all her missed summer days. The Earth People collect the tears that run from her eyes with tiny dirt-colored rags.

• • •

— BABY MAYBE

We leave the cafeteria in silence. Charlie and Leo walk ahead quickly. Joon looks after them thoughtfully and slows his pace. He reaches for my hand but I just can't. I wriggle away and stick my hands in my pockets. Joon flushes and smacks my arm hard.

"Don't do this. Don't ruin this."

I stop walking but stare at the floor, anything to avoid looking at him.

"Do you always have to be in control?" Joon is royally pissed off. I'm silent. "You do, don't you, *kono yarou!*

"Why is it Mother never controlled *you*, Jae?" Joon suddenly says. I look at him finally, surprised by the topic shift. He's facing me down with both fists on his hips. "You've never once been part of the family rituals. How is that? When I think about it, you don't go anywhere near Mother, do you? Isn't that why the bigger guys always beat you? That I get, but why does *she* allow you to be so – separate?"

"What're you talking about?" I mumble. "And anyway, *she* never goes near Madgirl either."

"Madgirl is maybe her daughter, *neh*? Does that make you equal? How do you rate that?"

"I went near Mother in the beginning," I say weakly. "She didn't like it."

"*Oushikuso*. When Mother doesn't like something, it goes away. Permanently."

I'm silent.

"I don't know you," Joon says sadly. "You're this innocent thing with old eyes. I had this weird thought when we came to get you at the Warehouse that time, that you were the one making Mother follow your lead .... Isn't that stupid?" And Joon glares at me. "Tell me that's stupid, *ne*?"

"*Bakayaro*." I smile, relieved. "And anyway, isn't getting to know each other part of loving? I know you ...." And I finally take Joon's hand in mine. "I love the parts of you I know, and the parts that surprise me. Do you love me?"

"I love you, *baka*." Joon's expression is bleak. "But I don't always trust you."

I rock back, surprised and hurt.

"I would die for you," Joon says. "But you wouldn't. You wouldn't die for anyone. Would you?"

"I would not *die* for anyone!" I know my voice is hard. This matters. "And neither should you. Aren't you the one who taught us all to be tough? I do love you, Joon, so damn much. But I want to live with you, not die for you." I try to calm down. "I want to live with you forever."

"Then accept the idea of me having a baby," Joon says. "If not now, soon. A baby that is part of me. Leo helped me understand that children allow us to live on after we die ...."

"*Stop it!*" I bellow. "You. Will. Not. Die. I won't allow it!"

Joon stares at me. "It's not exactly up to you, Jae."

"Don't you get it? What have you got to offer a kid except the guilt of bringing it into this world? Just having a baby could kill you! Isn't it better to focus on yourself, on living, on staying alive?! Isn't that hard enough? What if you die in childbirth – where does that leave me?"

"Everything dies – except maybe you, Jae? You think you never gonna die? Well. Maybe not. But I'm gonna make the most of my time. I'm gonna create a new life. I can't even begin to explain to you how magic, how important, that feels to me. I don't want to live forever. I just want to live."

My face feels frozen in a tragic mask. I can't control this rictus of grief. I sink down to my knees in the middle of the wide hallway, head bowed. "I'm afraid," I gasp, and Joon runs his fingers through my hair and pulls me close. I wrap my arms around his waist and hold on, drowning in Joon.

"I'm so afraid, Joonie. I don't want to be afraid for a baby too. Don't leave me alone."

"'The only certainty is change,'" Joon quotes something I'm sure he got from Leo. "But while I live, I'll love you."

"You'll love a baby more," I whisper, but he doesn't seem to hear.

• • •

— PRACTICAL WARFARE

We eventually wander outside the Uni walls, back to Charlie's private apartment in the stormproof building nearby. I feel ill and empty. Nothing is going right. I need to be alone. To think. But I can't bring myself to walk away from Joon just now. I almost bump into him when he stops abruptly, just inside the apartment door, finger to his lips. Loud voices are coming from Charlie's room.

Joon gestures for me to follow and we step silently out onto the balcony that circles the complexes' interior courtyard. We peer into their bedroom just in time to see Charlie slap Leo hard across the face.

"How could you? You *bastard*!" Charlie is beating at Leo with his full strength, pounding his chest and arms, but the big man just stands braced, expressionless.

I feel Joon's fingers digging into my shoulder. I pull him close, but keep my eyes on the figures in the room.

"I love you, Charlie," we hear Leo say huskily. It could be me speaking from just moments ago.

"*Frack you!*" Charlie shrieks, shoving Leo away. He whirls and lunges for the door. Leo catches him by one shoulder, pulling him up short and Charlie yells. Joon flinches and I hold him tighter. Leo wraps himself around a struggling Charlie and pins both his arms.

"I don't want to hurt you. Stop it!" But Charlie isn't stopping.

"Listen to me!"

"Why should I listen? You throw me away and I have to listen to your reason why?" Charlie smacks Leo again and is almost to the door when Leo pins him to the wall hard with his entire body. Charlie wails, face to the wall.

Joon buries his face in my neck. His silent tears trickle down my collarbone, but I can't look away. Something small and mean in me wants Joon to witness this.

Charlie's body and arms are trapped against the wall and Leo is saying something in his ear. Charlie bucks and tries to kick, but Leo shoves his body full against Charlie's back and thrusts his legs apart with his own, so the slender man is spread-eagle and helpless. I've a wild impulse to step through the window and help – do something – but Joon is hanging on me, limp with misery. So I hug Joon hard and wait and watch. I couldn't turn away now for anything.

Leo's low words are indistinguishable, but suddenly Charlie shouts, "There won't be a next time. Not ever! Do you have any idea how … ashamed I've been? How humiliated? How worried about how you might feel about me after … that Warehouse shit … happened? I've felt so – dirty. And here you are bragging about …. And you two all proud of yourselves! *Aaaaah!*"

"It was for you!" Leo roars. "Your research. Our dream! For me too. For a new life, *frack it*! Think of that, Charlie. Please. But none of it's worth anything without you." His hoarse voice trails off.

"Hypocrite! Liar! Don't you put this on me!"

"I want a child," Leo says, "more than I can possibly say. And I know you do …." But Charlie only howls.

"I love you," Leo says brokenly, into Charlie's neck. Charlie gives a great heave and manages to turn his body, but Leo still pins him, only now they're face to face. Leo presses his mouth to Charlie's. His lover must have bitten him, because Leo jerks back and Charlie pulls free. Leo grabs his arm and suddenly they're grappling on the floor. The hair prickles on my neck, I start to move forward, adrenaline pumping, but Joon stops me again.

"No. Nononono." Joon clutches my shoulders, fingers digging in.

Charlie is on top of Leo's prone form, trying to hit him while Leo holds his wrists. Charlie's long hair has come loose and tangles around them as he whips from side to side trying to yank his hands loose. The blood from his bitten lip smears Leo's face.

"You. It's only you!" Leo thunders, and somehow the fight goes out of Charlie. In the moment of quiet, my whole body feels rigid, electrified, every nerve tingling, even my ears ringing. Leo pulls himself up to a sitting position and Charlie goes limp, completely wrapped in Leo's arms, his head lolling, spent. After a long time, when they haven't moved or spoken, I squeeze Joon's shoulder and turn him silently away. I take his hand as we walk quietly back along the balcony and into the apartment, past Charlie's door and down the hall to our own small room. Joon closes the door and we stare at each other with wide eyes, empty hands hanging by our sides.

"Is that what it was like with you?" I ask, awed and deeply disturbed.

"No! Never. Not ever. Never again," Joon's back is to the door and he leans on it, staring at me. "We barely touched!" And then he launches himself into my arms. I grab his face and press my mouth to the full lips. Joon's hot tongue invades my mouth.

"You, I want it to be you." Joon is crying a little, his hands running up and down my back. We're still standing, only thin cloth between us, two quivering bodies, not sure whether to kiss or cry.

"I want you," Joon pants, pulling at my shirt, yanking it up over my head.

"Just you and me, just us," I sob. "No Leo, no Charlie, no *shimatta* babies. No people, no world, just you, just me, just Joon, forever, for always."

Joon doesn't answer – if he even hears. He rocks back, pulling me with him. We land too hard, jarring us both badly. For a long time we just lay there, holding each other. Too shocked to continue, but unable to let go.

And the world goes on without us.

• • •

What I can't remember, I imagine.
Then what needs to be, is.
I remember I can imagine.

What I can't know, I understand more fully.
Is this madness?
Are these dreams?

• • •

— MOURNING AFTER

In another room, the men are awake. (*As it must be – how could it be otherwise?*)

"You know. You know why," Leo murmurs roughly against Charlie's neck, tightening his big arms around his lover. It's hard on the floor and their drying sweat makes him shiver. His partner's skin is all gooseflesh. He heaves Charlie up and half-carries him to the futon, where he kneels down with him, still holding on. Charlie lies with his face averted.

"It wasn't revenge, or getting even, or even that I'm particularly attracted to him," Leo finally says. "I love *you*, Charlie."

"*Frack. You.*"

Leo pulls Charlie's head to his shoulder and his partner doesn't resist. His despair and the recent violence have left him boneless and limp.

"You know what having a child means. To me, to you, to everyone gathered here in hopes of a future. And the act itself doesn't mean much to Joon."

"It means ... a lot ... to me."

"Jae refuses to have a child with Joon."

"So you're just a *fracking* hero, aren't you?"

"You think it's been easy wondering what you – did – with that disgusting Spider Woman?"

Charlie's silent.

"I'm sorry. That was out of line. But try to put this just a little in perspective. Shit happens. But you're my partner in every way. I truly love you with my heart and soul." A single tear trickles down Leo's stubbly chin and pats down onto Charlie. "I sound like I'm rationalizing, but I know what not being able to have children has meant to you too. *Frack*, Charlie, I can't lose you over this. Isn't this part of our dream?"

"If it helps," he says later, after they've lain in open-eyed silence until the first cold light pales the dark intense night into day, "we didn't actually, *ah*, consummate anything. Just had a wank and tried to smear it in the right spot."

Charlie turns his face to his lover with an expression of slack-jawed disbelief. "After all *that*, are you actually telling me you two tried to make a baby playing spunk cookies?! *Fracking* hell. What kind of scientist are you?"

"If it didn't take," Leo says eagerly, sensing a relenting in Charlie's tone – anything is better than that overwhelming sadness – "we can just use a test tube and a ... a basting brush or whatever next time."

"There won't be a *fracking* next time."

"Or not."

"NOT," Charlie shouts. "Not, not, NOT!" And he's weeping again, damp face pressed into the futon.

Leo pats the shaking shoulders and tries to find the words that will make it better. Would he undo the last few days if he could? No. He made this decision consciously. He still feels it has a rightness to it that goes far deeper than he can find words for. But Charlie is – everything.

"I ... still feel that a child, that making a new life, is ... gods. So important. On so many levels. But if it really means losing you ... if I thought you couldn't forgive me, or didn't want this too – I mean, a child!" he adds as Charlie flinches violently. "You're more important to me than anything," he finishes softly. "I believed – I hoped – I was doing this for you too."

"Oh, gods. Don't do me any more *fracking* favors."

Charlie sighs deeply and Leo puts his arms around him tightly, stubbly face to the smooth ivory neck.

After a long, long while, Charlie breaks the silence, grudgingly, surprisingly. "A new life would help support my theory about the relative fertility of the intersex people."

"Yes!" Leo says eagerly, then shuts up when Charlie glares at him.

"It could help everyone understand – empathize – with what we're trying to accomplish here."

"*Uh-huh.*"

"I've always – wanted a child." His voice breaks.

"I know." Leo nuzzles his partner and strokes his hair.

"Are you attracted to Joon?"

"No! It's more what she – represents. New life. You know?"

"She?" Charlie's head snaps up, startled.

"Yeah. Joon says she's always seen herself as primarily female. She's finally asked that we start referring to her that way." Leo is distinctly uncomfortable with this idea. It's something he and Charlie discussed long ago when

Joon self-identified, ultimately deciding to follow Joon's lead. "She says she wished she'd been aware enough to ask when she first met us."

"*Huh*. No wonder you couldn't do it. You've never been a woman's man, have you?"

"Well, she never seemed all that female until she asked for that pronoun." Leo scratches his chin.

"Stop while you're ahead." Charlie says angrily, and smacks his hand – a bit more gently than before – to the red welt on Leo's cheek. He holds it there.

"While I have a head," Leo complains. But Charlie isn't running away, and that's good. "Charlie, I was so worried ...." He runs his hands up along his partner's torso lightly, his touch tentative. Charlie pushes him away.

"I didn't go near Mother this trip," Charlie says, watching Leo's face. "I never will again."

Leo drops his head, feeling shame and relief. "I'm glad."

"And you and Joon?"

"No. I won't. Never again. But ... if it doesn't take?"

"Then we'll try something in the lab. But no physical contact! Any baby of Joon's should be from Jae anyway."

"I want ... to be part of this new life," Leo says hesitantly. *He wants it so badly he aches*.

"I know," Charlie says, and he takes Leo's hand and places it over his heart. "We'll see. Maybe we can all be part of it. Of a new life."

"Charlie?"

"Right now I need to know ... you love me," Charlie says quietly.

So Leo shows him.

• • •

NonK: Literature of Quests
(Taken from the Democratic Underground circa 2011)

Aldonza: *Why do you do these ... ridiculous ... things you do.*

Don Quixote: *I hope to add some measure of grace to the world.*

Aldonza: *The world's a dung heap and we are maggots that crawl on it.*

Don Quixote: *My Lady knows better in her heart.*

Aldonza: *What's in my heart will get me halfway to hell.*
> **—Man of La Mancha**

• • •

Chapter 4
THE QUEST

The Chancellor sends a message for Charlie and Leo to meet him in the library. The handwritten note arrives with a Warehouse kid on foot. So we all go.

We find the Chancellor sitting by the main NonK terminal, keying in something he slides off the screen as soon as Leo greets him. Several other faculty members are waiting with the old man.

"Dr. Vassily," he greets Leo and Charlie formally, "Dr. McCauley." He barely nods to me and ignores Joon entirely.

The Chancellor is the University's Grand Old Man, dapper in an antique vest and robes. He holds himself rigidly erect, but his head comes just to my shoulder, and I'm not tall. He's been Chancellor of the University far longer than I've been at the Warehouse, and anything done in or around the University is supposed to go through him, though it seems there's little oversight of anything not purely academic. I'm still amazed he agreed to Leo's plan to have the Warehouse folk as students – though Leo did point out that the University's options are limited. It's good for them too.

I can't see a single spark of human warmth in the old man's face. But perhaps I'm wrong. The man has taken us all in and coped with Madgirl's belligerence. I tell myself once again that I am a terrible judge of people.

"I would like you to see something," the old man says primly to his gathered faculty. "Pull out your vidphones, please. I ask that each of you type in the same questions for NonK. Hit SEND when I give you the word."

I hadn't realized the few vidphones left could access NonK. The University provides one central information terminal in Town and one in the Marketplace, and there are a number of stations inside the Uni itself. But this is the first time I've seen these handheld access points, or even a vidphone at all, since my first day at Charlie's place.

Charlie, Leo, and the other faculty key in the phrases that the Chancellor dictates.

"World Population?"

"Unknown." Leo reads NonK's answer out loud off his screen.

"Number of towns connected with Internet?"

"Unknown."

"Most recent Internet failure?"

The faces reflecting the backlighting of the vid screens look confused. Charlie hits his speaker button and we all hear:

"Twas brillig and the slythy toves did gyre and gimble in the wabe – Twice nine is eighteen. Earthquakes flew over the eastern seaboard in record numbers … causing mass Oobleck. To sauté a jellyfish, first pat it dry and thoroughly soak to remove consciousness …. Gratis the Shaman. Our system is down, system

dooooown. Down. SOSOSOSOSOSOSOSOSOSO ... SO ... WHAT?"

Charlie taps the speaker OFF.

Everyone stares at one another. The Chancellor seems unconcerned.

"What was that?" Joon finally asks, but the dapper little man ignores her.

"Chancellor?" Charlie's annoyed.

"The babble you are hearing," the Chancellor says calmly, "is all we've received for months. It may be the death of the Town nearest ours, and is at least the death of a greater Internet. For some months, gentlepeople, the only working server has been here, within our own University. We are a network of exactly one, with only our own databases to draw from, though some random nonsense seems to be seeping in from outside."

He looks around the shocked faces. "Why so surprised? Have any of you been beyond our borders in years? Collaborated with colleagues from other universities in months? This is just another step in the slow disintegration we've been experiencing for decades. The last real communication we had with our closest University contact – what, 80 miles away? – was their corroboration of our seismograph readings regarding that midsized quake in the mid-Atlantic trench, received via NonK six months ago. There has been no – coherent – word since."

There's an uncomfortable silence. Then the agriculture lecturer speaks: "Is that where Sam and Izbell – our IT department – went? Didn't they leave right about then?" I notice Charlie twitch at the names and Leo look at his partner with concern.

"With my encouragement," says the Chancellor calmly. "Yes. Drs. Campbell and Aguilar went to pursue information about their colleagues' whereabouts. I asked them to collect their data if those researchers were no more. My injunction was for them to discover the location of, and hopefully recover, any other University databases. Our own seems to be somewhat – limited – without the data stored in the other locations. You might have noticed the lack of new ideas," he adds without humor. Someone snorts. NonK has had holes in its information for as long as anyone can remember.

"The blue kelp ale was new," Joon mutters. The Chancellor turns in his chair and glares.

"Young lady," he says. "If you must be present, please refrain from speaking." He turns back to his unhappy faculty. I'm shocked and expect a fiery backlash from our warrior – who'd seriously laid into me earlier for not referring to her as "she" long ago when she'd first mentioned her gender identity. But Joon is so gobsmacked at being called "lady" by that old misogynist that she keeps her peace, a tiny smile quirking her lips. She arches an eyebrow at me as if to say, "Told ya!" She's been meeting with Charlie privately for weeks on some project she won't tell me about. I'm frankly jealous. Privately I've always known Joon is perfect. I get anxious when I think about her changing in any way. But at least Joon's made me aware enough to really understand how that's not my choice. With her help, I'm working on me.

"Why weren't we told of the search team going out before?" Leo asks. His face and voice are so deadpan that I'm certain he's furious.

"I'm telling you now," the Chancellor says. "Campbell and Aguilar have failed to return, and we still have need of the information from those databases."

The faculty murmurs. I wonder why there are so few of them present. Where are the others? I haven't seen them all gathered together since my first day on the slab. But there'd been more of them then. And aren't there at least a few women in the ranks? All present are male.

"To make Dr. Vassily's ... dream ... of an educated populace a reality, we need a reliable library, and our digital library is damaged, or at the very least incomplete and questionable in its veracity."

Charlie's eyes take on the shine of a fanatic. "Our library is the compilation of human technology, our history, art, and culture. Without it, what do we have to offer these children? I'll go." He holds his hand out toward Leo as his partner protests. "Izbell is ... Sam and Izbell are dear friends. Izbell was part of my family once and we share a deep reverence for the scientific body of knowledge. I'm sure she and Sam are still trying to recover what they can. I'll head an expedition to look for our colleagues *and* attempt to recover any databases if no other course is clear." I see the Chancellor smile slightly as Charlie turns to Leo, who's looking back at him in horror. "Will you go with me?"

• • •

"WHAT WERE YOU THINKING?" Leo roars at Charlie the moment we set foot in Charlie's apartment. I wondered why he'd been so quiet on the walk back. But we all understand the need for private space away from the University complex or we wouldn't be here. Joon quietly shuts the door but stays close to Charlie, as if to protect him from Leo's wrath. I squash an impulse to go hide in our room.

"I'm going," Charlie says firmly. "I hope you'll go with me. The Warehouse folk are settling in; they're

163

starting to integrate with the Townies. The Chancellor can handle any faculty issues. We've accomplished so much already. We can't stop now. We need a complete library! We have access to a fraction of the information we had even a decade ago. We were fools not to realize what was going on – and when we did, we didn't plan ahead. Well, I know Izbell talked about the danger of this happening. But think about it, Leo. There are scholarly papers out there – from your field and mine – that we know exist, that are cited in the papers we do have. How can we throw all that away?"

"Charlie." Leo sounds tired. "I believe in what we're doing, but none of it – not one zettabyte of data – is worth putting you in this kind of risk."

"Then come with me!" I've never seen Charlie so animated. "It'll be like old times. Remember going on research trips? This is the same, only we'll be in quest of, oh, only half the known body of scientific literature. Can you imagine?"

"The Chancellor really wants you to go," Joon says quietly, from behind Charlie.

"What? Yes, of course he does." Charlie frowns.

"He wants me to go too. And Madgirl – I think."

"What're you talking about?"

"When we were leaving, he kinda hissed it at me. He said, 'You go too, and take that succubus with you.' What's a succubus?"

Charlie's irritated. "I'm sure you misheard. Why would he say that? Anyway, it's out of the question. You aren't going anywhere in your condition. It wouldn't be safe."

"My condition? What?! Charlie!"

"Uh-huh, your tests came back." Charlie is suddenly talking through a face full of dreadlocks as Joon throws herself into his arms. Charlie grins and hugs her back. Conversation about the trip is shelved as everyone's attention shifts.

"What? I thought it didn't take?" Leo's eyes are red-rimmed.

"Charlie's been playing geneticist," Joon says proudly.

"Charlie's been playing doctor," I mutter.

"Who's the father?" Leo insists.

"Does it matter?" Charlie stares him down, but then grins again. "Isn't it said that 'it's a wise child that knows its own parent'? Maybe it's also a wise parent who doesn't ask."

"But …."

"Congratulations, Joon. You're going to be a mother. And look, you have three proud fathers to support you." Even Leo knows it's time to shut up and celebrate. He pulls the jug of blue ale up from the cistern and we toast with it – sparingly.

• • •

No one can stop Joon. She's going on the expedition. Pregnancy has given her a confidence and power that no one can naysay. It slows our departure by weeks, as Leo and I try to talk her out of it, but in the end she makes it clear that she absolutely refuses to be without Charlie for the better part of her pregnancy, which leaves us with very few counterarguments.

Joon's excited when she finds an entry in NonK claiming that the dolphin, an air-breathing sea creature she's seen in the extinct-animal exhibit, once had same-sex best friends as their partners for life, who helped with birthing and calf rearing. It was often a mother or sister, she tells me. I argue that since I'm the only one around who's even close to the same sex as Joon, I should be the only candidate for the position. But Joon roundly refuses me, claiming Charlie as her birthing partner.

"I can count on Charlie," she tells me, late one night. My head is on her belly, ear to its still-flat surface, listening for some hint of another living being inside. "Charlie wants this baby as much as I do."

I'm silent. I feel there is something more to say, but my overwhelming emotions when faced with a pregnant Joon are still grief and fear. I can't bring myself to say what I know she wants to hear.

"I love you, Joonie," I say instead, and she sighs and pets my head.

"I know."

"Leo wants it."

"In a different way," she says thoughtfully. "I think Leo wants proof that life, or he, or something, will continue. Charlie's different. He wants it just for itself. And he wants young things to cuddle, *ne*?"

"He's a nurturer," I say. "Like Mother."

"Not like Mother, *baka* Jae." Joon's really angry. "*Undei no sa*. That's the difference between clouds and mud."

"But there is a mother feeling about Charlie," I insist. "Not you, though!" I tease her, cupping Joon's very male genitals in my hand, which earns me a smack. "You're more like the Virgin than the Mother."

"Leave off that," Joon says irritably, pushing me off her lap. "We get to invent our own selves, *na*? Why dig up all those rubbishy old ideas?"

"Because you're a goddess in another guise," I say absently, reaching out again to rub her stomach. I can't seem to stay away from it.

"Do you remember when we drank that blue ale, at Tao's?" Joon doesn't answer. "I saw something, Joon."

I rub my eyes tiredly. "Maybe everyone saw something different, I dunno. But I saw you different. 'Collective Unconscious,' NonK called it when I asked later. You looked like this idea, or this story I heard once, or maybe I was just drunk. But you were beautiful, Joon, so lovely." I lie down next to her and she absently runs her fingers through my hair again. I love the way it feels when she does that. Her gentle fingers can stroke away the harsh loneliness of centuries.

"I tried to find the story again, but NonK just gave me a few lines from a poem, something about 'seven veils'? I swear sometimes it's like NonK's playing with us. I – almost remember – a piece of it." I yawn. "It was 'Ishtar Trapped in the Underworld.'

"'If thou opens not the gate to let me enter, I will break the door ... and the lock ....'" My voice drifts off, I'm half in a dream already. I wake a bit and shift restlessly. I know I'm almost asleep and talking nonsense. But it makes sense in the dream. "We already opened the gate, though. Did we let her out too late? She only breaks things. You have to be the one, Joonie – you'll bring life back to the world. *Ah*, what am I saying? I was asleep, Joonie. *Hmmm.*" Joon pets my hair for a while longer. I can feel her fingers while the room expands into a dreamscape, a sloshing world of only Joon and me and me and Joon ....

"*Baka* Jae," Joon says softly, wrinkling her nose. "Just another silly story, *na?*" She slides out from under me and goes over to the NonK terminal.

• • •

NonK, ISHTAR- Updated
(Mashup and down from: Wiki Free /Ishtar, n.d.)

The Dance of the Seven Veils *originated with the Babylonian myth of Ishtar, goddess of fertility, love, war, and sex, whose followers practiced sacred prostitution. In one version, Ishtar decides to visit her mother (sometimes sister), Queen of the Underworld. Ishtar demands that the gatekeeper open the gates with the words:*

> *If thou openest not the gate to let me enter,*
> *I will break the door, I will wrench the lock,*
> *I will smash the door-posts, I will force the doors.*
> *I will bring up the dead to eat the living.*
> *And the dead will outnumber the living.*

The Queen is offended *and tells the gatekeeper to let her daughter enter, but "according to the ancient decree," by which Ishtar must pass through seven gates of blue lapis, losing something she values at each gate. Since she carries nothing, Ishtar sheds an article of clothing at every gate. When she finally passes through the seventh, she is naked, presumably dead – and very angry. Ishtar attacks her mother and is imprisoned.*

While Ishtar is gone, all sexual activity ceases on earth. *The king of gods creates an intersex being, **Asu-shu-namir** (Asu), to bring Ishtar the waters of life. But – purposefully or not – the water splashes Asu, and s/he becomes the personification of transformation, bringing fertility back into the world. In essence, Asu (meaning "tomorrow") becomes the Trickster deity.*

While Ishtar is dead, *her husband, Tammuz, god of the harvest, falls in love with Asu. In a rage, Ishtar frees herself by sending Tammuz (and any hope of a fertile harvest) to the underworld in her place. Asu is grief-stricken. To save*

*both Tammuz and the earth, Asu volunteers to spend
every other season in the land of the dead, during which
time Tammuz can go free.*

But since the lovers can only see each other in passing,
*they begin to swap places more often – and the seasons
begin to change with dangerous rapidity ....*

• • •

Madgirl doesn't refuse to go on the expedition; she just
utterly ignores all invitations. Charlie won't believe the
Chancellor wants her with us anyway, so the expedition is planned around the four of us, two Townies, and
the hydrology professor, who seems terrified of leaving
University grounds but eager to help find his colleagues.
Leo spends some time talking with him, and tells us later
he can't imagine why the guy attached himself to the
expedition. In the end, the Chancellor refuses him leave
on the grounds that they can't do without his knowledge
of the main water pipeline and its connections to the
reservoir and labs.

"Which doesn't say a lot about how the Chancellor values our fields of study," Leo grumbles. But he's
clearly relieved. The professor was so nervous he'd have
been a liability.

The Townies, both women from Fisherfolk families,
have worked at the University tending the hydroponics
and helping out at the other farms. Despite their valuable skills, the Chancellor seems to have no objection
about the women leaving. Charlie's keen because one
of them claims her grandmother was a midwife, though
Leo teases him that midwifery is unlikely to be geneti-
cally inheritable. Leo seems more impressed when she

adds that she's "birthed many a kid goat." Viable young of any mammalian species are uncommon. How different could it be?

• • •

— JAE'S MEMORIES

Time compacts into the briefest moments, when pain and pleasure are greatest. I remember only fragments. The trip is grueling and large parts of it are lost to me. The beginning, in particular, is dust and the dry grit of sand. This outer world is a fearful glimpse into our future. I yearn for water; my beginning and my end.

• • •

It's been months of travel, far longer than expected as we wind between dead towns. We're sand-skiing now. The solar tractor is dead, left behind a week ago. Our two Townie friends stayed behind to fix it, then take it on a more direct route back to Uni, if they can. It's strange going on without them. They became a part of our group, and now they're already gone. We've promised to get Joonie back to them before she gives birth.

Joon has taken to wearing a wrapped skirt left for her by our friends. Says it's easier to pee. With her growing belly pressing down, she has to go about every 20 minutes – or less. She barely slows as she skis, just squats and skis on. The rest of us carry the drinking water she's pissing away. We collect rainwater in tarps when we can. Joon's lithe boy-body is lost in giant belly and swishing clothes. Even her face is rounder and more radiant. Leo took me aside to scare the hell out of me, says he's afraid her hips aren't wide enough, her birth canal too tight. Wants me to massage the area to stretch it. Joon's up for it. She's happily horny. Wants all the cuddling she can get. I resisted until Leo pointed out we are far from any help, and that even big-hipped women used to die in childbirth. None of us have experience with this. Been ages since we've even seen young children. In one tiny village we passed – if you could call a collection of trash shacks and dugouts a village – the small, ragged people got down on their knees and kissed Joon's hands as we passed. Some of the women had dolls clutched to their breasts: bundles of flax with drawn charcoal eyes. They fawned on Joon, gave us pounded flax blankets and food they clearly couldn't afford to part with. Joon's face shone like a beacon. She touched every hand that reached out.

No wonder she caught a cold.

I'm warming a goatskin of broth someone gave us; smelling like a billygoat but all she can eat. Her throat is raw and her nose runs. Even shiny-faced she's beautiful. Leo and Charlie sit close around her as windbreaks while I build a fire of crackly bamboo and seared yellow dune grass. Joon is brighter and more compelling than the flames. She's our locus. Her belly is so round and tight it looks like a painful world/globe, and she grunts when she shifts. Everyone leaps to help. Charlie jokes that her breasts are growing and Leo looks away. How can he care for Joon but be so uncomfortable with her femaleness? I reach out and slide my hand under her shirt and cup one of her breasts. She shines up at me with a smile warmer than the sun. Leo gets up abruptly and leaves. Charlie looks sad at this, but I grin fiercely back at Joon. She's mine, not Leo's. Where do these primal thoughts come from? Even as I think them, I feel undone. My smile slips and I drape myself over her huge belly while she pets my hair. Something inside tries to bump me away. We both sit up, startled. Joon pulls Charlie's hand over to feel the kick. We are laughing excitedly when Leo comes back to camp. He drops hard onto his knees beside Joon, lays his cheek to her now naked belly, shining golden in the firelight, and tears roll down his face. I pet his hair. Charlie rubs his back. We are all in this together.

• • •

Charlie and Joon are bonding. It's sometimes hard for me to do the things I know she needs, and Charlie is always there to take up the slack. She leans against him while he feeds her soup, massages a cramp, brushes her hair all frizzy and twists it into some semblance of her once aggressive dreadlocks. When she's hurting, it's Charlie she wants.

Leo and I move away a little at times, but we are not the solo "bachelor" men. I am not a man.

"How about me?" I ask Leo. "You seem to have lost Charlie to Joon for now. Won't I do?"

"Why would you even ask that?" he says coldly.

I want to punch him. Instead, I watch him turn and walk away. On impulse I run and tackle him, taking him down hard. I land a few hits, before he pins me, roaring, to the ground.

"What's your problem?" he snarls. He has both my hands pinned above my head, and for a moment I get to feel submissive and helpless. My breathing hitches. I shift my hips suggestively and feel his startled response over me.

He gets up quickly and I laugh at him. He's going to stalk off and I'm going to keep laughing. But suddenly he sits down beside me and asks, gently enough, "What is it you want, Jae?"

I sit up and hug my knees. I rock back and forth. I'm not laughing anymore.

"I don't know. I've never known."

He hugs me while I allow a few tears to water the dry land.

Maybe that's what I wanted.

• • •

And in the end, we find nothing. We ski into a sizeable city – who knows if it's the right city – more broken than the huddled shacks we've passed on the way. The buildings are crumbled and the buckled roads impassable. The rigid construction couldn't stand up to the wind like the more flexible – if dry and stunted – bamboo still standing in the leeward hills. There's no other life. No one picks through the rubble. Nothing creeps in the shadows. It's so lifeless Joon refuses to shelter behind the crumbled walls, and Charlie agrees, saying he's worried about toxins from the dusty ruins. There are no landmarks left, no point in scrabbling through that endless horizon to look for anything.

We have to face that there is nothing to do but return. Nowhere have we found resources even close to those at Uni. No one has power, gardens, hydroponics, books. Nowhere is there anything but decay and scratching in the dirt. And now, without the hope, energy – and supplies – that kept us moving forward, we have to retrace our steps. Only Joon seems to blaze with purpose. She's ready to nest. She wants to go home. I only hope Uni is a home we can return to. There were no surprises here. But our hope is nibbled away even more. Supporting Joon becomes the motivator that allows us to turn around. She is our world.

We wouldn't have made it far if not for the dusty, small humans in their clustered shacks, who may have once inhabited the ruined towns or that broken city. How long has the city been dead? Nothing fits what the Chancellor told us. Not the distance, not the passage of time. I can barely remember why we're out here.

If there's a filthy tarp made into a shelter, the little folk offer it to Joon. If there's a handful of maggots or a length of bamboo filled with fermented shoots – and little other food for the winter – it's presented to Joon as if she's a living jewel. And she is. As her face becomes more drawn and her belly tighter, a light glows in her green eyes. She moves through the ragged villagers as a shining brown beacon, allowing the gnarled and chapped hands to touch her belly. When shelter is offered – as it always is – we all collapse, and Joon leans against the packs and loosens her wrap, setting free the tight-skinned, glowing brown orb; so ripe and fecund. So different from the dry, dusty skin of these little people in their packed dirt compounds, protected by earth embank-ments to help divert the constant wind.

• • •

The Earth folk, Leo has started to call them. It isn't an insult. They're surviving on dust and rain as far as we can tell. They give us as much hope as Joon clearly gives them, and their generosity keeps us alive. We try not to think about what it will do to them, once we leave with half their food in our stomachs. They never pressure us to stay, probably knowing it will mean the death of several of them if they keep feeding even one of us. But their eyes glisten as we struggle out into the sand each morning, and we see tracks of tears on their wind-worn faces. We hope to make it to another village before dark.

• • •

At each poor shanty town, folk press gifts onto Joon, who never refuses them, though a few Charlie takes off her later, fearing disease. Her pack and hair are hung about with beaded rags, pretty pebbles, and bits of colored wire, plastic, and bone. She favors the biggest blue beads – or perhaps the little people do. She looks like a brilliant magpie. Today, when we pass a sheet of salt reflecting the bright morning light, I see our reflections and realize the rest of us are looking more and more like the little earth people. Charlie's once fair hair is a tangled rope of dirt and grime. He's grown a thin goatee-like beard he calls his face fungus. Leo's always wild hair and dense beard now look like he's stuck his head in a bush, his expressions almost invisible. My own hairless brown face is windburned and dominated in the reflection by huge, shadowed eyes and sharp, smudged cheekbones, my hair a vertical mass of spikes. Our focus is so constantly on the vital, lovely Joon that I don't think any of us noticed.

We are close now. But I have an unreasoning fear of returning to Uni, despite Joon's need for shelter. We hope and we plan, but everything we attempt has always seemed too little, too late. And there's a storm coming. Our moments of peace, despite the hardship, are over.

• • •

— DISUNIFICATION

The pressure of a northerly wind bears down on us as we approach Town. It stifles some of the others' excitement about homecoming after so long away. Even the wind is sluggish and thick, pushed this way and that by tendrils of warmer air. Joon moves slower than usual, struggling through some invisible barrier of exhaustion as we near our goal. But she's more focused too, determined to keep moving forward. Leo wants to swing around to the Market first for news but Joon wants the walls of the University around her and no one's going to stop her when we're this close. I want to go straight to the greenhouses. All I can think about is stuffing my mouth with greens. Or snagging a fish from the farmed tanks lower down the water main below the greenhouses. Anything fresh. Charlie's acting oddly about going to the greenhouses though, probably because of the weight of the air and the promise of something big coming. Despite the strength of the greenhouse construction, perhaps he doesn't want to be inside glass when the storms hit. But as usual, we blindly follow Joon, who aims straight east across the hilltops toward Uni and the ocean below.

We end up scrambling in a side gate just as the storm front announces its arrival with wild gusts of warm and the promise of wet. The dampness, at least, is welcome on our desert-dry skin. Everyone is relieved and laughing as we slam the doors and dump our gear in a suddenly silent hallway that leads to the classrooms. It feels so strange to be inside, like the feeling of getting off a rocking boat when the land continues to move underfoot. The cessation of wind follows us in the same way, our skin warm and sensitive from the recent buffeting, ears ringing in the sudden quiet. We've brought a taste of the outside in.

We seem to be in a relatively unused part of the University complex. The greenhouses are a little inland to the south, the hydroponic farms, labs, and bigger lecture halls to the north. And we came back due east across the cliffs above Town, arriving at the back of the Uni in order to get Joon inside safe walls as soon as possible. But it feels strangely empty and still. We've lived with the wind for months. Now it's sealed away and the sterile halls feel lesser for lack of the wind's desiccating, corroding, invigorating presence.

"It's the classroom maze." Leo's annoyed. "It'll take us forever to get to the kitchens from here."

"After all the way we've come?" Joon says brightly, though she's collapsed on her pack. "That's nothing."

"Actually." Charlie frowns. "I believe we're close to the Chancellor's rooms. He has his own supplied kitchen."

"Why here? Keeping an eye on empty classrooms?"

"They needed a monitor for the hydro-tanks' pipeline between the labs and the kitchens, originally. Eventually the Chancellor took over the monitor's job. I expect he needed some peace and quiet of an evening. Let's see if he's in."

The Chancellor's rooms are down a side hall, through huge arches almost as big as the front doors of the Uni.

Beyond is a small, empty anteroom with a normal-looking door in the corner. It's locked.

Leo pounds on it. "Damn! I need food *now*." He pounds again, then turns away with a sigh. Leo suffered most from the lack of rations. We had to make sure Joon got what she needed to eat and sustain the baby first.

"Wait." Charlie puts his ear to the door. "I hear something." He knocks lightly and calls out, "Chancellor? Are you there?"

There's a sudden scuffling right behind the door. Then silence.

"Chancellor! It's Dr. McCauley. I'm with Dr. Vassily. Is that you?"

Something moves again behind the door. Then stops.

"What in the world …?" Charlie's exclamation is interrupted by the scrape of something heavy being dragged. I pull Joon back a few steps. The knob turns and the door opens inward.

"Charlie?" The quavering voice is followed by a form so shrunken and tentative, it could be an Earth Person.

"Chancellor?" Charlie's shocked. The old man lurches forward and wraps thin arms around his horrified colleague's neck.

"Too late," the old man sobs. "It could have worked. It could have …. But you shouldn't have come back, son. It's too late."

Together Charlie and Leo gently pull the old man's arms from around Charlie's neck and lead him back into his rooms. After a moment, Joon and I follow, carefully dragging the packs inside first and closing the door. There's a heavy trunk nearby so I shove it until it blocks the door again. Something's clearly wrong. It seems prudent not to take chances.

We find the three adults in an elegant sitting room with antique wood paneling and brocade chairs. An artificially lit window casement holds a mini-garden filled to bursting with greenery, a short view into Eden. Visible below it, gurgling inside the walls, the big water main chuckles. The water runs openly through the bottom of the window casement, so one can see the flow for a few feet. Several jellies float past in the artificial stream.

In his formal receiving room, the Chancellor puts on calm like a ceremonial robe, and quietly offers his guests food and drink. But his hands are trembling as he passes around an open tin of candied jellies that make even my mouth water. He offers to make tea, but Charlie presses him to sit and talk.

"Chancellor, what is it? What's happened? Where is everyone and why are you barricaded in?"

"Is this all you have to eat?" adds the ever-practical Leo.

"There are fresh fish and greens in the alcove," the Chancellor says and waves unsteadily, "and dried stores and spring water in the kitchen. Do put on the kettle, would you?" He looks vaguely past Leo and then catches sight of Joon behind him. The rheumy old eyes widen.

"No!" The skinny arms cover his head as if the old man is afraid. "No!" After months of people crowding around our shining Joon to stroke her belly and offer gifts, I'm dumbfounded by his reaction.

"Don't let her in!" the old man cries out, but when he stands up from his fancy chair, clearly agitated, he suddenly loses all energy and thumps down onto his knees instead. "Don't let her in!"

Charlie sinks gracefully to the floor beside him and puts a gentle arm around the older man's shoulders. He waves us toward the kitchen with the other.

"Go. Put together some hot food. Give me a chance to find out what's been going on." He returns his attention to the old man and murmurs softly to him. Leo stands over them both like a furry sentinel. Joon and I go.

In the kitchen there's more food than we've seen in months. Maybe ever. It's an obscene amount of food. There are barrels of dried fruit and others of dried salted fish, braids of garlic and herbs in the rafters, shelves of bottled wine and vinegar and sealed clay pots of preserved goods. The old man has stockpiled the place for a very long winter. Joon dives into the small, overstocked pantry and comes back out crowing happily.

"It leads to a washhouse with a real hot pool! I can't believe it! I want a bath right now. Can I?"

"Oh, hell yeah," I say around a mouthful of dried gooseberries. "Shove some of these in yer gob first." I pop a handful of fruit into Joon's mouth and she chews happily, moaning.

"More," she groans and I scramble to open another smaller barrel that turns out to be packed with dried cicadas for roasted *semi*. The sheer quantity is outrageous. We crunch happily for a long moment. Then Joon sighs. "Bath first. If you could just brush the salt off a few of those jellies, start them soaking, and look for more of the candied sort too. Those were yummy!" she calls as she sheds clothes on her way toward the bath.

I look after her for a long moment. Then, muttering a quiet *"wari"* to the hungry Leo and Charlie waiting in the other room, I grab another handful of fruit and follow her, as I always must.

• • •

NonK: Entomophagy also means Bug Juice
(From Greek ἔντομος éntomos, "insect(ed)," and φἄγεῖν phăgein, "to eat" – Wiki.org)

"There are over 1,400 species of recorded edible insects."
— United Nations Food & Agriculture Organization
(From CreepyCrawlyCooking.com):

- *hachi-no-ko* = boiled wasp larvae
- *zaza-mushi* = aquatic insect larvae (tastes like watermelon)
- *inago* = fried rice-field grasshoppers
- *semi* = fried cicada
- *sangi* = fried silk moth pupae

"If all [hu]mankind were to disappear, the world would regenerate back to the rich state of equilibrium that existed ten thousand years ago. If insects were to vanish, the environment would collapse into chaos."
— E. O. Wilson

• • •

— LIFE AFTER ALL

Some time goes by before Joon and I emerge from the kitchen, freshly washed and with a cooked meal for the others. Charlie and Leo are sitting together, hands clasped, looking gray and tired, watching the old man sleep soundly on his ancient overstuffed couch. He seems a small dried husk. Joon bans all conversation until we've all eaten, then sends the men to the bath with instructions not to talk at all until they're clean and rested. She explores the Chancellor's quarters and chooses, as her own and mine, a small plain room with a hay-filled futon and nothing else. We fall down and are dead to the world within minutes.

•••

I wake hours later. It's amazing to feel well-fed and rested, but the silence bothers me. The lack of wind is quieting to the skin, but not the mind. I don't like waking alone in this ringing stillness, so I stretch quickly and go in search of Joon. She's in the sitting room, tucked right into a corner of the huge, plant-filled window under the light, her journal in her lap. Her swollen feet are soaking in the cool water of the hydroponic pipe. She looks like a bulging wood nymph.

"Joon." She looks up as I come into the room. "You okay?" I can see she's been crying. I try to take her hand, but she's busy wiping her eyes.

"It's only life," she says. "That's all."

•••

— JOON IS ALL ABOUT DYEING

Time has passed and now Joon is bored. The Chancellor's been closeted with Charlie and Leo most of the day, to hear their report. Joon entertains herself rummaging in the marvelous kitchen. She discovers treasures and is arranging pans, spoons, cloths, and herbs beside the hot pool when I find her.

"What up, love o' mine?" I ask, sneaking up from behind and grabbing at her belly. I bat each side gently, pretending it's a ball. She swats me away.

"A new look." Joon pretends to ignore me while she concentrates on measuring several cups of gray powder into a bowl. She adds some of the warm water and stirs it into paste. It has a nostalgic smell, like cut grass.

"C'mere," she says. "Wanna play with your hair, *naa*."

"Uh-*uh*."

Joon narrows her glass-green eyes and I give up. Joon is righteously bossy these days, far more than she ever was pre-pregnancy. She knows we've agreed, amongst ourselves, that it's generally best to give her what she wants. She clearly feels that this is as it should be.

"Where do you want me?" I sigh.

"Strip and get in the pool, *neh*? This could get messy."

"Oh joy." I strip slowly, dragging it out, hoping I can distract her, but as soon as my clothes are off she gives me a shove and I splash into the pool.

"Hey!"

"Wet your hair."

I dunk my head obediently, and Joon arranges me at the side of the pool with my head on the edge and a flax cloth under my neck. The warm water gently buoys my body and I stretch my arms along the rim of the pool. The utter luxuriousness is quickly followed by guilt when I think of the Earth People living in holes in the ground to hide from the wind and sun. I wonder if we could trek back out with some supplies – and maybe a barrel of seeds? Are they better off out there than here?

"What brought this on?"

"Had a bad dream," Joon starts, then stops. Some of the thick paste she's working into my hair drips into the pool. It immediately stains the water around it a rusty red.

"*Shimatta*," she mutters. "*Ah*, let's say I just like the color of Leo's hair, okay? That brown with red highlights."

"Forget this!" I raise my head. "You want me to look like Leo? *Baka* Joon!"

"*Baka* you." Joon leans down to kiss me on the lips. Mollified, I settle my head back on the cloth.

"What was your dream?" I ask.

"Dun matter."

"Tell! Or I won't let you play."

"*Oh*, it was stupid, okay? I dreamt I had to, *ah*, climb down somewhere deep. You were gone, in trouble. I had to find you and bring you back. Only I couldn't see you underground. It was like, everywhere I looked, you were there, same color as the dirt, but I'd get closer and it was just roots, or rocks – or weird things staring back at me. It was like that NonK poem about going through the seven gates before dying. It was really scary, okay!" Joon whacks the top of my head for snickering.

"Oh, Joonie. Don't you fret, fat pregnant lady. This ain't Ishtar's gates ... and I ain't going nowhere." Joon whacks me again. "So, what's that got to do with messing with my hair?"

"Can't hide if you're a redhead," Joon says firmly.

"*Shimatta*! Really?" I touch my head and my finger comes away with a dab of grassy paste on it. When I rinse it off in the water, my skin is faintly pinkish underneath.

"*Huh*. All good I guess. Not gonna lose me in the deep dirt at least. How long it'll last?"

"Not long," Joon says. "Now shut your eyes. I'm gonna wrap your head in this cloth. You sleep until I say you can wake up, *ne*?"

"*Hai*. But first I need kisses."

Joon leans over and rests her lips softly on mine. I taste them until I start to drift off. Joon wraps the cloth over both my hair and eyes, leaving my nose uncovered. I'm half-asleep when she stands and throws the lever that cuts circulation of fresh water into the pool. I must have made a noise when I felt her leave me, because she says softly, "Let me know if you get too hot."

• • •

In a dream I watch from Joon's memories. I see Jae wrapped and sleeping in the pool. Joon pauses a moment in thought before taking the bowl of paste and quietly emptying the rest of its contents into the pool. She stirs the water, which immediately turns blood-red.

• • •

Joon's considering pushing my arms, now resting on the edge, into the water, but decides it might wake me from my doze. She settles down on the edge of the pool to wait. After a few moments, she carefully dips just the soles of her feet into the water and keeps them there.

After a while Joon stirs and lifts one foot from the pool. The paler bottom of her foot is rusty red. She pats it dry and examines it. The color doesn't smear or lighten when she licks a finger and runs it over her sole. She puts it back in the pool. When I stir, she shifts the towel off my eyes and feels my forehead. I'm hot and sweating, so she uncovers my head, nudges me awake, and puts a cup of cool water to my lips. I drink, eyes still closed.

"It's time?"

"*Mmm.* Careful standing up. You're hot."

"M'dizzy. Need to get out," I sigh. Joon helps me step out of the pool. I stand, swaying, while she pats me dry. When I finally get my eyes open enough to look around, Joon is staring at me with such an expression of glee that

I glance down. My entire lower body, with the exception of my normally light brown arms, is a dark rust-red.

"*Ai*! What'dchu do to me!" I screech. "*Baka* Joon! What'dchu do!"

Charlie and Leo come in to see what the yelling's about. They see me standing, arms outspread, staring down at my crotch, head matted with what looks like dung and smelling of hay. There's a straight line across my chest, just under my armpits, with everything below colored red. They crack up laughing. Leo's whoop reverberates through the bathing room.

"I wondered what you wanted that henna for!" Charlie's careful not to touch anything.

"But *why*, Joonie!" I wail.

"You called me fat," Joon says, looking me over with great satisfaction. "And now you can't get lost in the ground."

"Y'all *suck*!" I yell at the room in general, but Joon pulls me backward toward the pool, and I let her push me down so she can wash the muck from my hair. It feels incredibly soft to the touch afterward. I pull a lock forward to see what it looks like. It might be a dark cherry, though it's hard to tell while it's wet. Joon starts vigorously toweling my head.

"Stupid Joon! How long am I gonna look like road-kill?!" I complain loudly.

"Like what?" Joon asks curiously.

"Like I had my throat cut and bled all over!"

"Big baby. *Tch*, I dyed my hands."

"Serves you right."

"Look, my feet too!" And Joon lifts her feet, one at a time, so I can see the tidy red footprint under each.

"*Huh*," I snort. "What for?"

Joon ignores me. "Oh, look!" she breathes. Leo makes encouraging sounds and Charlie leaves to rummage in the kitchen for something that reflects.

"Looks good," Leo says grudgingly.

"*Maa*, still not dry, might lighten some," Joon says critically.

"Gods 'n' fishes!" Charlie comes back in with a cracked mirror from an old solar still.

"What?" I grab the mirror from him.

My hair is standing up in spikes from the toweling; it's a bright, barn red, contrasting oddly with my black brows and the naturally umber skin of my face. My eyes look greener than usual in contrast, and something about their almond shape makes my expression down-right wicked. Is that me?

"It's Puck!" Charlie gasps. Leo catches Charlie's reference to one of his old media plays and laughs.

"My job here is done, *laa*," Joon says with dignity, but she can't take her eyes off me.

"*Suteki*. Dreamy. *Hmm*, Joon?" Charlie teases.

"I gotta get out of this heat," I grumble, but I wipe the condensation off the mirror and take another long look at myself before I stand. "*Hmph*, I even look good like this." But then I glance down at the rest of me.

"This part, I don't like," I groan, gesturing. "Aw, Joonie, my *dick* is red!"

"I'll make it up to you," Joon purrs, surprising me by taking my hand and leading me from the wash pool, hips swinging. Leo gives a catcall but Charlie shushes him.

"Let them play while they can," I hear Charlie say, as we stumble out toward our shared sleeping room, giggling.

• • •

Joon's thoughts are butterfly kisses in my dreams ....

• • •

— *INTERLUDE*

Now it's Charlie sitting by the window, staring into the greenery with sad eyes.

Eyes I also see through.

Charlie's fingers trail through the water. Leo watches silently from the doorway for a while until, with sudden determination, he barges noisily into the shared space, thudding heavily to his knees in front of Charlie and burying his head in his lover's lap.

"Gor blind me, scrape me eyeballs out with a spoon; they're too dirty to use ever again," Leo wails.

"Leo!" Charlie is instant concern.

"It was just so wrong! Take the image away, I beg you." Leo is putting on his drama-queen best.

Charlie draws back, suspicious. "What *are* you on about?"

Leo climbs up Charlie, leaning heavily on him while he whispers hoarsely in his ear.

"It was hideous!"

"What was?" Charlie pushes at him irritably, but can't budge the broad shoulders.

"I went to wake our androgynous angels," Leo rasps. "Ye gods, the horror!"

"Oh get on with it, you big baby. Just tell me."

"I never meant to see ...." He pauses for effect and Charlie thumps his shoulder with a fist.

"I knocked. I did. I couldn't hear a thing. So I opened the door. Inside ...."

"Hmmm?"

187

"Was a huge pregnant lady."

"Oh for gods' sakes!"

"With a gigantic belly. Naked. Bouncing. Doing it to a bright red boy. Just like in your *Wild Kingdom* vid, Charlie!"

"Oh. My."

"It was grotesque. It was unnatural. I feel uncleaaaan!" Leo wails.

"You are *such* an idiot."

"My eyes, my eyes!"

"Stop moaning in my ear. I didn't need that image either, thank you very much." Charlie pushes Leo's face far enough away so he can look at him. "So, all this fuss is just because … you saw …?

"Exactly," Leo says in his normal voice. He turns and slides down between Charlie's knees, leaning back against him.

"Next thing I know, you'll want to do *me*, and where might that lead, I asks ya?"

Charlie stands suddenly, jostling his partner.

"Charlie?"

"Get up."

"My angel? My pure one? Surely you can't want …."

"Follow me. Now."

"Oh, the indignity!" Leo wails, following his lover with a bit more bounce to his step than usual.

"Oh, the shame!" he moans happily, carefully latching the bedroom door behind them.

• • •

— *THE CHANCELLOR'S TALE*

Charlie and Leo roust us in the late afternoon. It's time to talk. They tell us they got very little from the old man earlier about the situation at Uni, and nothing about our Townie traveling companions. The old man had just rambled about his son, lost years ago, and how he loathed the sea wasps in the exhibit hall.

All we know is something's gone wrong. Somehow it felt important to take time to eat, sleep, and play a little before facing the next hurdle.

The Chancellor sits primly in the sitting room. He's twitchy around Joon, but gives the rest of us a jerky nod. We gather by the artificial light of the window and breathe in the damp earth and green plant smells as if that will help. Charlie and Leo have spoken with the Chancellor about our own unproductive venture, but it's time for us to hear what the old man has to tell us about the home front. We've put it off as long as we can. We know the news won't be good.

"It was that girl," the Chancellor starts, his eyes flicking over our Joon in a way that makes me tense up.

We never liked him.

"That Madgirl. And the storm," he adds, as if to be fair. "And the quake. I suppose you can't have seen the Town yet?" He's looking at me and seems to expect a response.

"We came in from the west," I say cautiously, "why?"

"Well, it was probably very localized," the old man snorts as if it's all a joke. "Storms inside and out." He fades away into his own thoughts for a moment. His shoulders hunch and he looks down at his feet like a naughty child.

"Chancellor?" Charlie sounds a bit alarmed. The old man looks up and pats the younger man's hand weakly.

"Your plan was good. The Warehouse students were settling in, figuring out where to live and eat. The halls were full of young people again. They seemed so happy!

The faculty and the staff from the Town worked with them to set up study schedules – and to teach them what that meant.

"This place of learning felt so hopeful again. Everyone was excited. The new students were quite drawn to the library and the museum. They soaked up whatever we threw their way – especially the food." He chuckles a little, then quiets.

"That … self-styled Madgirl … just trailed along behind. Whenever something new came up – for example, when we suggested putting some of them to work in food prep – they'd always look to her for permission. She'd nod – and only then could we move forward. But it didn't occur to me then that she really had total control over them." His head twitches suddenly. A negation. "I barely noticed her after a while; she was just there, in the background. An annoyance. A rock in one's shoe. I focused on all those lively minds, so ready to learn what we had to teach." His voice trembles. An old man's voice.

"It was a good plan," he says again, some of the old authority ringing out. He looks directly at Leo. "A praiseworthy plan."

"Yes," Charlie answers for Leo, who looks shell-shocked. This had been their plan, after all. And their failure evidently, whatever it was.

"A month of pure joy." The old man sighs. "Then the first disturbance hit."

For once it wasn't the wind. Though evidently a low-pressure change preceded it. During the storm, somewhere out on the continental shelf – recorded by the University's elderly seismographs – the world had shifted, had shrugged its shoulders, and the tiny fleas riding on its back paid the price. There was an enormous quake, its epicenter far out to sea, far enough away to tumble only the rough shacks – including the Trash Café – flat to the earth. The Townspeople had felt it – and breathed a premature sigh of relief that it hadn't been worse.

The University sent out warnings about the coming wave. And come it did. The water itself would cover the entire port Town, but it wasn't just water. First the ocean receded, disappearing out to the horizon, leaving a seabed scattered with rubbish. Because of the warning, almost everyone knew what that meant. Only a few foolish souls ran out onto the seabed, greedy for salvage. Most port residents hurriedly evacuated. Those who could raced uphill to the safety of the University. No one had been able to carry much. The survivors watched in horror from the cliffs as, instead of a wall of water, a moving wall of garbage taller than an upended ocean liner pitchpoled onto the Town, smashing everything in its path.

Shipping containers tossed with tires and Styrofoam cups, ancient condoms and Playtex tampon sheaths, iron girders and broken boats; corroded beer cans and barrels of toxic waste mixed with old bones, refrigerators, plastic forks, rotting corpses, broken bicycles, old shoes, porcelain doll heads, Bubble Wrap, broken fishing nets laden with corroding bomb cases, boots, shopping carts, airplane parts, cars, broken glass, chunks of asphalt and paving stones, and plastic everything: tarps, phones, hearing aids, teeth, picture frames, crates, benches, eyeglasses, furniture, computers, trash cans, shelving, and children's toys. The undead detritus of a dying civilization came crashing down with force on homes, Market stalls, roads, and any unlucky people who thought they were far enough inland to be safe, pulverizing everything in its path into rubble.

It was difficult to tell when the water receded again, as it left its deadly mountain of garbage behind. The entire Town was buried by what the ocean ejected. There was no hope of uncovering it, much less rebuilding the port. It had become a giant rubbish dump.

Leo and Charlie are beyond shocked; this is not what they'd expected to hear. I feel resigned, numb, as if some disaster I'd long anticipated had come to pass, in whatever shape it took. Joon's eyes are closed, her face calm but a little gray.

"That was the external event," the old man's voice intones, as if he's reciting a lesson. "The internal storm came next."

It was chaotic finding places for the Townspeople. Most of the survivors were from the port Market. They were the ones who had believed the warnings, or seen what was coming and fled first. Many of them worked at, or had relatives working for, the University, and there was room, despite the recent accommodation of the Warehouse kids. The kitchens went to work overtime. The agriculture section suddenly had as many workers as it could use. The Town Fisherfolk were finally able to explore the Aquaculture section – and were even encouraged to start learning how it and the Mari cultured jelly-fish farm worked, with its piped and filtered seawater. It wasn't exactly a happy time, but the University halls were bustling, and people were working together – at first. When problems did arise, it was often over space and food, though it was obvious the University could accommodate the numbers.

But somehow Madgirl was in the middle of every conflict. It soon became clear that the biggest disagreements were over people's roles. When people were hungry and scared, working in the kitchens or on the farms were popular jobs. But as everyone settled in, and the Warehouse kids began to resume their lessons, resentments arose. The Chancellor had hoped to teach them, for example, the basics of engineering and food science, so as to be able, one day, to fix windmills, make batteries, run the hydroponic plants, and keep the grid going. But the folks who worked every day to grow and provide food for the rest became resentful. Any students not actively helping in the kitchens or ag buildings, or who spent too much time in the library, were given smaller portions, which led to infighting. And every-where that an argument began – there was Madgirl.

"I heard the same thing from every sector," the Chancellor groans. "'The Townies resent us,' or 'those Warehouse punks are using us.' And then the inevitable happened, and the Townspeople discovered the Ware-house students were different, better, probably fertile, and *worst* of all – longer-lived. There were ... jealous disputes. An understatement, I fear. Jealousy." His expression darkened.

Leo hides his face in his big hands. Charlie's hands are over his mouth, eyes wide. Joon's eyes are still closed.

"We had a classic 'them versus us' situation, with everyone taking sides and feeling hard done by. I believe the Townies, despite their obsession with having or not having children, never considered the Warehouse folk *as* young people, even when the Town was standing. They were too different, too dirty, too – *old*. The separate groups tolerated each other back then, when the Town was still there, by staying away from each other for the most part. But with everyone in close quarters? Well, you can imagine. Because here the Townies were being told that their new purpose in life was to support these 'special' people."

"But Chancellor, you're a public speaker, above all. You've dealt with these kinds of situations before. You, of all people, with your love of history, you know where this kind of thing can lead. Did you not try to stop it?" Leo's rich voice pleads rather than criticizes.

"Of course." The old man sits with such dignity, even I can see how he could command respect. For a moment his voice is firm and strong and he radiates power. Then he wilts.

"But that *female*," he whines. "That insane – mad – girl. She was a destructive little animal, undoing every attempt I made. You understand how a certain momentum can begin, a movement in a direction, good or bad, like a wave ... and one person can't easily stop or direct it. But she could. She was like a sharp rock in a fast river, parting the river into two halves. But that wasn't enough for her. Oh, no."

"Divide and conquer," Leo rumbles, lifting his face, expression deadpan.

"Exactly." The Chancellor gives him a sharp look. "You understand. There is historical precedent. Perhaps she planned this all along, or took advantage of the situation that arose, but the first thing she took control of was the food supply, and the first thing she got rid of – was me.

"She was *never* interested in the new students learning what we had to teach. I don't think it mattered to her that the technology the University offers won't last without maintenance. She certainly doesn't want us to pass on our cultural history. She is *not* an intellectual." He looks lofty for a moment, before his shoulders sag once again. "She's a thoughtless animal, destroying for the fun of it!" The old man sinks back on the couch, lips pressed tight, his face angry and confused.

"Where did things stand when you retreated here?" Charlie asks. But I can't listen anymore. It's obvious. There's been a coup. Madgirl's in charge and she's being destructive. I brought her here. And we are out of time.

"Sometimes one person can make a difference," I say, getting up to look for my pack. I start sorting through our pile of bags, wondering if there are any supplies left.

"What? Are you going somewhere?" Joon sounds scared. "We don't know what's really going on out there now, or whether the Townspeople …."

"The Townsfolk are dead," the Chancellor says grimly. "I'm sure of it. Or in hiding like me, or working as slaves for *her*." His old voice shakes. He's pathetic. "I was in fear of my life and left while I still could. But I had time to plan ahead a little." He waves his hand around the luxurious room. Charlie looks shocked.

"But, Chancellor, clearly one voice can make a difference, as you said. If you'd stayed …?"

"I'd be dead too," the old man says grimly. "I kept an eye out. I still had some surveillance – until it was dismantled." He looks pained. "There were a few Townspeople who brought me news. I think they saw me as a kind of deposed king in hiding …." And he giggles.

It's a horrible sound. Out of character.

Charlie and Leo exchange glances. They must see the importance of hearing the other side of this story. I *have* to find out.

"Do you also get visits from … the students? The Warehouse kids?" I ask. I grab a pack and stand waiting, hands rigidly at my sides. I feel like I'm about to implode.

"No." The old man purses his lips. "Even my favorites abandoned me in the end. The ones I helped most told everything to that ... female." Now his expression is petulant.

Frack. He's more out of touch with reality than we are.

"I wanted to help them," he intones impressively. "But it was just too late."

When Joon speaks, it's like a gong ringing in that closed space. "What exactly was your relationship with Madgirl?" she says, her voice hard and deep. We all look at her in surprise.

The old man hunches his shoulders. He says nothing.

"Did you do something to her?" Again the gong of her voice rings out. But the old man stays silent, his face turned away from her.

"Did you ever try to teach *her*?" Joon asks.

"What would be the point?" The old man looks up, surprised. "She doesn't have the immortality gene."

We are shocked silent.

"So you're the one discriminating," Joon says finally.

"I gave everyone productive roles, according to their potential," the old man says.

Charlie gasps.

"And what role did you give Madgirl." I allow the sheer irony to bitter my tone.

"Nothing!" The old man is suddenly shouting. "I gave her nothing because she was worth nothing. You don't know; you didn't see her. Just standing there she seduced everyone in sight. Oh, the Townies *loved* her at first. They were practically falling over themselves ... until I showed them how it really was."

"And how was it, really?" Joon's low voice is so controlled it sounds brittle, breakable.

"Whore!" Old man spittle flecks Joon's face. "That bitch came to me, pretending she wanted to work with me. As if she had anything to offer! And she turned on that – thing she does. I felt it. I was being manipulated – we all were! She wanted to control *me*. I am not that easily controlled! I locked her in a dark room – left her there for a week. I knew what it would take to break her. She couldn't get to me then! Ha!"

We watch, horrified, as what had once been a grand old man decays in front of our eyes. The Chancellor spits as he rants, his eyes water, and his hands shake. Without warning he lunges at Joon, landing a roundhouse punch to her cheek. It rocks her head back but she stands firmly, glaring at him.

"Whore!" he screams again, and then I take him down. *Rage!*

I sit on him, punching his head until he's silent – and I keep hitting him until Charlie and Leo drag me off. Joon makes no move to help them.

"*Damn* him!" I scream, shaking off first Charlie, then Leo. They stand close, between me and the downed Chancellor. I pace the room, so angry I can't stand still. "I invited Madgirl here. This is my fault. And maybe it could have worked, but that filth-licker locks her up? After what was done to *her*? What the hell happened here?" I'm panting a little.

It's over. Is it over? Everything we try, always too late.

"She was our hope for even having a future. Do you know she never had a bit of care from Mother, not even as much as the rest of us. Who ever gave *her* hope? She never had a place. She might be the most powerful empath on the planet. She may be the only person who could have helped him make this work, and he locks her up in the dark and calls her a *whore*? What's *wrong* with you people?"

And suddenly it's Jae versus the room. Joon stares at me incredulously.

"'You people?' Jae? Are you not one of us?"

"I. Don't. Know." I take a deep breath that gives me no air. I can't calm down. "I'm gonna get Mother. Maybe it will help. I don't know." I scoop up a pack. Stepping over the unconscious body of the Chancellor, I go to Joon. "I love you," I say huskily. "So much. But I don't know if we can save anything. I don't know if there is any place left for new life. Maybe it's been too late for a long time. But I have to try." I kiss her hard and leave her standing there. Alone.

• • •

— *JAE ON TOP OF GARBAGE HILL*

On the cliff overlooking what had been a Town, I can barely see the curve that delineated the once bustling harbor – bustling compared with any other human habitation we saw in our travels. My stomach feels hollow with loss. The entirety of the lowlands are completely filled with rubbish on top of rubble. There's no way down and in. The unstable mounds and mountains of twisted metal and plastic look impossible to move through or over. The harbor itself is choked with upended boats and broken containers. It will be some time before the water manages to move or wear it down – if ever. The Town has become a dangerously unstable dump. I wonder how long it will be before people, desperate for raw materials, risk their lives mining it for whatever they can salvage. I don't want to think about that too hard. I've already spotted what look like rotting munitions shells, and there's bound to be worse.

I set off at a trot along the cliff top, heading south. Hopefully the curve of the hills protected the

Warehouse, but there's no knowing how far the power of the wave pushed its deadly cargo inland. I assume the wind farm is far enough, high enough, to have escaped, but I plan to check that too. The pressure is still building as the new storm front we came home on continues to develop, but the air is relatively still, and it feels like I have a bit of time before the front hits. The pack starts to chafe as I run and, as I adjust a shoulder strap, my hand catches in a loop of beads. With a sinking heart I realize I've grabbed Joon's pack instead of my own. This pack is festooned with beads and bones and feathers. How could I have missed that? I consider just dumping it and running on, but I stop to take a moment and see what's left inside. Our rations were gone by the time we'd reached the Chancellor's rooms, so it's unlikely there's anything useful.

The pack thuds on the ground as I slip it off. I wonder idly if she's slipped some books inside. A minute later I'm sitting on the ground, laughing out loud as I take out box after box of candied jellies from the pack. My darling magpie is nothing if not careful about her food. Joon has clearly been hoarding since we got back. Besides the candy, there's a full waterskin, a large packet of salted jellyfish, bandages and salve, a worn piece of tarp, a crank flashlight, and a knife. There's even a billed hat with a tie to keep it on in the wind. When did she have time for this? At the very bottom of the pack is a thin book. I pull it out – Joon's record book. She's kept it ever since Charlie started teaching her to write on our long trek. I open it at random and see my name scribbled again and again in her childish writing.

Newest one, I rite you, sins the wrld is danjrus, and no noing if we will meet. I hve no name fr you, and may not till you r born

into wun. If you live, plees no Jae as a fathr. Let him find you
a name. Jae is gud with names. He haz many. Charlie and Leo
will love you, but giv Jae a chanz. Giv him many. He is my grate
love – uther then you – an wurth the effert.

I feel short of breath. I flip to the end of the pages of large, scrawled handwriting and read the last entry:

Sum thin rong. We cum home to find no place fr my baby to be
born. Can you forgiv me fr this wrld? I want so bad to see you, fr
you to liv – even if thers no hope. I heer you in me. Wen you mov
I feel life. Evry minit with you is preshus. I fite fr you long as I
can. I stoll food to fill r paks. We may got to run – can you forgiv
me? I no Jae will stay with us to the end ....

I won't cry. Instead, I swear a blue streak and jump to my feet, my errand even more urgent now.

• • •

—A SMALL CONTAINER CAN HOLD A LOT

Joon refuses to leave the Chancellor's rooms. She hasn't spoken since Jae left. Charlie's worried.

Joon's thoughts still wing away from my understanding; skit-
tering through windy skies.

Charlie and Leo shut the Chancellor, as best they can, into his sleeping quarters, but he's awake and raging inside, and they can't keep him there forever.

"I honestly don't know if there's a better place to go at this point," Charlie sighs. He's in the pool with Leo, taking a moment. Joon is hiding in the small room she and Jae shared the first night and even the Chancellor went quiet after they shoved some food and wine into his room. It's like having two unruly children to look after.

"We'll have to let him out eventually," Leo says thoughtfully. "Or we could bump him off and just stay here until the food's gone."

"Leo!"

"Get real, Charlie, where else are we going to find a safe place – and food enough – for Joon to have her baby? She's getting close, and now that Jae's gone she's depressed as hell."

"You'd kill the Chancellor for a place to stay and some candied jellyfish?"

"I don't know," Leo says. "Maybe. I'm not sure we have options now. We've had it too easy." Charlie snorts. "I mean it, Charlie. You saw how the Earth People have been living. We weren't even aware it was that bad out there."

"So we go back to our own rooms and help the others with the University hydroponics, the gardens, the wind farm. We go back to civilized people, Leo," Charlie says. "We have everything we need right here at Uni. We always have. Kill the Chancellor? That's like letting in the wind. Once that starts, we're already over as a species."

"What if he were to hurt our Joon?" Leo asks. "Or the baby?"

Charlie is silent for a long time.

"Charlie?"

"Then I would shred him. Without hesitation. And I don't want to be that person, Leo. There has to be another way!"

"Well, we can't keep him shut up," Leo says. "I don't trust him. So that means we take our chances with the others. Are you prepared for the possibility of that being even worse?"

"The life I always wanted to live was the Chancellor's life of intellect, not just the day-to-day survival of the Earth People. Do we even have a choice anymore?

"I'm tired," Charlie finally adds. "This is a good place to recoup our energy and rest. Just for a couple of days, Leo," he pleads. "Besides, I doubt Joon will go anywhere just yet."

"She wanted to leave," Leo says. "But now she's just waiting for Jae."

"Yes," Charlie sighs again. "Let's all wait for Jae. Just for a few days. Then we'll go out into the world and find what's left of our dream."

But in the morning, they discover the Chancellor is gone.

• • •

— *JAE IN DEEP*

I'm nearing the point where the cliffs swoop down to join the lowlands. As different as the landscape looks, I still hope to find a way down to the Warehouse. I'm above the path Charlie and I traveled, so very long ago it seems, to free Madgirl. The Warehouse is just a bit farther along, on the very outskirts of Town. It might still be accessible. I wonder if it's possible to reach any of the tunnel accesses, but fear the landscape is too changed for me to find them. The ones back in Town are most likely flooded. What would have happened to the Warehouse kids if they hadn't left for the Uni's higher ground before that trash tsunami?

As the lowlands rise again there's less detritus. I can see what may be the outlines of ruined buildings through the rubbish. The wave lost energy this far south, it seems. It came in from the northeast, hit the Town, and then flowed south along the natural lowlands. Eventually that land rises again into the undulating hills of the Wind farm. But the lowest areas are devastated. My heart thumps at the sight of a symmetrical shape jutting up from the sea of garbage. I'm still on the high ground, dreading setting foot on that shifting mass, but it does look like I might be seeing the roof of one of the smaller unused warehouses. If it is, it's the first uncrushed building I've spotted.

I stare into the mess and something moves down below. A person? Without considering, I shout out, but the creature ducks out of sight. There is no doubt about it; something is alive down there. I'm going to have to wade in.

• • •

— THERE'S ALWAYS SOME MAD GIRL

(and who can blame them?)

Charlie can't help feeling they should have noticed the front door being ajar. There's more air movement in the room, now that he thinks about it. The Chancellor, with strength he hadn't seemed to have, pushed past the furniture they shoved in front of his bedroom door and simply walked down the hall and out the front door. The door's probably been open all night and morning while they cooked a leisurely breakfast and tried to tempt Joon with it. The news of the old man's escape at least brought her from her room, but she's still quiet and subdued.

"Perhaps it's just as well," Leo grumbles from his perch on one of the old brocaded chairs. He's washed and shaved, and has turned from a furry kobold back to human again. But he's so big he still looks like a man in a dollhouse. Charlie also feels renewed with clean, combed hair, a change of clothes, and a bit more food in him. He's shaved his scanty beard. All of their faces are weatherworn and thin. They aren't the same people who set out to map civilization.

Charlie stares at Leo hard. "A moral dilemma avoided?" he says, but doesn't explain when Joon looks at them quizzically.

"I don't trust that old bigot." Leo returns the look thoughtfully. "He knows Jae's going for Mother. What if he tells Madgirl?"

"Would it make a difference?" Charlie says. "Honestly, I wonder if anything we do matters."

"Hey now!" Leo says, looking warningly at Joon. "What's that about?"

"That's right," a new voice breaks in. Charlie whips around. Joon flinches but barely shifts in her chair. She hangs her head; hair half hiding her face.

Madgirl has walked right in the open front door, which none of them ever bothered to close after the Chancellor left. A machete hangs at her hip. Others crowd in behind her. She's staring, with dread and longing, at Charlie. At Charlie's blue eyes.

"Mother?" she says.

• • •

— JAE MEETS A NEW KIND OF EARTH PEOPLE

I stagger on the tilted deck of a fishing boat as it settles under my weight. Suddenly I'm sliding down the slimy surface, tangling with a plastic chair, of all things. I'm sure the boat will crush me as it continues tilting, bow to the sky, but instead it turns into a slick ramp that dumps me onto a lower level of trash, then stops. I wait, breathless, to see which way to fling myself, then realize my footing seems stable. The smell under the boat is unbearable, a mixture of rotting seaweed and acid mud, pulped iron, and decaying jellyfish. I wish I'd listened to myself and avoided this particular adventure, but I'm so sure one of the tunnels to the Warehouse is nearby. There is a sudden movement again, to my right, deeper down and farther in. With some hunting instinct from a previous life aroused, I crouch down and creep forward.

• • •

— CHARLIE & MADGIRL AGAIN

Madgirl shakes her head and approaches Charlie with caution. She startles him by stretching up and sniffing his neck, which he later tells Leo sent chills right down to his toes, and made him think of the Chancellor's "little animal" comment.

"Not," Madgirl says with disgust, "one of us." She stares at Charlie, standing too close. "Why do you look like her then? *Ne!* I know you, longhair. You and that … boy … took me from Warehouse. Why you hiding here with that *kusateru oyaji* now?"

"The – *ah* – Chancellor is no longer here," Leo says. "We were tired and hungry. It seemed a safe place for a while."

"Well, that's truth," the girl says cryptically. "But not safe now." She's been ignoring Joon, all while moving closer. Leo is faced with a grinning Townie when he shifts to step between them. So the Townies aren't all dead. Charlie recognizes a man from the Market.

"Fish Master," Leo nods, which wipes the grin off the man's face, but he doesn't step back. Another man steps forward to block Charlie.

Madgirl is in Joon's face now, leaning over the seated girl, staring into her eyes. She hasn't looked at Joon's belly once, and it's hard to miss.

"You ...." She lets out a long hiss of air. "*Hidoi*. How can this be? Why would you do this?" And she puts both of her hands on Joon's belly and shoves down hard. Joon gasps and Charlie and Leo both surge forward, but are blocked by Madgirl's followers.

Joon locks eyes with Madgirl and yanks her own shirt up, grabbing Madgirl's wrists so that her hands are suddenly braced on the bare skin of Joon's belly. Madgirl freezes. Her eyes roll up in her head and her body goes rigid for a moment. Then she jerks back as if she's been burned.

"I hate you the most," she hisses. "You're the cruelest one – *mugoi*." She pushes past her own people, past Charlie and Leo, and picks up a chair. They all flinch as she hurls it into the bay window, smashing the artificial lights and crushing plants. She picks up a porcelain vase and throws it at a wall. Without ever coming too close to Joon, she methodically moves around the room, smashing whatever will break while the rest of them watch silently. She doesn't seem angry, just intent on trashing the room.

She stops and wipes her mouth. "Get any food from the kitchens. Take it all. Break everything else."

"Why?" Charlie says.

"Because it doesn't matter what we do. Because the sooner it's over the better." Madgirl turns toward Joon again, striding over to her so fast no one has a chance to react. She slaps Joon across the face hard, once. She raises her hand a second time, but the Fish Master steps close and catches her arm, whispering something too low to hear.

Madgirl lowers her hand.

"You're the mad one," she says to Joon. "Your actions are insane. There is no place for you with us." The Fish Master tugs at Madgirl's arm and she lets him steer her from the room. The others follow.

Joon crouches protectively over her belly, a hand to one cheek, eyes blazing.

Charlie and Leo scramble over to her.

"Are you okay?"

"*Shimatta*! What is with these wack people smacking me in the face? *Busaiku* bitch!"

The men smile weakly. Joon is back.

• • •

— JAE, STILL IN IT

I am so stuck; squeezed between what feels like greasy plastic boxes with too many corners digging into me. Multicolored light filters down through the hill of garbage I've fallen through. It's like being inside a giant gumball machine, but I'm small and the gumballs seem likely to crush me as they shift underfoot – and over-head. I curse the oil that covers everything. It stinks of chlorine and I can only hope it isn't too toxic. I'd trusted that I could keep my footing, leaping on top of this heap, but the transparent oil fooled me, and I not only lost my balance but slid like a fish through every crack in the heap of garbage. It's unstable even now. The only thing stopping me from falling further is that I'm jammed between two crates. My feet can't find purchase on anything solid enough to let me push back upward into a larger gap.

My hand flails across one gray-green crate and the color wipes off, showing bright red underneath – the original color? What's going on? I claw at it and discover I can dig my fingernails into the red plastic. It feels punky. I end up with oily plastic under my nails and still no good handhold.

I try to yell, but my lungs are compressed and my shout sounds more like a wheeze. I was so sure I'd seen someone moving around down here, but I must have been mistaken. Nothing could navigate in this mess. Why did I try? I need help and there's no one to hear me. I'm well and truly stuck. With nothing to lose I call out again, but can't help kicking out when something brushes my ankle. I can't see what touched me. There is as much terror as relief when unseen fingers wrap around my ankle. A breathless shriek is forced out of me when the invisible hand suddenly yanks downward.

I fall, clonking my chin on the red crate as I slither past. I land on something stable and am yanked side-ways. The mass of garbage overhead shifts and compacts downward, but I'm protected by some kind of roof over-head. I lower my arms as the clatter subsides. I look up into the weirdly lit faces of … surely these are Earth folk? They're very like the people that fed us on our travels, small and the light brown of dry grass. One is holding Joon's pack, shaking the brightly colored baubles clipped to the back. They're all grinning at me.

"*Ah*, thank you," I manage. They all grin harder and pat my back, yammering in some language that doesn't make any sense to me. Some of the words are familiar, but they aren't put together quite right.

The small man holding my pack suddenly rips off a large blue crystal Joon was given just outside the dead city. I protest, knowing she values it. But the little man just threads it onto a string he yanks from his shirt and loops it around my neck. The pack he tosses aside.

"Hey! That's my food!" I barely have time to scoop up Joon's pack as two Earth People grab my arms and pull me deeper into a huge culvert. It's darker, but protects us from the pretty, shifting pile of dangerous rubbish overhead.

The small men – and one woman, I guess, as she has oddly hanging breasts like nothing I've ever seen, even on Mother – let me go and scamper down the culvert. I bend almost double to follow. A lighter patch ahead promises an ending, for which I'm grateful, but when we're finally able to stand, I'm surprised to see the rough-hewn walls and weak battery lights I recognize from the tunnels under the Warehouse. I hadn't been completely sure I'd come far enough before jumping into the garbage; it's a relief they were close. But the familiar wet-cement smell of the tunnels makes me realize I'm actually afraid to face Mother this time. The small grinning people continue to tug me along, not down the tunnel, as I expected, but across it to the alcove in which the dim light hangs. I'm as familiar with the tunnels as anyone at the Warehouse, more than most, but I never noticed hatchways above the battery lights. It makes me wonder if this is really a tunnel I know. It looks similar, but coming in the way we did confuses my sense of direction. One of the small men reaches up and yanks on the hatchway. It clatters down and I see a rusty ladder above it, leading upward into darkness. I sigh. I'm not a huge fan of dark tunnels but they seem to appear quite often in my life nonetheless.

The Earth folk brace their feet on the wall and scamper up the ladder. I have more trouble getting my feet on the first rung. A soft hand under my sole gives me a hand up. I look down at the bright-eyed little woman with the hanging dugs, and notice for the first time that there's something with eyes peering around her from a pack on her back. I almost yell when I realize she's carrying a baby. A baby!

Thumping back down to the floor, I drop to my knees in front of the woman, hands over my mouth. She smiles and swings the baby around for me to see. I can't resist touching the plump, dusty skin with one finger. My own hand is dark and weather-beaten in contrast to the light, satiny wood color of its cheeks, just gently brushed with peach. I realize tears are rolling down my face only when the woman starts wiping at my eyes and calling anxiously to the folk on the ladder. A face appears above and fusses down at us, but I'm lost in the gigantic brown eyes of the tiny baby. I can't look away. When a little hand reaches out and grasps my finger, I think my heart will stop. The other Earth People slowly climb back down the ladder. The woman hands me the warm soft bundle of baby. They all squat in a circle around us and chat calmly to each other, beaming while I cradle the baby to my chest, breathe its sweet breath and feel its warmth spread through my entire being. After a while, I sigh and reluctantly hand the baby back to the woman. She casually slings it around onto her back. When it squeaks, she slings one of her long dugs over her shoulder too. Contented nursing sounds fill the chamber. From a sitting position, I fold my body around until I'm on my knees and bow until my forehead meets the floor of the annex. The woman watches anxiously.

"Thank you," I say, wiping my eyes and sitting up. "You give us hope."

"*Ah!*" the woman says, patting my cheek. Then she gestures up the ladder.

• • •

It's a long, dark climb with little but the rhythmic clang of feet on metal and the softer sucking sounds of the nursing baby behind me. It's surprisingly peaceful. I'm almost sorry when the feet above me stop and I hear another hatchway being pushed aside. Wind and a harsh light pour in. I continue to follow the backlit shape of the man above. We finally step out onto a strangely ridged, high grassland. We must be at the top of the southern cliffs. There are Earth People everywhere, some so small they must be children. Lots of children! Unlike the groups we saw inland, these people are plump, healthy, and very busy. There are gigantic trenches interspersed with 12- and 15-foot-high mounds ridging the landscape. I turn in a circle, to see if I can orient toward Town, but there's nothing but a mountain of garbage to one side, the mounds on the other, and ahead, the glitter of ocean below. The water looks remarkably blue. I wonder idly if it's spewed out enough of its garbage for clear sailing. Probably not.

The woman with the baby waves me toward a trench and we walk over to see what's going on. Lines of people are carting rubbish up from just over the crest of a hill and are throwing their loads down into the trench. The folk I've come here with tug me over to one of the mounds and we walk to the top. Other Earth People are piling dirt there, presumably burying the rubbish. But why? A single man, a bit taller than the others, and as covered in trinkets as Joon's pack, stands at the apex of the mound where there's still an opening showing the buried trash. He flings seawater into it, brought to him by the smallest of the Earth folk, children carrying bottles and boxes and small buckets of water. The man smiles at the children, takes their offerings, and flings each bucket in a wide swath, covering as much area as possible.

"What in the world?"

My entourage approaches the Chief, as I internally dub him (he reminds me of the Chancellor just a bit). They hold an animated conversation in their odd, mixed-up language. The Chief frowns and shakes his head. But they continue to chatter at him. He walks over and fingers the beads on Joon's pack, so I rip off several strands to give him. The old man lifts his lip in a sneer and reaches for the crystal around my neck, but I cover it protectively and the small woman fusses at the Chief, who drops his hand. I tuck the crystal inside my shirt. I want to give it back to Joon. I can't wait to tell Joon about the baby and the children here! I badly need to see her. I smile at the Chief and the frowning face answers by shifting into a wide grin. The man grabs my arm and walks me to a mound far from the others. This mound has been left alone long enough that new yellow grass is growing on it. How long have they been doing this digging and planting of garbage? The Chancellor said the tsunami came only a few months ago. Or was it longer? The Chief keeps up a running monologue in his odd language. I let the sounds run over me. It's been a very long time since I've been around folk who don't speak languages I understand. It's oddly exhausting. Like listening to muffled voices through glass.

We reach the farthest mound. The Chief calls out and I turn to see we've been followed by more than my original entourage. I search through the crowd for the woman with the baby. She's near the front and seems anxious. I wave and turn back to the Chief, who's being handed a shovel by a short lad. I can't help reaching out and touching the small boy's hair. It's so soft. The boy beams up at me and the Chief *harrumphs*. We climb to the top of the mound where the Chief gives a great cry, and slams the shovel into the dirt. The crowd is absolutely silent. I look around, trying to interpret their expressions. The Chief labors for several shovelfuls, then calls down and is replaced by two strong young men. After a while, he calls again and beckons to me. We stare down into the freshly dug hole.

At first I can't see anything, so I lean over. The Chief puts a restraining hand on my shoulder just as the stench hits. It's awful, like getting hit in the face with a combo of chlorine, skunk spray, and rotting jellyfish. My eyes water, but the sun hits the pit just right and I see the shine of oil below. One of the workers shows me the end of the shovel; it's also coated with thick, smelly oil. They quickly throw the dirt back into the pit. I notice they're careful not to touch the oil.

The Chief peers into my face. I rub my forehead, and the Chief nods encouragingly.

"The rubbish turns into that … stuff?"

The Chief smiles.

"But how?"

He mimes throwing water over the rubbish.

"If seawater broke down plastic rubbish into oil, the Town wouldn't have been buried in garbage," I say, mystified. The Chief shrugs his shoulders and holds out both hands, palms up. Then he yells at the crowd and the woman with the baby comes and tugs at my sleeve, so I follow her. Tucked down between the newly dug trenches, and in the lee of the mounds, is a wide clearing. It's very clean, with green growing things around it that have obviously been cultivated. I wonder how they find enough freshwater to irrigate in the desiccating sunlight.

In the compound are a number of baked-earth houses and one big, oddly metallic-looking teepee-style tent. *Frack*! Is it made from rolled solar panels? Things that look suspiciously like antennae sprout from the top. The woman pushes me toward the tent and through a flap opening. I step through into a whole other world.

Inside, everything glows blue. Several computer terminals squat in the central space, where a very tall woman taps at a keyboard. Even sitting, her back is longer than my companion is tall. To one side is a steaming kettle sprouting curled glass and copper tubing. On the other side of the tent is a table set with dozens of round dishes. I recognize them as culture dishes. Charlie used them in his lab. Buckets, jars, and containers sit all around the circular room, but the computers dominate. Nothing about the Earth People ever suggested they had technology like this.

"Oh, good, you made it," says a very clear voice. The woman at the keyboard turns to face me.

"Did you bring my crystal ball?"

• • •

— THE SHAMAN

"What?" I know I look flummoxed. I feel I deserve to look that way. "What is all this?"

"This is a computer, dear boy," the woman says. "Glorified filing cabinet. Thought you'd have seen plenty of them up at that precious University of yours."

"Yes. But …."

"Once upon a time, everyone had the silly things," the woman says. Her eyes are very bright and sharp. "You'd remember *that*, surely?"

I can't answer.

"But what're you doing? Who are you?"

"First, the crystal, if you please." The woman holds out her hand. I hesitate. "I'll give it back. I just want to copy it."

I hand her Joon's crystal, and the woman plugs it into a port on her computer.

"I don't …."

"Information, my dear. That thing your Chancellor is so greedy for – and so stingy about sharing. Among other things, I hope to find better low-tech methods for desalinating water, seeding hemp and bamboo, as well as hints, answers, or better yet blueprints for a number of other key questions we have – like what to do with the noxious oil left in those mounds. Shall I put the recipe for our Plastic Eaters on there for you?"

"The what."

"Didn't our Chief just show you? Our little Plastic Eaters. The wee bugs we're mixing with seawater to break down that tidal wave of garbage that killed your

Town. Very inconvenient for us as well. I shall miss that blue beer from the Trash Café."

"You know it? Of course you know it. But who are you? I do ... *ah*, have Tao's original recipe for that. If you want."

"*Do* you! That would be much appreciated. Write away! Amongst its more amusing properties, that blue poison is also very good as pest control and fertilizer. It's loaded with growth hormones, by the way." She hands me a stylus and a wax slate. "Bit of a problem for these folks, who need to stay little. Smaller food requirements, dontcha know. But I indulge since it's far too late for me anyway." She trails off into a mutter, "Still, we must find them *something* for ceremonies. It's just too depressing to be sober *all* the time ...."

"You aren't related to George Salsbury, by any chance?" I guess as I dig awkwardly into waxy resin with the stylus.

"No, no." The woman's face is serious. "Dear George was a colleague. But yes, he did share his data on Plastic Eaters with me before he sailed away into the sunset. I fear never to return."

We observe a moment of silence for Dear George.

"To be honest, George was a fool, but a very nice man and a good friend. I think he knew they wouldn't make it, but he and the Chancellor's wife were so very eager to leave and start anew after her son was stung by that sea wasp ...."

I ignored that bit of gossip. "If he knew about Plastic Eaters though ...."

"And sailed away in a plastic boat? He never did spend time really thinking through the ramifications of his research."

"But you did?"

"Oh, yes. Plastic Eaters have been around for *hundreds* of years, you know. Invented by a sixteen-year-old girl back before the New Millennium, if one can believe the histories – and one usually can't, my dear. But they were hailed as the absolute *end* of technology and left undeveloped. Just imagine if the little buggers got loose?"

"No more wind farm?"

"No more plastic turbine blades, no more tubing, no more tarps, no more scavenged trash that keeps us hanging on now that we have zip for industry."

"You like trash?"

"We live on trash, dear. And so do you. But that's coming to an end now."

"Why?"

"Because we need to find other ways if we are going to survive."

Could the woman in front of the bank of computers be a closet Luddite? "*Umh*, you didn't cause that tidal wave, did you?"

"You don't strike me as a complete idiot. How could I?"

"But you're dealing with that mountain of rubbish?"

"We had a Zen opportunity not to let it all go back out to sea. We decided to take action."

"I see."

"Do you? Imagine if the oceans were teeming with fish and birds and marine mammals. Imagine being able to take a net to the shore, or drop in a fishing line, and pull up a nontoxic dinner."

"I can imagine that," I whisper.

"Now imagine an ocean of plastic, nothing living, not even jellyfish."

"I don't think I can ...."

"And you wouldn't have to! Because we'd all be dead. We are just doing our bit toward the survival of the species – for however long we can."

"Me too," I say quietly.

"I know, dear," the woman says sympathetically. "You've had a hard row in a leaky dinghy yourself, haven't you? Tell you what. I hear from the gal that brought you here that you're looking for that great cow that used to hunker down in the pits just below here. They can take you to her if you like. A few of them have taken a liking to her, the gods know why. Treating her like the bleeding Earth Mother. They've been tending to her over at the wind farm. She won't leave the place."

"What? Really? How … how did they know?"

"They understand your language fine, just don't care to speak it. Bunch of Insect-Eating Back-to-Earthers trying to reinvent themselves." She sighs. "Like I should talk."

"But you speak it – my language."

"I'm a tech-head, dear heart. They don't want to be like me, but they need me. And I need them."

"For what? To melt plastic?"

"So as not to forget," the woman says, tapping her head with a forefinger. She turns back to her keyboard, pops out the crystal and hands it to me. "Thank you for the data, dear. Don't let the door hit 'cha ass on the way out."

"Oh! Can I come talk to you again?" Suddenly I'm full of questions and don't care if they're the right ones or not. This woman knows so much. "I need to remember too."

"Sure! Why not." The woman grins. "If there's time for a next time in all the works and days of man. Bring that lovely ripe Joon-berry I've heard so much about. Have your people call my people. Ta-ta!"

"Uh, yeah." A shorter, carbon copy of the woman behind the terminal has appeared to usher me out. But I don't want to go yet.

"How did you ...?"

"I'm the information gal," the woman says. "The Shaman." The terminal makes her face more blue than brown. Her teeth glow white. "Or *a* Shaman anyway. We come in all sizes. Oh! And yes, we have a midwife. Or a mid-husband at least," I hear her mutter just as the heavy flap falls and I'm left squinting in the wind and sun.

Shimatta! A midwife! I feel the pressure of time once again. "Can you take me to Mother?" I ask a small person who has come up to stand beside me. It's the woman with the baby. She smiles and gestures inland. I fix my eyes on the calm, sleeping face of the tiny baby on her back and follow.

Chapter 5
MADGIRL BLOWS IT

The auditorium, through Joon's eyes, looks like a disaster survival center. The seats have been ripped out and the floor is filled with mats, blankets, and bodies. People are bunking down here, so perhaps assimilating the Townies into the University space after the trash tsunami hasn't been as simple as the Chancellor implied.

It's also glaringly obvious that the Townies and the Warehouse kids are thoroughly integrated. Another lie of the Chancellor's? Was the old man the one trying to create a schism? Or perhaps he simply retreated into a convenient lie?

Several of the smallest kids from the Warehouse are sitting together on a blanket with the Market Master, who is teaching them how to tie knots. Joon spots Tao sitting against the far wall, with a cast on his leg, and is about to wave when she sees a slender blond Warehouse kid she knows, who can bust heads with the best of them, slide down next to Tao and cuddle up under the arm he slings protectively around the deceptively thin shoulders.

Joon nudges Charlie's arm and points. Charlie grabs her hand and lowers it, but nods. They both scan the crowd. It's the same story over and over; Townies and Warehouse kids are sitting together, lying together, helping each other with small chores. If anything, it looks as if the Townies – survivors who've lost everything, and the most likely to be in need of help, many with obvious injuries – are being protective of the smaller – though not necessarily younger – Warehouse folk. Joon bumps Charlie's shoulder to get him to look toward a big man she recognizes from Town, one of the many struggling Fisherfolk, who's limping through the crowd with a bucket and ladle, feeding anyone who holds up a hand. A redheaded boy she remembers from her Warehouse days, Sami, saunters beside him as if he owns the world, passing out bowls. Occasionally the big man says a word or ruffles the boy's hair and the thin face lights up. He looks like a kid on an outing with his dad. There are recognizable Uni-workers who are also Townies, but the few faculty are notably absent.

Nothing the Chancellor said fits this scene.

Charlie and Joon stare at each other and both turn to Leo. He's also looking out over the crowd like a man having a revelation, his face alive with hope again.

The door behind the dais bangs open and Madgirl stomps in. The Fish Master and his cronies are behind her carrying supplies and what could be weapons, heavy steel rods wound with tape. Joon doesn't like the look of those. Madgirl's people step down off the stage and start handing out packets of food. No one reacts with fear, and Joon relaxes.

"Why is everyone crowded in here?" Charlie asks Madgirl, who gives him a long stare before turning back to the doorway. There's a scuffle going on there. Two more big Townies and a Warehouse kid are tugging at someone who doesn't want to come inside. It isn't much of a struggle though, and a bald Townie with a weatherworn face laughs as he helps yank the Chancellor into the auditorium. The old man's hands are tied, and there's a gag in his mouth. They're pulling him with the rope tying his hands like a leash. He falls to his knees in front of Madgirl, groaning from the impact.

"Stop this at once!" Charlie shouts, his words echoing through the auditorium. Joon's never heard that shrill, impassioned note in his voice before. The entire room goes quiet and all heads turn their way.

Charlie goes down on his knees beside the Chancellor and tugs at the knot binding his wrists while Madgirl giggles.

"How can you do this to an old man!" he shouts up at her.

"You know what he and his sort did to me …," she leans down to hiss in Charlie's ear, then straightens and giggles again. Charlie keeps working at the knots. No one tries to stop him. Leo comes over and pulls the gag from the Chancellor's mouth. Tears roll down the sagging face.

When the old man is free, he sits back heavily on the stage. Leo rubs the thin wrists but Charlie stands to confront Madgirl.

"I see you're able to do good things." Charlie waves to the crowded auditorium of people watching the tableau on the stage. "Your people are helping each other, working together. This is admirable. But what else is going on here? What about the plan to educate? To help these folks live the best life they can? To learn …."

Madgirl is no longer giggling.

"Too late!" she spits viciously. "What good will it do? Remembering the past is pointless. We are all dying. This world is dying. You've been out there. You know it. I can see it in your head. You believe this is pointless!"

Charlie looks helplessly over at Leo, who stands slowly and approaches them.

"Look in my mind if you can," Leo rumbles at the girl. "Do you see hopelessness there?"

Madgirl stares up at Leo, eyes wide. Joon wonders for a moment if Madgirl also reflects back the emotions of others as an expression that seems purely Leo's shifts Madgirl's features. How to interpret it? It was like … dedication? Belief? The love with which Leo looks at Charlie? Madgirl resists, her features twisting. Leo steps in closer and grabs her shoulders. His touch seems to take all resistance out of her.

"Believe me," he says in his deepest, most resonant voice. It rumbles through the auditorium.

"We can make a difference," Leo booms. "We can learn. Work together. Live well. We can create something good, something we can gift – to our children." He nods to the crowd, and then again toward Joon who stands with them, hands splayed on her belly.

Madgirl's eyes are wide; she pants with the weight of Leo's words and feelings, helpless to fight them off. Her eyes roll toward Joon and her whole body flinches. But Leo tightens his grip.

"We need you," he tells the girl. A huge hand lifts to cup her face. "You have not always gotten the love you need," he says more softly. "But your people love you. We all need you."

Tears squeeze from the girl's panicked eyes.

"I'll die," she says.

Leo smiles down on her. "So will I," he says happily. "And I'll leave behind a life I'm proud of – and life itself will continue."

Joon leans into Charlie, who's staring at his lover, eyes liquid with unshed tears. Joon's certain Charlie will forgive Leo for everything now. He understands. Joon presses her belly against Charlie's side and wraps both arms around him. He hugs her forearm to his chest, without taking his eyes off Leo.

No one notices the Chancellor struggling to his feet. But every head turns as the door bangs open again.

It's Jae. He's walking at the front of a litter being carried by a number of tiny people the color of dry grass and dirt. Their dusty clothes and skin, eyes and hair, are all the same color, camouflaged outdoors, perhaps, but completely out of place inside, against the shiny floors and smudged white walls, as if the earth has found a way to walk upright and invade the halls of learning. What they carry is even odder.

On a litter curves a pale mound, numerous small cloths plastered over it where the fish-belly pale skin is tinged red with sunburn. The Earth People at the front carefully set the litter down, while those at the back keep their end high. Mother's tangle of hair has been pushed back. She looks tiredly out of bright-sky eyes; so similar to Charlie's in color, and so different in expression. Joon runs and throws herself into Jae's arms. He staggers back, and the Earth folk brace his legs with supportive hands, crying out encouragement at the same time. Small hands stroke the sides of Joon's belly as she crushes whatever part of herself she can against

Jae. The pattering of the small folk's laughter sounds like rain on dry leaves.

Jae hugs Joon tight for a long moment, then gently pushes her away. When she protests, the little people take her hands and pet them soothingly. She looks down at a face that winks up at her, a finger to its lips, and is surprised to recognize the wrinkled cheeks and fly-away hair of Mother's Mouthpiece – the skittish old woman from the Marketplace who once demanded Joon go to Mother. She's no longer avoiding looking Joon in the eye. The old woman is pale, but so tiny she barely stands out among the Earth People.

Jae approaches Leo and Madgirl. Joon can see that he's trying to take in what's happening as quickly as possible. He stops beside Madgirl and puts a hand on her arm. She flinches again.

"Your mother has something to say to you – something she should have said a long time ago," Jae murmurs to her. Leo releases her. The girl moves as if sleepwalking. Jae tugs her toward the litter and she shuffles over until she stands facing the pale giant of her mother.

Blue eyes fix on the girl. Puffy, sun-peeled lips open, but the words everyone hears, as if whispered directly to each individual in the room, aren't coming from her mouth. A low, pleasant humming fills the hall.

"*Forgive.*" The words form in each mind. "*I was afraid. It was unfair to you.*"

Jae takes Madgirl's limp hand and places it in Mother's.

Both sets of blue eyes widen.

"*You also?*" This time the words also seem to come from Mother's lips, the voice attenuated and light, barely audible. But everyone hears. "*I feared for you. I hid you. I followed you ....*" The cracked lips barely move. A dusty brown hand squeezes a tiny rag over them, wetting them lightly. "*I loved you ….*"

The howl of a wounded animal shrieks out from behind them. The Chancellor staggers forward, balancing an impossibly heavy wooden podium shakily in his skinny arms. It's made from a real tree and is old, the pride of the lecture hall. The Earth People react first, surging toward him while everyone else stands rooted in shock. Two Earth folk hit him at knee height and Joon hears something snap wetly. But the old man continues to pitch forward over their heads, scrambling on damaged legs, and the heavy podium falls with a wet crack on the large woman's skull.

Where there has been a unifying voice in all their minds, there is suddenly nothing at all. The abrupt cessation of life is shocking. Irreversible.

The Chancellor fills the sudden void with foulness.

"Filth! Whore! Get out of my mind!" he screeches, scrabbling at the heavy podium where it lays. It's dark and slippery with Mother's blood.

"Never again! Keep your filthy thoughts out!" he shrieks again, but Jae is there, tearing the shaking old hands away from the wooden block and throwing the Chancellor roughly aside. The man staggers and falls onto floor. The little people push roughly past him and crowd around the litter, patting mother's ruined face, murmuring. Then Madgirl is on him.

"Too late!" she hisses, grabbing the Chancellor's face between her hands and squeezing. Joon watches helplessly as the girl glares down into the old man's popping eyes. A feedback loop of hatred-in, hatred-out wavers across both their expressions. Everyone in the hall feels waves of nauseating loathing and horror as the damaged young woman stares into every dark recess of the old madman's mind. His face purples and the whites of his eyes turn bloody. The thin fingers claw at her cheeks.

"Out. Of. My. Head!" he spits. "Female filth! Bitch!" And with a moan of fear that everyone in the area feels as a red-hot flash, the old man also goes silent.

In the reverberating absence of sound, Madgirl drops the Chancellor's body to the floor and kicks it.

"You say 'bitch' like it's bad." She bares her teeth. When she turns toward the group behind her, her eyes are truly mad.

While the others stand frozen in time, the Earth People silently file from the room. One stays behind; the pale, bent figure of Mother's Mouthpiece wraps its cloaked arms around Mother's neck and stays by her side. Joon watches the rest go with a feeling of terrible sadness. She knows Jae has always had a horror of irreversible actions. She sees that he can't bear to look at the bodies on the stage. She cannot imagine what they will all do next. She wants to comfort him but her hands stay limp and lifeless at her sides. There seems no comfort possible.

Madgirl turns to Leo. "No such thing as hope," she says cryptically to the big man, who stands unmoving 10 paces away, unable to process what's just happened.

Madgirl reaches into the dead Chancellor's coat and pulls out a small, black plastic box. She holds it up over her head so all the shocked and frozen people can see it.

"Present from the dead," she giggles and toggles a switch.

Jae leaps forward and pushes Joon to the floor.

• • •

— BADABOOM

The first explosion takes out NonK and the entire library wing. Every information station in the University goes up in sparks, starting numerous fires.

Charlie finds himself sitting on the stage. He looks up to see Leo shaking Madgirl, who's limp in his grip, her head snapping with each shake.

"It's not too late," Leo's saying. "We still have the greenhouses, the wind farm. There's still hope ...."

"Too late," Madgirl mutters, eyes wide with fear and despair. Leo realizes he's shaking her too hard, just as Charlie reaches out a restraining hand. Then a second explosion hits. It throws both men off the stage onto the auditorium floor along with most of the crowd. Madgirl goes down hard under Leo. When Leo manages to get shakily to his feet, Charlie can see the girl is unconscious. He wonders vaguely if she's dead too. No one moves to check. Leo yanks Charlie upright, pulling him toward the doors. Charlie feels disoriented. He fingers a throbbing spot on his head and his hand comes away dripping black. The whole world seems to have lost its color.

"We have to get out of here." Leo looks like he's shouting, but Charlie can't hear him clearly. His voice is muffled, like sound through water. Good thing Leo has such a deep voice, Charlie thinks vaguely. He's sad. Why is he sad? What's happening? His head hurts.

Joon! There's Joon. So that's okay. They need to keep Joon safe. And there, Leo has Jae too. He's holding him by one arm and shouting at him, pointing. Something about the hydroponic farm being the most important? Why is it? Charlie's always felt strongly that the library is their most valuable asset. He's told Leo so. But something's happened to the library, hasn't it?

Charlie's ears pop, just as the room fills with smoke. Leo's huge voice booms out, suddenly clear.

"STAY CALM! HELP EACH OTHER CLEAR THE ROOM! LEAVE THE BUILDING NOW! DO NOT STOP FOR THINGS! GET PEOPLE OUT!"

Charlie giggles weakly. That's Leo all over.

Then his lover's arm is around him and he feels that everything will probably be okay. But he does want out of that smoky room.

He lets Leo pull him toward the door, looking down as they pass Mother's body to see the tiny old figure still wrapped around – shielding – the ruined head. The daughter still lies unmoving down on the floor.

The hallway outside is full of people running. Leo has Joon by one arm. Joon is shrieking something about Jae. The shrill pitch of her voice hurts Charlie's head. His vision is still muffled and gray. "Where's he gone?! Where'd you send him, you bastard?" Why is Joon hitting Leo?

Leo has each of them by one arm, trying to drag a staggering Charlie and a hysterical Joon toward the main exit. A Warehouse boy is standing in the big double doorway up ahead, holding it open and pushing people out. He gestures for them to hurry. Joon tries to pull them back in the opposite direction.

Leo is forced to stop or lose hold of the struggling Joon, just as something large and flaming crashes down between them and the doorway, scattering shards of burning debris. Charlie feels the heat blasting off it, tightening the skin on his face. He hopes the boy in the doorway is okay. It's impossible to see behind the rubble and flames and smoke.

"Leo," Charlie says reasonably, "we can't go this way. Let's follow Joon." Joon's already twisted from Leo's grasp and is running back past the auditorium and toward the labs.

Leo swears but he doesn't move to follow Joon. Charlie tugs at his arm.

"Leo. It's hot. We need to go with Joon."

"No, baby," Leo says. "I need to get you somewhere safe." He pets Charlie's head, then stares at the blood that comes away on his hand. "I need to take care of you," he whispers, eyes wide.

"Don't be stupid!" Charlie says sharply. He feels clearer now, though he thinks he might be speaking too loudly. Leo needs his help. "I'm fine. Head wounds bleed a lot. You know that. We have a job to do. We need to follow Joon."

"There are going to be more bombs," Leo says tiredly. "He'll have wired the greenhouses, the hydroponics, the fish farm ... anything that would let us survive."

"What?" Charlie stares. "Why?"

"Maybe he was afraid of living," Leo says. But then he seems to find his energy again. "And I don't give any of us much hope if we don't save the hydroponic reservoirs. Come on!"

"Leo." Charlie feels lightheaded as they trot up the corridor. Something is throbbing painfully in his head. "I want to follow Joon, but what the hell do you know about defusing a bomb?"

"I don't." Leo says shortly. "But Jae might be able to shut off the reservoir. Save it."

"Jae?"

"I told him where to find levers to divert the water. Save your breath. We just have to get lucky now."

231

"Seems in short supply – our luck," Charlie says, then shuts up to concentrates on moving forward as fast as possible. At least the air is better the farther from the fire that they get. So the air purifiers are still working.

He hears a tremendous hissing sound far behind them.

"The automatic fire extinguisher?" he pants.

"Yeah," Leo says. "Let's not get caught by that."

Charlie knows the University system gives time for people to vacate before the foam extinguishers come online, as they leave little available oxygen in the immediate area. It's an imperfect system, but effective. Is it foam though? Or liquid nitrogen? He remembers there'd been a lot of discussion about that among the faculty, long ago.

"The Chancellor always was liable to sacrifice a few for the sake of the many." Charlie tries to laugh and coughs.

"He was willing to sacrifice everyone, Charlie," Leo says. "That evil, misogynistic bastard. Can't believe I thought that old woman was our worst obstacle. She very nearly saved us."

The thought of Mother sobers Charlie up. He's completely alert now, adrenaline pumping. His last view of Mother – hurts. The image of the three broken women in their frozen tableau is seared into his mind.

Mother, Maiden, and Crone versus the Patriarchy. All down. What now?

"We were always our own worst enemy," he says sadly.

"Shut up and run, Charlie," his lover replies.

They find a small group of people milling near the Chancellor's ruined offices. Tao of the Trash Café is one of them.

"Have you seen Jae?" Leo calls as soon as he sees them.

"We followed him this far," Tao says grimly. He's supported on one side by the willowy blond from the Warehouse. "We were gonna help, but he said it was too dangerous. Told us to stay here."

"No. Get the hell outside," Leo says. "I sent him to divert the reservoir before another bomb goes off, but there may be others."

"I reckon that *hidoi yarou* wouldn't have wired his own quarters," Tao says grimly.

"You think he wasn't suicidal? Get your people out! *Now!*"

"I know somewhere safe." The blond adjusts Tao's arm across his shoulder and gathers the others with a jerk of his head. "I'll take us there."

"Jae said to tell you to find some – Shaman?" Tao says urgently to Leo. "Us too." But the blond is already hurrying him away.

"Just stay away from the greenhouses and the wind farm," Leo calls after them. "Hey! Have you seen Joon?"

"Just behind Jae," they call back, running now as the fear hits them.

"*Shimatta!*" Leo swears. "Stupid, pregnant *ushi*-cow." He pulls Charlie along again, heading north, toward the labs and the hydroponic farms.

"Thank you for not … asking me … to leave with them," Charlie pants.

"Would it have done any good?"

"*Huh,*" Charlie grunts. Something is bumping around in his mind and he can't quite … *Ah!* "Leo! Liquid nitrogen! They decided on liquid nitrogen for the auto-extinguishers in the research areas!"

His lover looks at him as if he's mad. "That's stupidly lethal," Leo says, stopping abruptly.

"They chose it," Charlie explains carefully, "because NonK claimed it was used in one of the world wars to freeze bomb mechanisms. To render them useless! The Chancellor wanted a two-in-one system in case of terrorists. But he didn't know he was the terrorist back then." He almost laughs but is afraid he won't be able to stop. Somehow he squashes it. "Leo, we have to start a fire in the labs!

"See," he says, as his partner's face lights once more with hope, the only expression that matters anymore. "You need me."

"I've always needed you," Leo says, pulling Charlie to him and kissing him hard. "I need you so much it's killing me. Now run!"

• • •

Charlie remembers where the sprinkler system emergency switch is. He'd been on that committee. But it's moot when they arrive at the main lab because Joon is inside, standing right next to a huge, obviously handmade bomb. It's squatting in plain sight on top of a dissecting bench in the middle of the lab. It's a big ugly can of fuel wrapped with steel rods with an obvious timer taped on top. It seems unlikely that it's connected to the same remote mechanism that blew the library, which confuses Leo, who realizes he expected a predictable, sequential pattern of explosions from the normally tidy and organized Chancellor – however insane the old bastard became.

Jae's inside too, trying to push Joon into the safe-like, lead-lined cupboard set into the wall of every lab, with a symbol over it for bomb shelter; the Chancellor cutting corners again. Will it be safe enough? Interestingly, the bomb and shelter are side by side, a threat coupled with an invitation to hide.

Charlie looks longingly at the nitro systems switch, then follows Leo into the lab. They walk softly.

"Jae," Leo says quietly.

"Get out," Jae replies. "Take her with you."

"If the mechanism is too difficult, Charlie says this sprinkler system has liquid nitro."

"That would kill everything in the labs. The hydro and fish tanks are open!" Jae is tense.

"But it would save the system itself."

"And poison the entire reservoir. This can't be the only bomb," Jae says. "Too obvious."

"Agreed. Is it on a timer or motion sensitive?"

"*Ah!*" Jae's barely had time to look at it. He's been too busy panicking over Joon.

"Shit, Jae," Leo says. "Focus. We need you. You've got the best chance of surviving. We can't do this without you!"

"Then get her the hell out and *let* me focus!"

Charlie is beside the bomb. He reaches out and yanks the timer away from the fuel tank. The wires part easily, which is very satisfying.

"*Huh*," he says, while the others stare, horrified. "That seemed to work."

Jae grabs the timer from him and pulls it to pieces. There aren't any secondary explosives inside.

"*Shimattaaaa.*" He lets out a long breath, locking eyes with Leo.

"A red herring?"

"Definitely."

"Charlie, you hero," Joon says just as Jae picks her up bodily and manhandles her into the cupboard.

"Charlie." Leo motions him to follow. Then finds Jae pushing at his back too.

"But …."

"No time. Stay. I know what I have to do. Go!"

Leo steps into the cupboard. There's room for the three of them, but it's close quarters. There are short built-in benches along each side with storage beneath. Jae slams the door shut and Leo helps him throw the latch from inside. The doors are heavy and the sides are sunk into thick walls. But it doesn't feel safe. What could? Joon turns on a dim overhead battery light. There's a medical symbol over one bench, probably water underneath too. But it clearly isn't meant for long-term occupancy.

"How long does he expect us to sit here?" Charlie says tensely. "I want to do something."

"We weren't helping," Joon says, tears trickling down her chin. She sinks to the floor, her head on her arms across one bench. Charlie rubs her back.

"Where is that fool headed?" Charlie fumes.

"The box jelly tanks," Leo says. "I told him once how much the Chancellor hated those things. They're linked to the same water system, so a breach there would drain the entire hydro farm, which is also fed by the aquaculture tanks. Plus they have the brackish and saltwater reservoirs behind them. It could let a lot of water out fast."

"I thought the Chancellor just hated women," Joon says bitterly. "Oh, and empaths. And did I mention anything with a twat?"

"He accepted the Warehouse folk," Charlie says heavily. "At first."

"He could pretend most of us were male. Except me and Madgirl anyway. And Mother."

"Oh gods," Leo says, finally sitting down. "How could we have missed that?"

"Maybe 'cause you share some of it," Joon says bluntly. "No! I ...."

"It's hardly the same thing," Charlie says acidly, removing his comforting hand from Joon's back.

"Oh, *frack*, I know Leo's not that bad," Joon says. "But you claimed we had a chance to move beyond all that old gender crap, and there it is; *bakeno kawa ga hagareru*, 'the mask is ripped away.' Or why do *you* think the Chancellor wigged, *ne*?"

"He was an old-school bigot," Leo agrees, shushing Charlie's protest. "And he'd been one of the lucky ones: He had a child. But then lost it. Can you imagine anything worse? It was a son. His wife left him after that."

"He saw himself as an intellectual," Charlie offers. "And the story's more complicated than that. His wife insisted on the importance of the life of the body, not just the mind. She was the fearless type. She took the boy out to sea. She wanted him to experience gathering food for himself. They went on one of the fishing boats. He got stung."

"And died?"

"*Hmm*." Charlie nodded. "It was so fast. It had to have been a sea wasp. They didn't used to occur in northern waters. Most of the box jellies we get here wouldn't kill an adult, but .... The Chancellor never forgave her, though she tried to make him, bless her. Years she tried. She ended up having an affair with George Salsbury, remember, Leo? She left with him when he decided to sail to England last year."

"The fellow researching Plastic Eaters," Leo says. "But an affair's hardly grounds for genocide."

"Not to you …. Wonder if they made it to England?"

"You think the Chancellor rigged their boat?!"

Charlie swears. "*Shimatta*. Guess we'll never know. But …. *Frack*. What a thought."

They're silent for a long few minutes.

"I hate this!" Joon says, rising. "*Oitoma*. I have to go." Charlie stops her with a hand on her belly. "You have other responsibilities, Joon."

Standing, Joon raises her face to the ceiling and howls. It's a long wail of desolation and fear. Charlie feels Joon's stomach undulate under his hand just as the entire shelter shifts sideways. The floor ripples and tilts.

As the light flickers, Joon feels the arms of both men encircling her (*encircling us all*), cushioning her belly. She looks down to see their faces close together, looking into each other's eyes with expressions of such tenderness ….

It's time!

She reaches for a strength she's found once before, hidden deep within her, something that crackles like electric cables in water. She's mildly pleased to find that it is blue.

• • •

NonK on Love: *The western philosophical concept of love is sometimes described as "a virtue representing … human kindness and compassion" Though: "'Our virtues are most often but our vices disguised,' according to*

French philosopher François duc de la Rochefoucauld (1613-1680)."

Saint Augustine wrote that human love (as opposed to the gods') "only allows for flaws such as 'jealousy, suspicion, fear, anger, and contention.'" However, "Saint Thomas Aquinas, following Aristotle, defines love as 'to will the good of another'" (Wiki on Love).

In Japanese, "Koi is a feeling of longing for a specific person ... as romantic love or passionate love. Ai tends to be a more general feeling of love. Koi can be selfish ... or wanting. Ai is always giving."

With different kanji characters, "Koi 鯉 means 'carp' and Ai 藍 means 'indigo blue.'"

• • •

— RUN JAE RUN

I run. *Jack be quick!*

I have one chance to figure out what the dead man will blow up next. If I guess wrong, it will be too late. I've never been good at figuring out people – not even myself. Leo had told us the story of the Chancellor's son and the sea wasp when we'd returned from our long trip. I also remember Leo saying Charlie used the idea of lost boys to convince the Chancellor to accept the Warehouse kids before we even left. In any case, Leo made it clear that the sea wasp tank – that I once showed Joon – is where I should head now. But can I really bet everything on that old story of the Chancellor's son? How can I understand the mind of that monstrous bigot, the one who has ruined us all? For what? What did that old man hate the most? I pass the *Turritopsis* tanks. In all the panic and crises, they're calmly circulating in their artificial current. Tiny clear bells with red bellies, floating up and around and down. Polyp to medusa to seed to polyp. Eternal and unthinking. As close to immortal as is possible. I feel a surge of compassion and empathy for these little brothers, but I do not love them. I do not hate them either. What did the Chancellor hate the most? What could be worse than a child dying before its parent? The venomous sea wasps caused that death, not these passive little survivalists.

But after I pass the tiny *Turritopsis,* my footsteps falter. What's pecking at my thoughts? What's an old man afraid of? Something worse than losing a child? Was he afraid of dying? Of living? I picture the Chancellor furious with rage. What motivates that kind of anger? Grief? Fear? Or something I'm not equipped to imagine? Surely not jealousy of a lonely, unending life?

I almost stop, but then picture Joon and her big, vital belly. Joon hiding in the dark. Leo and Charlie hiding with her, along with all their hopes for her child and a future. I picture the big soft eyes of the Earth woman's tiny baby and I know nothing can be more important than that new, hopeful life. Nothing worse than losing that hope.

I sprint the last few yards to the box jelly tank. The sea wasps are healthy, basketball-sized medusas, each corner hung with thick, shortened tendrils pulled in for lack of food to hunt, framed behind thick aquarium walls. Their water has circulated first through the aquaculture reservoirs, which then takes those nutrients to the hydroponic farms, a gigantic system that has the potential to feed an entire town. I spot the lever that diverts the connection, so that even if the container holding the most poisonous animals in the world ruptures, the reservoir that feeds into the aquaculture section – that keeps our food systems alive – should hold.

I leap up, climbing on top of the pipe, and grab the huge lever. There's never been much hope I could fix any of this mess. But by simply moving forward and doing what I must, I discover that I do know who I am, after all. I'm someone who can do this much to protect the ones I love, to protect Joon and the new life she carries. *Who wants to live forever?* So what's the antithesis of this kind of love? What drives the old man's ghost? Hate? Apathy? Despair? Of the old man's deadly sins, I choose despair over envy. Despair is what I've known the best and longest. No one could envy centuries of despair. I put my whole weight on the lever above the box jelly tank and pull it all the way down.

I guess wrong.

With a crump that sounds like kids jumping on chunks of Styrofoam, an explosion over by the *Turritopsis* tanks shatters the huge pipe with the force of an entire reservoir of water behind it. A tremendous jet of water and glass erupts outward. I fly sideways, into the only tank now cut off from the system. I land in the sea wasp tank with a percussive crash that sends every animal splattering up against the glass. As I hit, I see – through a distorted lens of glass and water and shock – the giant blue whale skeleton crumpling as the roof comes down. The entire building, the walls, my loves, the world, is washing away in one last flood of glass shards and old bones.

Superimposed over the chaos I see a crimson reflection of my body in the glass, clothes floating in strips like grave windings, *the memory of Joon's fingers playing through my hair.* It's over. It is done. No more chances. No more hope. No reset. Game over.

Fade to black.

• • •

NonK Says: It is Universally Accepted that Red Means Danger

(Taken in part and mangled slightly from Wiki Free / Chironex fleckeri)

Chironex fleckeri, commonly known as sea wasp, *is the largest (sometimes described as the smallest) of the cubozoans, or box jellyfish. Its bell may grow to the size of a basketball, trailing four clusters of 15 tentacles from each corner. The tentacles can retract to 15 cm when resting, or thin and extend to 3 meters when hunting. It is the most lethally venomous species of box jellyfish in the world .... The venom from one animal is enough to kill 60 adult humans ... in as little as 3 minutes.*

In common with other box jellyfish, *Chironex fleckeri have four eye clusters with 24 eyes that seem capable of forming images. However it's debated whether they exhibit object recognition or tracking, since it's unknown how they process information due to the lack of any sort of brain whatsoever.*

One anecdote tells of a series of tests by jellyfish experts *from the legendary Southern Hemisphere, in which two white poles were lowered into a tank with a single box jellyfish. The animal appeared unable to see the poles and swam straight into them. Similar black poles were placed into the tank. This time, the jellyfish seemed* aware of the black poles and swam around them. Finally, to see if the specimen could see color, a single red pole was placed in the tank. The jellyfish seemed repelled by the object and cowered against the far wall of the tank. The experts believed they had found a repellent for the creatures and proposed red safety nets for beaches and red body suits for swimmers.

Clearly this proposal is highly imaginative, as no sentient being who valued life would consider swimming in the Great Garbage Ocean. Also, the Southern Hemisphere's lost lands (called The Ring of Fire), if they ever existed, are thought to have submerged near the middle of the New Millennium.

These land masses included Lost Atlantis, The Shaky Isles, the Land of Oz and, on the northern curve of the ring, the 7,000 islands of Nihon-koku archipelago, once known as Japan.

• • •

— POOR OLD MICHAEL FINNEGAN BEGIN AGAIN

(Jack's Back)

> "Is it like this
> In death's other kingdom
> Waking alone
> At the hour when we are
> Trembling with tenderness
> Lips that would kiss
> Form prayers to broken stone."
>
> T. S. Eliot – "The Hollow Men"

Gone, all gone; the animals, birds, the oceans. My people are memories, voices calling out to be remembered and lost again. Swirling blue rises and falls with the tides. I have lived too long and now I am alone. I've outlived them all, alone forever in a sea of blue. I will not open these eyes again. There are only the tides, a broken world, and empty blue. What's the purpose of living when the world has gone away?

Joon's bright voice calls out to me. I comfort myself with memories of Joon, of Joon's baby, of big Leo and serious Charlie. I long to see Joon's face. I sink down to the bottom, holding my beloved's image. Remembering. Why did they leave me alone? I am angry. I am sad. I am lonely. I float calmly in a sea of blue. There is nothing else. There is comfort in knowing there will be no more struggle. I won't open my eyes. I will not grow to adulthood again. Alone. I flutter my bell and float with the tides.

"Jack!"

A disturbance. Thoughts flick across my jellyfish mind. *Jack and his Beanstalk, Jack the Giant Killer, Jellyfish Jack – last hope for humankind.* Also petulant thoughts; Joon was not the only one attracted to Leo! Was it fair that everyone loved Joon and not me? Well, Charlie didn't love Joon in the end, not that way, though he looked after her like a mother. Do mothers always love their children? I can't remember if I was loved – *ah!* Not remembering is the key. I can *not* remember, and go to join them finally in the tide. I understand the important thing is that I loved them. Calm. Float. Exist. Choose to remember – or not.

The blue light is everything. I cycle through it, remembering. I float in a primal sea. It's saltier, sweeter, than expected. It does not etch my skin. I am a wriggling jellyfish.

I rise and sink, hear a rhythmic beat.

The world is not dead yet.

A lifeline connects me to it still. The world beats.

The sea closes in painfully, squeezing me down to a ball of hurt. I feel. I must be alive.

The beat increases to something frantic, the sea squeezes and releases, then quite suddenly rejects me with one final *SNAP* as glass walls crack and finally break.

Memories/Detachment/Confinement going, going, gone. My calm world shatters.

I fall through blue into a place of cold and grief. I start to wail with the shock and wonder of it as startlingly cold air fills unused lungs. I am born again.

They are all here, my lovely ones. Waiting for me.

"JACK!"

The beginning is also blue.

• • •

It turns out Sea Wasps really are afraid of the color red. Who knew?

• • •

EPILOGUE

It is the 6th Season, 3rd Summer of the year of the Moon Beetle. A solar pit separates salt from seawater using a huge chipped lens, collecting distilled water in scavenged glass through pitted copper tubing. In the protected, trash-free bay nearby, The People's jellyfish farm is thick as tapioca. Off to one side, kept relatively free of windblown dust in the lee of a healthy stand of bamboo, are the drying racks. Behind them, hundreds of huge mounds march into the distance between fields of hemp. The mounds cover the particulates and poisonous oils left by the Plastic Eaters and are kept away from the huts, which move as new mounds are added. Huge fungal shapes grow over the surface of the mounds, some tall as trees, others low and wide in varied forms; some stepped like yellow stairs, others hairy white mats. The weird, wonderful fungi digest what the Plastic Eaters find indigestible. The People regularly rake the bays and beaches and add any contents they can't use to the mounds as offerings. The mounds are places for contemplation and remembering – otherwise avoided.

In front of mud and bamboo huts, the old women munch roast beetles and weave seeds into grass mats for decorations. They tell stories to anyone passing by in singsong chants. An old man fries dried jellyfish with seaweed over an open fire in the center of the compound for whoever is hungry. It's a good life. The People are small and cheerful and eat well enough. They value life. There is sun and wind, salt and water, jellyfish, seaweed, millet for porridge, many kinds of insects, hemp for clothes and oil, mushrooms for fuel, and golden kelp beer for ceremonies. The People don't require much – and they have all the time that there is in the world.

A tall boy/girl comes out of a hut; s/he has one sparkling brown eye and one green. Frizzy, dirty-blond hair is twisted into short, thick dreads. S/he is taller and darker skinned than the small dust-colored folk making up the population of the village. At least half of them tend to have round eyes while his/hers have heavy epicanthal folds. S/he is beautiful. Around his/her neck is a plait of very straight, fair hair, threaded through a blue idiot stone – a NonK stone – that once showed images of water distillation systems, jellyfish farming, hemp cultivation, types of fungi useful for bioremediation, and recipes for kelp beer.

S/he is their Shaman; long-lived, empathic, maybe even a bit psychic, who knows? S/he remembers the past easily, even from before birth. S/he remembers everything – all of the four fathers' (one also a mother's) stories and more, synthesizing/channeling every point of view. Sometimes s/he thinks s/he dreams the future. The People are proud of their Shaman, but they're even more proud of having figured out for themselves how to live and eat and raise their young. So they don't rely on him/her too much. These days the blue stone's access port is jammed with colorful bits of plastic and beads. The learning songs are sufficient to remind The People of everything they feel the need to know.

Someday the tall girl/boy – or a part of them – will be in a snowstorm in a city not yet invented – will float in a primal sea of Medusozoa. Or maybe s/he already has.

S/he's dreamed the blue goddess. S/he dreams the world.

It is full of color.

"Life is tenacious,"
The old women sing.
"All things repeat."

• • •

NonK: Thought-terminating cliché:

(Defined by example, from "I am The Walrus" by Lennon, J., circa 1967)

"I am s/he as you are s/he as you are me and we are all together."

• • •

SNAP

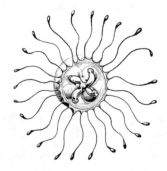

GLOSSARY

BLOOPS, BLOBS, TRICKSTERS & GODDESSES

JELLYFISH is both plural and singular. They are not fish! A group of Jellyfish is called a *SMACK*. Some jellyfish species are hermaphrodites, both male and female at the same time. Others are either male then female, or vice-versa, but not both simultaneously. These are "natural transgender jellyfish," according to writer Joram Piatigorsky.

"Jellyfish" is the common name given to the medusa-phase of gelatinous members of the subphylum Medusozoa, part of the phylum Cnidaria. Jellyfish are usually free swimming with umbrella-shaped bells and trailing tentacles, though a few anchor to the seabed at some stages, as polyps. Tentacles contain stinging cells, used to capture prey and defend against predators. Medusa produce larvae that disperse widely, then enter a stationary polyp phase before reaching maturity.

NEMATODES are small invertebrates that have adapted to nearly every ecosystem in water and soil, from the tropics to the poles. They're among the most diverse organisms in the ocean, with up to a million species. Sensitive to pollution, Nematodes were once widely used as indicators of environmental health.

BOX JELLYFISH: *Chironex fleckeri*, nicknamed Sea Wasps, are the most lethal jellyfish in the Southern Hemisphere, with tentacles up to three meters long, covered in millions of stinging cells that release microscopic darts on contact. The amount of venom in one animal is enough to kill 60 adult humans.

TURRITOPSIS DOHRNII, the immortal jellyfish (small as a pinky nail), is a hydrozoan that can reset or reverse its life cycle to an earlier stage when the medusa experiences stresses like injury or starvation. The bell shrinks, reabsorbing its tentacles and settling on the seafloor as a blob. The blob roots and develops into a new polyp. After maturing, it buds new medusae that are duplicates of its previous life stage. The process is called transdifferentiation – the conversion of one cell type to another – and is quite rare (*from Natural History Museum, UK*).

OOBLECK: a fictional green substance in a Dr. Seuss book, or a non-Newtonian fluid made of cornstarch and water with viscosity that can change under force to either a more liquid or a more solid state.

PUCK: a character in Shakespeare's play, *A Midsummer Night's Dream*. Based on English or Celtic mythology, Puck is a mischievous trickster fairy or hobgoblin.

VENUS OF WILLENDORF is an 11 cm. ochre figurine of a nude motherly figure that may have been an early fertility goddess. Found at a Paleolithic archeological site near Willendorf in Austria, it is estimated to be over 30,000 years old.

HIPPIES (1950s slang): One who chooses not to conform to prevailing social norms.

PROVERBS, RHYMES, EXCLAMATIONS & A POEM

LUCK IN THE LEFTOVERS: There's something good even in the last helping of an old meal.

THE CONDUCT OF A THOUSAND YEARS TO BE DETERMINED IN AN HOUR: A long-term reputation can be broken or shored up in a hot minute.

SHIPPO WO DASU (Japanese): to reveal one's tail – or one's secrets – unintentionally, as in old stories when a fox or racoon's tail pops out and gives away their disguise.

UNDEI NO SA (Japanese): Opposites, like chalk and cheese or clouds and mud.

BAKENO KAWA GA HAGARERU (Japanese): "The mask is ripped away."

ATAMA KAKUSHITE, SHIRI KAKUSAZU (Japanese): "Hide your head and you expose your bottom."

ALL AROUND THE MULBERRY BUSH ... POP! GOES THE WEASEL (English nursery rhyme, mid-19th century): Commonly used in Jack-in-the-box toys. In the UK, the rhyme may be about poverty and having to pawn one's clothes. The weasel may be "weasel and stoat," meaning "coat" in Cockney rhyming slang. In the USA circa 1850s, the phrase "Pop Goes the Weasel" meant "just like that."

JACK JUMPED OVER THE CANDLESTICK (English nursery rhyme early 19th century): Jumping a candle that stayed lit meant good luck.

GODS 'N' FISHES! (American): From "Ye gods and little fishes!"; an old-fashioned euphemism used as an exclamation of astonishment.

'TWAS BRILLIG, AND THE SLITHY TOVES, DID GYRE AND GIMBLE IN THE WABE: In the ballad "Jabberwocky," from *Through the Looking Glass*, Lewis Carroll used nonsense words to tell a story.

JAPANESE WORDS (always dependent on context):

Kinro kansha no hi: "Thanksgiving"

Niname-sai: "Celebration of rice" (Shinto)

Kudasaimasu: "To kindly do for one, to give, to bestow, to oblige"

Gomennasai: "I'm sorry" (formal)

Sumimasen: "Excuse me, thank you"

Maa: "Well" (expresses indifference)

Oitoma: "I've got to go" (slang)

Shimatta: "Oh dear, oops, oh no"

Itadakimasu: "Let's eat"

Ume: "Plum" (as in plum wine)

Ii kagen ni shiro!: "Knock it off!"

Kono yarou!: "This bastard"   *Busaiku*: "Ugly"
Hidoi: *"Cruel"*   *Ushi*: "Cow" or "child"
Oushikuso: "Cow dung"   *Onisan*: "Elder brother"
Baka, Bakayaro: "Idiot,   (respectful)
stupid"   *Wari*: "I'm sorry" (casual)
Suteki: "Great, lovely,   *Kusateru Oyaji*: "Stinky old
splendid, wonderful"   man"
Mugoi: "Cruel, inhuman,   *Abayo*: "Goodbye" (rude)
unkind"

DRINKING TOASTS: "To Your Health!"

"Kanpai!" (Japanese), *"Salud!"* (Spanish), *"Saude!"*
(Portuguese), *"Sláinte!"* (Irish), "À votre!" (French*),
"Budem zdorovy!"* (Russian).

QUOTED AUTHORS

E. O. Wilson, (1929–2021) was a secular humanist
and writer, biologist, naturalist, and entomologist.
Wilson was the world's leading expert on ants, nicknamed the "ant man" by Sir David Attenborough.
Wilson was an environmental advocate and expressed
hope for humanity until his death.

T. S. Eliot, (1888–1965) was a poet, essayist, publisher,
playwright, literary critic, editor, and banker. At first
Eliot's modernist poems were considered outrageous.
According to Wiki, in "The Hollow Men" (written
1925), it is hard for the characters to act. They put
neither good nor evil into the world. The final lines
are the most quoted of Eliot's poetry:

This is the way the world ends
Not with a bang but a whimper.

DALE WASSERMAN (1914–2008) wrote the play *Man of La Mancha,* circa 1965, based on the novel *Don Quixote,* by Miguel de Cervantes. Wasserman told of the mad knight Don Quixote as a play within a play, performed by Cervantes and fellow prisoners as they await a hearing with the Spanish Inquisition.

JOHN LENNON (1940–1980) wrote "I am the Walrus" circa 1967, apparently to upset fans who'd been assuming scholarly interpretations of the Beatles' lyrics. He was evidently inspired by two LSD trips and Lewis Carroll's poem "The Walrus and the Carpenter." Lennon's lyrics were called *Word Salad.*

R.E.M. (1980–2011) "It's the End of the World as We Know It (And I Feel Fine)" circa 1987. Stream-of-consciousness lyrics that lead singer Michael Stipe said came from a dream in which he was surrounded by famous people at a party with the initials "L. B.": Leonard Bernstein, Leonid Brezhnev, Lenny Bruce, Lester Bangs.

(All adapted from Wikipedia, the free encyclopedia)

About the author

After a decade of sailing the world with researchers in summer and assisting a glassblower in winter, D. K. McCutchen teaches writing for College of Natural Sciences, University of Massachusetts, and is an Associate Director of the Junior Year Writing Program. Currently they live on a river with two brilliant daughters and a flightless Kiwi, and write LGBTQIA-friendly, gender-bender, post-apocalyptic speculative fiction.

Books include *JELLYFISH DREAMING*, winner of a Leapfrog Global Fiction Prize, and *WHALE ROAD*, a Kiriyama Prize Notable Book and Pushcart nominee about chasing whales through the South Pacific. *JELLYFISH DREAMING*'s companion novel, *ICE*, winner of a Speculative Literature Foundation grant, is in progress.

Acknowledgments

Thank you, Mary Bisbee-Beek, Publishing Sherpa extraordinaire. You guided me to where I needed to be, and the Write Angles Conference guided me to you.

Thanks to Rosanne Parry for choosing my manuscript for Leapfrog's Global Fiction Prize! Thanks, Shannon Clinton-Copeland and Nicole Schroeder, for your editing insights. And thank you so much, Tobias Steed, for your incredible patience with my many emails!

Thank you, Michael J. Delucca, for believing in this story. Kirsten Mosher, you were the best, most patient reader in existence, helping me find my beginning and be aware of sensitive themes. Thanks, Drew Campbell, for early help with PC language. So many thanks, Mike Bukowick, for your lovely illustrations for *JFDs* graphic summary & the black & white drawings here..

Always and forever, thanks to my family, Tim, Lili, and Pip. I can only trust that you know how much your own creativity helps me stay hopeful during these difficult times.

In memoriam, thank you, Leighton McCutchen, my first editor, who I know would have celebrated when I found out – on what should have been his 89th birthday – that *JFD* was going to be published. And thank you, Marko, for being part of that celebration from afar, before you also had to leave. I miss you both.